Sophia Nash

THE ART OF Duke HUNTING

AVON
An Imprint of HarperCollinsPublishers

This is a work of fiction. Names, characters, places, and incidents ar[e] products of the author's imagination or are used fictitiously and are no[t] to be construed as real. Any resemblance to actual events, locales[,] organizations, or persons, living or dead, is entirely coincidental.

AVON BOOKS
An Imprint of HarperCollins*Publishers*
10 East 53rd Street
New York, New York 10022-5299

ISBN 978-0-06-202233-2
www.avonromance.com

First Avon Books mass market printing: April 2012

Printed in the U.S.A.

10 9 8 7 6 5 4 3 2 1

To my mother

Acknowledgments

Warmest thanks as always to Helen Breitwieser/Cornerstone Literary and Lyssa Keusch, Executive Editor at HarperCollins, for expertly shepherding to publication this second book in the Royal Entourage series. No one does it better than the two of you! And to the entire HarperCollins family, especially Liate Stehlik, Carrie Feron, Pamela Spengler-Jaffee, the sales force, and the art department, thank you for your outstanding support.

And to my family, and to my circle of friends, especially Amy, Kathy, Jean, Laurie, Jeanne, Kathy A., and Cathy M.: The love goes round and round.

Prologue

Roman Montagu, the seventeenth Duke of Norwich, knew he would end up at the bottom of the sea. He'd known it for almost two decades.

Yet, he never complained about his fate. For God sakes, no. Why, he had cheated death longer than most of the devilishly long line of Norwiches before him. He even considered himself lucky.

For a Norwich.

Indeed, almost everyone in England knew why there had been a dizzying number of Norwich dukes in two hundred years. They were cursed. Every last one of them had found death prematurely.

It was said the first bloodthirsty duke had

damned the family by publicly accusing a young lady of witchcraft after she had refused his ham-handed offer of marriage. But really, who could blame her for her less than enthusiastic response? The duke had not brought jewels to profess his affection. No, he had brought a half dozen ill-plucked fowl to her family and proclaimed her the luckiest lady alive due to the honor he would bestow on her. That did little to impress the young lady, or rather, the young witch, whose powers might not have saved her from persecution, but had managed to thereafter damn each and every Norwich duke, whose blood matched Norwich I, the Duck Hunter.

Roman had learned to live with this familial noose by adopting the blackest sense of humor concerning his forebears' early visits by the Grim Reaper. Indeed, he could recite the family's history by rote.

1. The first duke stuck his spoon in the wall when he choked on a giblet in his favorite duck stew not two days after his not-so-beloved burned at the stake while cursing all Norwich dukes.
2. The second unfortunate duke ate grass for his last breakfast when a bolt of lightning struck his duck blind in which he was silently perched at dawn in the pouring rain. It was then that the whispers of the curse began.

3. The third, fourth, fifth, and sixth dukes vowed to give a wide berth to all fowl to stay alive. Instead, they dampened their insatiable thirst for hunting by pursuing the dangerous fairer sex in London's ballrooms. While they might have been well-endowed with passion for the wives and daughters of their class, sadly, they were not well-talented with dueling pistols or swords borne by the husbands and fathers. The line devolved to a far less romantic branch with better aim.
4. The seventh duke tried to avoid the curse by daily readings from Johnson's sermons. He tumbled from the rolling ladder in Norwich Hall's famous, but mostly unread (especially by dukes III through VI), library while looking at an illustrated guide to geese hidden between Johnson's pages.
5. The adventurous eighth duke tossed away all sermons and took his dirt nap after sinking in a Scottish bog in search of a rare merganser, which barely looked like waterfowl at all. He had wrongly assumed the curse would not cross the border.
6. The ninth, tenth, and eleventh dukes were never seen or heard from again when they heroically went to war against the French. At least they were brave. Then again, when you knew you would die young, why not em-

brace your fate and die like a hero instead of a demented birdbrained predator?

7. The twelfth duke refused the call to arms. Indeed, he refused to put one toe out of bed in an all-out effort to avoid his fate. He cocked his toes in an acute case of gout within a twelve month. Most said it was the duck paté enveloped in goose fat.
8. The thirteenth duke knew he stood not a ghost of a chance given his number and family history. He went out in a blaze of pleasure, at full cry, with one of his seven mistresses, who tickled him with duck feathers.
9. The foppish fourteenth duke sacked a host of valets before he inadvertently strangled himself whilst fashioning a new knot for his Widgeon-colored neckcloth the scandal sheet dubbed the "Norwich Noose."
10. The fifteenth duke decided to confound the curse by befriending the enemy. He raised a pet mallard, who quacked on command and followed him everywhere. But while taking a short lie-down under a willow tree, a poacher aimed for the sitting duck and killed the dreaming duke instead.

Only Roman Montagu's father, the sixteenth Duke of Norwich, had lived past his fourth decade. Some said it was due to a tragedy of which he never spoke, or his avoidance of all spirits and hunting. Indeed, the stern aristocrat refused to sin in any fashion whatsoever.

But Roman knew better. The man had avoided a premature rendezvous with his maker by sheer bloody pigheadedness. Yes, the sixteenth duke had been nothing if not inflexible. But even the most wary and stubborn Montagu man could not avoid his destiny. At least Roman's father's death had been dignified. It was hard to find humor in a fall from a horse. Then again, the sixteenth duke had not possessed a shred of wit. Roman never told his sister or his mother that there had been feathers nearby, indicating his father's horse had most likely bolted from the sudden appearance of a migrating flock.

And so Roman Montagu, "Seventeen" to his intimates, did not worry overmuch about his future since it was already written. He would be the first Norwich to sink to the ocean floor—just like his elder brother before him, who should have been duke. He did not know how a duck would cause it, but of his fate he held not a feather of doubt. The other point on which he was decided, was that he would be the last—the very last—Norwich. There were no males left in the line—not even a fourteenth cousin twenty-four times removed.

And so, Roman Montagu, went about the process of life in a simple manner. He avoided ducks, and he did not enter bodies of water larger than his bath. The rest he left to chance. He worked on his grand schemes, and seized every moment of every day with gusto for who knew when the lights would go out.

But at this very moment in time, it appeared he was about to break the record of shortest title holder. Well, at least it did not involve a damned duck.

Or did it?

Chapter 1

Sheer unadulterated terror rained down on Roman Montagu, the Duke of Norwich. He was in the grip of a hellish nightmare—on the one thing he had vowed never to set foot on again . . . a ship. He shook his head, and it seemed to spin endlessly in the gale wind. Seawater lanced his eyes as waves crashed and retreated over the railing, while clips rattled against the masts over the roar and whine of a storm.

Hell and damn. 'Twas not a dream. His brother was not some ghostly figure haunting him. No. Roman was wedged in the windward corner, unable to move. His fingers clawed the quarterdeck, only to find one hand tied to the sodding taffrail. His blood seized and stood still in his veins.

Blindly, he freed his wrist, and managed to crab-walk away from the stern. The vessel rose and violently shifted on a massive wave and he slammed into the mizzenmast. The blow sent a shower of white hot pain sparking through his brainbox. He lunged for the aft mast again. It was his only chance.

Safety was up in the rigging, where he would wait for the hair-raising crack of the deck's wooden beams giving way to shoals—when the sea always won her game with foolish mankind who tried to tame her. Up one of the three masts, he would be the last to lose.

As the ship violently creaked and rocked in the kaleidoscope of the summer storm tumbling through the inky darkness, he tried mightily to make the muscle of his brain flex. He had not one particle of an idea of how or why he was on this bloody wreck in the making. Flashes of insane evening revelry with his fellow dukes in the royal entourage crackled through his mind as he was tossed away from the mast.

Well, damnation, he knew how to swim. He'd once proved he could outswim fate. Maybe he could do it again.

It was worth a try.

Esme March, the Countess of Derby, peered out of the rain-riddled porthole of the door leading to the ship's deck. She was probably the only passenger not terrified or ill. Yet.

But at least she was not afraid. The captain had warned of an approaching storm when they set sail, and the vessel was a very fine ship. The greatest deterrent to any sort of fear was excitement. She was finally embarking on the trip of a lifetime. All by herself, despite everyone's pleas to the contrary.

But she might become as green as a pea if she didn't inhale a few gulps of bracing sea air instead of remaining in her small cabin. Her gaze swept the murky seascape as she gripped the door handle to keep her balance.

For a moment, she thought she saw something odd—likely just a poor sailor whose task it was to secure a line. The deck would be impossible to negotiate given the pitch and sway.

There he was again—an eerie image of a man, his hair whipping his face in the storm. She inhaled sharply as he slammed into a mast and fell back.

Good God. The man regained his footing and swayed dangerously as an enormous wave crashed over the railing. He reached wildly for the mast but the wave dragged his body toward the edge of the ship.

Esme bolted past the door, knotted a line about her, and dashed for the stranger about to be lost to the sea. She couldn't breathe for the ferocity of the wind and the freezing sheets of rain.

She grasped the man's wrists just as he would have been tossed into the deep blue. Esme prayed for strength. His hands gripped her arms as another wave crashed over them both, the white foam glowing in the darkness.

As the seawater receded, for just a moment hanging in time, she chanced to see his face; harsh lines etched the corners of his mouth and forehead. But it was his translucent pale eyes that frightened her.

She recoiled. It was the second time she had spied death in less than two years. The ship pitched to advantage, and they were hurtled in the direction of the door to the cabins.

For some odd reason, the gentleman appeared to pull away from her. She used the last remaining strength she possessed to navigate him over the threshold before he sagged. She had but a moment to open her door before he lost consciousness.

Esme struggled to move his leg from the doorjamb, and then shut her cabin door and locked it. She paused, dripping puddles on the bare wooden floor. She pushed back her wet, tangled hair from her eyes.

Lord, he was so deathly pale; his lips waxy and almost blue. Wind-whipped strands of dark hair threaded with premature gray plastered his vaguely familiar, noble profile. He looked like a weary archangel felled to earth while she probably looked like a drowned rat.

Please let him not be dead. It would be too much to witness again. Finally, his chest rose and fell. By habit, she slipped the door key into the top of one of her sodden calfskin half boots.

She grasped his nearly frozen hand and felt for his pulse. Not that she'd know what to do if she found it. She had not an idea if it was too fast or slow. She was tempted to slap his face to revive him since cold water would likely not work on someone who'd just endured a wall of seawater.

Just then, with a rushed gulp of air, he came full awake, scrambling like a wild animal looking for escape. The unearthly pale blue eyes that met hers were intensified by an intriguing web-like line weaving through each iris.

Lord, it was he. Only one man had eyes like that. They were unforgettable. It was unfortunate and obvious that none of her features had the same unnerving effect on him.

Lurching to one knee, he flinched away from the touch of her hand and half crawled toward the door. He wrestled with the brass lever.

For some absurd reason, he wanted to get out. Thank God she'd hidden the key just as she had on so many other occasions with her husband. But this gentleman was another case altogether. She had not a chance of holding him back. He might be her height, but his torso was immense and he was clearly as strong as a bull stampeding the corridors of Pamplona in August.

"Please stop," she said, gripping the back of the one sturdy chair in the cramped cabin. "Wait a minute."

He again rattled the handle, his shoulders flexing with the effort to rip the door from the frame.

She had a terrible thought. "Is there someone else out there?"

"Key," he shouted. "Where is the bloody key?" They both stumbled sideways when the ship heaved starboard.

"But you'll die out there." There was not a single melodramatic note in her words—just stated fact.

He didn't deign to turn to face her, but at least he paused, a sign he was finally listening. He then jammed down the brass lever so violently, a screw gave way and the handle failed to return to its position. The oath he swore was so blue it made Esme cringe.

"Fool," he gritted out, still not looking at her. "Death is in here, not out there."

Esme stared at the back of his coat. The stitches at the center seam were stretched to the limit. The drenched blue superfine clung to the striated muscles of his shoulders.

"Please look at me," she said quietly.

"I'll find it myself," he choked, finally turning to stare at her. His eyes swept down her tall frame.

"What is so important out there?" She'd never backed down from a threat in the past, and no matter how intense his glare, the clothes of a gentleman were a good calling card.

He marched toward her, his black riding boots with the arched outer edge molded to his calves. The seawater-soaked leather soles made smacking sounds as he walked. He extended his palm for the key.

"All right," she said. "I'll tell you where it is if you tell me what you were doing."

"I'll have the key and then I *might* tell you." He grasped her arms and Esme felt the strength in him as his hands squeezed her. He was a mere half inch taller than she, so she looked almost directly into his light blue eyes, which almost glowed in the static air.

"Are you going to growl now?"

His eyes narrowed.

"Look the storm is waning. There's no need to go out there." And, indeed, it was true. Even the howl of the wind seemed muted.

He released her abruptly, but the wildness in his eyes did not disappear.

"You've a cut on your forehead."

He refused a reply.

She continued her tried and true methods of

speaking calmly in the face of insanity. "I'm freezing." She reached for her two blankets and offered him one. "You must be too."

He muttered something incomprehensible and didn't take the blanket. She set both back down.

"Oh pish. Do tell me what's going on, Lord . . . ?" She might know exactly who he was, but she was not in a fawning frame of mind.

"Grace . . ." He barely paid her any attention.

"Lord Grace? Hmmm, I've never heard of a Lord—"

"No," he sighed, "Duke."

Yes . . . that explained it precisely. All dukes were overbearing. Too much power. Too much deference. She raised an inquiring eyebrow. Too much inbreeding.

"For Christsakes . . . I'm Norwich."

"I see. Are we sure?"

He sighed heavily. "Roman Montagu, *not* at your service."

She smiled inwardly. There was always such a darkly humorous side when past and present collided. "Really? How lovely. I didn't know we had such refined company on board."

Again he muttered.

"Would you be kind enough to speak louder, Your Grace? I guess I must be becoming a bit hard of hearing in my advanced years."

When he didn't refute her, it irked her, which annoyed her even further.

"I said," he articulated clearly, "I didn't know such refined company would be aboard either."

"I'm merely a countess, Your Grace. I'm—"

He interrupted. "I was talking about me."

She frowned. "Of course you were." She lowered her voice. "It's what dukes do best."

"I beg your pardon," he replied. "What did you say?"

"I see old age has affected you too, sir," she said sourly. She would not kowtow to him. He hadn't even thanked her for saving his life. That reminded her. "I saved your life."

"Sorry?"

"I'll enunciate better, Your Grace. I. Saved. Your. Life."

"What is your name, madam?"

"Esme March, Countess of Derby," she dipped the smallest curtsy possible, "at your service even if you aren't at mine. May I see to that gash?"

"No." He showed not an ounce of recognition.

How lowering. "It's the least you could do since I saved your life."

He rolled his eyes. "Look, I'll tell every last sodding person in London you saved my life if you give me the key." His voice rose with each syllable.

She smiled and hoped it didn't appear sincere.

"But the winds have died. Why are you acting so oddly and what is so bloody important to you out there?" She was proud of herself for swearing. She so rarely had an opportunity to try it unless she was in private. And blasphemy was much more fun with two.

He stared at her and those strange eyes of his bored into hers with an intensity she felt down to her toes—just like the first time she had seen him in a ballroom, and he had not noticed her.

"Ships sink." He shrugged his shoulders. "If you can swim, you are far less likely to drown if you're on deck. You won't be able to open that door"—he nodded to hers—"with the weight of water pushing against it. It's simple science."

His words made a small amount of sense, and so she locked away the schoolmarmish tone from her words. "Of course. But I really don't think we have anything to worry about now. Don't you agree? *The Drake* is new and well built—such fine craftsmanship."

He closed those unnerving eyes of his. "*The Drake*? This ship is named *The Drake*?" He seemed to moan.

He might be a handsome devil with that ancient noble mien, but his wits were scrambled. Right. She walked to the secured water jug, poured a good portion in a bowl and dipped a piece of linen in it. Crossing the space, she faced him. "May I?"

He didn't move. She wiped his face with clean water and dabbed at the cut on the upper edge of his forehead. She almost recoiled when she noticed a familiar licorice scent almost oozing from his being. *Absinthe*. One of her beloved deceased husband's poisons of choice. She held her breath and forced herself to say not a word lest she lose her grip on common civility.

When she was done, she dropped the linen and he stepped on it so she could upend the bowl over his head to sluice the salt from his face and clothes. Silently, she repeated the steps to cleanse herself. After scrubbing her face dry, she offered him a new scrap of linen too.

"Are you ever going to tell me what was going on out there?" she finally asked.

"I was preparing to die, madam. You must be one of the few in England who hasn't heard of the Norwich Curse."

"Oh, I know all about the 'Duke of Duck Curse.'" Why, she knew more about it than anyone. But now was certainly not the time to tell him she was a direct descendant of the initiator. She certainly didn't want to play, ahem, ducks and drakes with his sanity.

He pokered up. "We prefer the other reference."

The vessel immediately dipped ominously and both stumbled sideways. His eyes glazed over as his face paled. He looked ready to lose his bearing again and so she dragged him to the sole bunk in her cabin to urge him to sit.

"Rest for a moment," she urged. Esme crossed the space to pour a tin cup of water for each of them and then returned to offer him one.

As she watched him drink, she suddenly remembered. Remembered hearing what had happened to his brother all those years ago. The duke had every right to be terrified, especially since he obviously had not an idea why he was on the ship. If she had to wager on it, she would guess it had something to do with the royal entourage, the infamous rapscallion band of dukes who walked hand in glove with the Prince Regent, and of which he was a member.

Every English lady worth her weight in smelling salts had a favorite member of the royal entourage, and Norwich had always been Esme's since the night many seasons ago when she had first spied him entering a gilded ballroom in Mayfair—his mother on one arm, his ravishing sister on the other. His intelligent, regal face full of angles had mesmerized her, and she had silently prayed his cool eyes would meet hers. But they had not. He had swept the room with a casual, arrogant gaze and she had not caught his eye even though she had been standing in prime view. And he had barely glanced at her later that evening when the Duke of Candover had introduced her along with a bevy of his sisters. Then again, this gentleman's indifference to ladies with matrimony on their minds was legendary. Like all the other events she spied him attend afterward, he danced once with his mother, once with his sister, and then disappeared with members of the royal entourage. He was the most mysterious one of the tribe.

But right now, there was not a hint of pride in the duke's stark expression. He drank the last bit of water and returned the cup to her hand. His unguarded expression met hers and she could not stop herself from moving a step closer.

She set the two cups on the side table, and then paused, trying to fight the intimacy of the moment. But the black despair she spied in his face broke her. She sat on the bunk beside him.

Roman's thoughts were perilously close to getting the better of him. He was even allowing a tall, spindly countess beyond the first blush (and second blush, most likely) to order him about. He'd be damned if he'd spend another second here, except that he was beyond weary to the bone and his head ached from slamming into the mast and suffering the ill effects of drinking too damn much.

And she'd been wrong. The storm was regaining intensity now. The sounds of creaking wood made the blood pool in his ears and block his thoughts.

Someone was speaking to him. He wasn't sure

if it was the countess for he was lost in the past, his brother's last words swirling in his mind. He looked up to see her studying him and noticed she was shivering.

Without thought, he grabbed the blanket at the end of the bed and draped it over her slim shoulders. He secured it about her, and a small sense of calm invaded his gut as he tended to her.

A great horrid boom buffeted the air. He closed his eyes and listened so hard for the sound of breaking beams that he couldn't breathe. Instead, he felt something ever so smooth course down his sideburns and cheek. And again. And then he felt it on both cheeks. He exhaled deeply. Roman opened his eyes to find her stroking his face. God, was he nothing but an infant to be coddled? It was not to be borne.

"Listen to me," she whispered. "It's all right. Just take my hand in yours."

"Don't cosset me," he gritted out.

"Why would I want to do that?" she replied with a casual shrug. "You're as cross as a bear and half as pleasant."

She was damned good at dissembling. A crack of thunder broke his momentary lucidity. He jumped up and hit his head on the low hanging portion above the bunk and fell back. He eased onto the length of her bed as dizzying darkness retreated from the edges of his vision.

Her gown rustled and he felt the small dip of the mattress as she lay down beside him. His head pounded with a vengeance.

"Look," her voice was so soft. "I know your story. It's all right. Just lie here with me." Her thin hand slipped into his.

An ache in the back of his throat would not allow him to speak. The waves were crashing faster, and the pitch and sway of the ship made him feel like the jaws of death were within a hair's breath. He fought the overwhelming desire to get the hell up. Find the blasted key. Sprint to the deck and climb the damned mast. Like before.

"Please don't," she whispered as if she could read his mind.

He turned his head toward hers. She had the most intelligent, tranquil face—a sense of calm and kindness radiated through every pore. Her wet and tangled light brown hair framed a face with large gray eyes that were fixed on him with compassion and ageless wisdom. Her eyes made the chaos beyond these walls almost fade into a static hum. She shivered again and primal instincts rose within him.

Instinctively, he released her hand and pulled her into the crook of his shoulder before wrapping his arms around her thin frame. That was when he felt her gentle lips graze the edge of his jaw. He'd never felt anything like it. It was pure comfort.

The storm had reached a pitch of intensity and he gripped her tightly, barely realizing she might not be able to breathe properly. She reached and stroked his sideburn and jaw again and he exhaled.

And suddenly, desperately, he wanted her.

Roman groaned. For Christsakes, it was insane. And impossible. For some confounded reason he was aroused and the touch of her hands was bewitching him to a blinding degree. She was soft and gentle and he felt like a wild animal.

The ship heaved to port then fell so hard that Roman felt his body hang in the air.

She exhaled roughly as her body jolted against his.

He regathered her to him and without thought lowered his head to press a kiss on her forehead. He felt far more in control with this woman in his arms. But it wasn't enough. He wanted to lose himself while he was locked inside here. He felt paralyzed, unable to find the effort to break down her door. There would be nothing but a wall of water behind it.

She looked up at him, and he felt the tension of desire fire through his veins. He still could not believe this countess was allowing him to hold her. For some odd reason, she made death feel farther away than it was.

A deafening crack of thunder rolled through the air and it broke the moment. Before he could react, she moved halfway on top of him, grasped his face and kissed him. He latched onto her like a man gasping his last breath. He could not stop his arms from binding her to him.

He should be a gentleman. He should stop. He should not take this gentle woman. But he could not change course. He could not let her go. She felt like a life raft. The best he could do was to utter one word. "Please." And then he could not stop from repeating it. He prayed she would not see reason.

He felt her head bob on his shoulder, and then he pulled face-to-face with her and kissed her again, long and deep. Only once did she turn her face away for but a moment.

He reached to touch her cheek but could not stay the shaking in his hand. He lowered it.

She grasped his hand and brought it to her lips.

"I want you," he said in a dark voice he didn't recognize.

She slowly ran her fingers down his chest. Instinctively, he knew it was all the answer he was going to get. Her soft hands were now unbuttoning his damp waistcoat and the top shirt buttons. His neckcloth was nowhere in sight—surely lost in London, where he should be.

Without another thought, he pulled down her sleeve and swept aside the top of her dark blue bodice where the swell of her breasts hid the fast beat of her heart. Her skin was so soft, unlike anything he'd known. She inhaled sharply when he cupped her lovely breast. A hard crest formed at the tip as he touched her.

A howl of wind brought him back to reality. He started to breathe unevenly and it was all he could do not to jump toward the door. And then shockingly, her hands were fiddling with the button on the falls of his breeches. Her hands found him and he could not breathe.

Time stood still and the sounds of the tempest faded.

Roman had thought he had experienced it all when it came to seduction. It was a fairly simple game played by jaded ladies of the Upper Ten Thousand who wanted to be led astray; charming widows and married ladies who exuded an air of fatigue and a desire for something to distract them from their lives of lassitude. But he had never ever had a lady attempt to take the lead once the bedroom door was closed. It was the last thought he had as her hand encompassed his arousal. He was as hard as a cannon and the small of his back tightened, poised for release.

The ship dipped sharply and Roman used the momentum to roll on top of her. The great, damp mess of her skirting was in the way and he bunched and pulled at it until it was above her slender waist. He stared at her kiss-bruised lips, the flush of her cheeks, and her stark expression before he parted the slit in her drawers, and drove into her without pause.

She exhaled with the most erotic sound, and pulled him closer.

He forged deeper as the vessel rose, and held tight as the ship bucked in the wild sea. Roman worked her tight passage, lost in her instead of the raging storm. Each time he reached a peak and longed to go over she stilled and held him back. There was a method to her madness, and soon he understood her game.

And so they prolonged it. Prolonged it until there were no more peaks to ascend and descend. He was so close to the edge that every movement was pain and pleasure.

"Go on then," she whispered.

"With you," he replied raggedly.

But his nerves were all at once at such a pitch that he could not let go. Never in his life had he found himself in such a state of terror and arousal. During this time out of time, they continued as before—giving and taking, pausing and continuing, yet rarely speaking. Instead he stared at her face, her eyes dark and unreadable. And then she traced her fingers from the base of his spine, down his backside to caress his sensitive, tight sac—an action that was his undoing. He made an inarticulate sound and felt her contract around him. He pulled out of her tight, warm wetness and emptied himself on the linen in long bursts that drained him. The pulsing was unbearably pleasurable as he tried to regain his breath.

Utter exhaustion engulfed him, almost comforted him, as he rolled and pulled her back into his arms. Filled with something that felt like gratitude mixed with confusion and mystery, he tenderly kissed the top of her head. Who in hell was this lady? Had he been introduced to her at any of the hundreds of the ton's entertainments he'd attended over the years?

His exhaustion and curiosity were short-lived. She was no-nonsense. The countess dragged herself to a seated position and swung her legs off the bunk.

"Where are you going?" He tried to regulate his voice.

"To the deck." She pushed her tangled locks of light brown hair over her pretty shoulder.

He was dumbstruck.

"Are you coming?" She was rearranging her bodice.

"Now you want to go?" Ladies really were the most capricious creatures.

"I think it a good idea, actually."

Speechless, he stared at her.

"I think one of the masts is down. We should decamp as you said." She peered at him over her shoulder with those huge gray eyes of hers that were eerily familiar.

"I beg your pardon?" He rasped out, his mouth cottony from the spirits.

"Didn't you hear the crack and the splintering a few minutes ago?"

He lay back down and covered his head with a forearm. *Christ.*

"Well?" she urged. "Look. I know your head must feel wretched, but we've no time to dally. It was absinthe, right?"

Just hearing the name of that poison made him nearly retch. He held up his hand. "Please don't say that word."

He heard her footsteps walking away.

Her calm voice floated back to him. "I don't know why gentlemen insist ladies are the inconstant sex. Do you or do you not want to go on deck?" She paused. "I, for one, am not going into the rigging even if a mast is still standing. But I'm going to search out one of those small boats on deck, just in case."

Roman refastened his falls, feeling like an idiot in the face of her cool head and courage. She was not at all playing this game the way it ought to be played. She was the fair maiden and he was supposed to be the savior. She should be weak at the knees and instead, he was the lunatic. He rearranged his shirt, buttoned his waistcoat, and awkwardly shrugged back into his blue superfine coat, damp and misshapen from a thorough drenching. He raked back his hair, and pretended to be the collected aristocrat he was on dry ground. He crossed the small chamber and bowed as cool as you please. He would not hurry even if every pore of his ravaged body screamed to rush.

The mysterious Countess of Derby bent down to retrieve a key from her boot.

The devil. No wonder she hadn't bothered to remove her boots during their interlude. Wasn't she the cool one?

And again, wasn't he the bloody idiot.

Chapter 2

Esme wasn't at all sure how she managed to keep her façade in place the next morning. Inside, she was all raw nerves and shock. She hadn't known she could possess a shred of aplomb after almost two hours of lying in a cabin bunk last night with a reined-in wild man, exuding equal measures of feral passion and intoxicated fear. And all along, the shock of such intense pleasure washed over and through her. The way this man had taken her had shaken her to the depth of her being. There had been none of the gentleness, none of the loving words she had known in the past. There had just been raw carnality with a touch of terror on his side and intense emotions on hers. He had been like a bull, stretching her, taking as much as he could and pushing her harder until something had happened to her that had never happened before. She still wasn't certain what had gripped her but for several long moments the most extreme sensations had coursed through her. Did he know? It was absurd. The entire experience had unnerved her so that she did what she did whenever she felt too exposed, she hid inside of herself and presented a calm front to the world.

Right now, standing among the flock of other bedraggled persons on the deck of *The Drake* as it limped into port, she felt as if it must be transparent to everyone what she had done.

She prayed she wasn't blushing. She glanced from the tips of her practical boots to the captain of *The Drake*, who was conversing with the Duke of Norwich. The latter was gripping the railing off the bow, his gaze focused on the port they were approaching at a decidedly uneven pace. The duke turned suddenly and his blue, blue eyes bore into hers. He gave her a knowing glance. And a smile that spoke of intimacy shared. It was the look she had dared to hope he would give her the first time she had seen him so many years ago in that ballroom.

She immediately turned her attention to the older man beside her. Mr. King, also known as the Master of Ceremonies in Bath, and also known as a man who liked nothing better than to peck at gossip until it barely resembled the truth at all.

"My dear countess," the gentleman opined. "Such a fine day, no? And after such fireworks last night."

Fireworks, indeed.

The old puff-guts was dissembling, trying mightily to have everyone forget that he hadn't blubbered, "All is lost! Every man for himself," several long hours ago at this same spot on deck.

"Who would have guessed," she replied faintly.

"My dear, I should like to offer you my services this bright morning," he continued. "I shall take the trouble to secure a room for you as soon as we set anchor."

"Thank you, sir, but I shall see to myself."

"Dear me. But I should insist, Lady Derby. A lady traveling alone? Without even a maid? It is not at all the thing, don't you know. Why, if your husband were alive, he would—"

"But he is not and I am very capable of seeing to myself." She always had.

The older gentleman cleared his throat and muttered something.

"Sorry?"

"I said, Lord Derby should have shown more restraint and taken better care. You would not be alone in the world if—"

She interrupted and stood straighter. "My husband always spoke very highly of you, sir. And my family and Lord Derby's rarely leave me alone." She smiled at the humor that was lost on the gentleman in front of her. "Indeed, I have never understood why solitude is so frowned upon."

"I'm not speaking ill of him," Mr. King harrumphed. "Merely stating the truth and coming to your aid, madam. I'm certain he would want me to help you in your hour of need."

Esme had hoped to escape the endless years of defending her husband Lionel. It never satisfied, for no one ever believed the love she had held for him. "You are too good, Mr. King, but I've already plans for accommodations." The lies were mounting now.

His bushy gray eyebrows rose a notch. "Really? And how did you accomplish that when we're at a port that was not our destination?"

"Why, Mr. King, are you doubting my word?" She prayed she was not blushing.

Mr. King cleared his throat. "I say, in my day, ladies did not just go traipsing off alone on a ship."

She gaped at him in mock surprise. "Mr. King, whatever are you suggesting? Have I ever given anyone cause to question my character?" *Until the last four and twenty hours.*

He studied her and tutted. "Of course not, my dear. Your character is without blemish. You are a model of propriety. It is a shame the same cannot be said of everyone." His eyes gleamed with delight. "Did you not see that the Duke of Norwich is mysteriously among us this morn? I assure you he did not board this vessel in the usual manner. I was given a list of passengers prior to sailing, and well . . . What can one expect from one of the royal entourage? I feel it necessary to warn you off this duke, madam. He brings ill luck and worse to our respectable group. I for one shall—"

She nodded to the gangplank. "Good day to you, Mr. King."

"Ah, we're ready to . . ."

Esme twirled her parasol and strolled away from the blowhard in mid-sentence. It was the best she could do for if she had stayed another minute he risked a whack on his head by her parasol which had been known to have a mind of its own. She felt a smile forming and then paused.

It had been a long time since she had felt relaxed and playful. It had been a long time since she had felt a plume of anything but duty or the passion of her art unfurl in her breast. She stood beside her two trunks at the end of the queue of weary passengers anxious to debark.

What on earth had come over her? What had she done? If someone had told her she would do something so outrageous, she would have denied it to the end of her days. Yet, she did not regret it. When first widowed, she had wondered if she would ever lie in a bed with a man again. She had very much doubted it. She was old at four and thirty, and worse, she was plain. And too tall. A wretched combination for a lady. At least she had independence, a rare enough thing for any female, widowed or not.

Norwich had left the cabin after her, insisting she leave first despite his poorly hidden desire to flee. They had not shared one word since. She had only heard him tell the captain that the ladies on the voyage must be given the two rowboats if the ship sank, which at one point had appeared a distinct possibility. But the crew had chopped off the downed mast and morass of rigging that had been dragging down the ship. She had kept an eye on him throughout, but he had seemed able to marshal his fears, with only one hand gripping the aft mast.

They were blown far south of their course. That, combined with the felled mainmast, had forced them to put in unexpectedly at the Isle of Wight. Who knew how long they would be stuck?

It didn't matter, really. Any place but London or Derbyshire or actually, any place without a *shire* or a *ville* attached to an English hamlet was fine with her. She just needed to cast her eyes on new vistas and inspiring venues.

Lost in reverie, watching the last of the canvas secured high on the spars by sailors, who appeared like a flock of industrious birds in the leafless branches of trees, she failed to take note of the duke's approach.

"Penny?" he said.

She whirled about. "Sorry?"

"For your thoughts." His eyes appeared so different from before. Now they sparkled with good humor, and he looked unbearably masculine. Why was it that a man could take a dunking, have salt encrusting the tips of his hair and even his skin not to mention his ruined Bond Street clothing, and look like a rugged, aristocratic prince among men? It was entirely unfair. She didn't need a looking glass to know she looked like a wretch.

He smiled, which made her lose track of the conversation.

"Ermmm. What did you say?"

"It's the age problem, right?"

"I beg your pardon?"

He laughed, and it made her insides turn to half-cooked preserves.

"Your hearing. You're hard of hearing. I am so sorry."

She loftily flitted one hand in the air. "How ridiculous. I hear perfectly well. You're the one who didn't hear the mast splinter."

"Thank you," he replied.

"For what?"

"For not rubbing my nose in it. You're to be

commended. Most would not have been able to resist making sport of my abominable behavior last night."

"I make it a habit never to tease a man with whom I will soon share a name," she declared with mock seriousness. "By the way, when shall you send the announcement to the *Morning Post*?"

His smile slipped and he hemmed and hawed for a moment before he stopped. "Oh, you're, um, well. You are just . . . funning." When she did not immediately reply he halted, horror-struck.

She regarded him with her best version of innocence. It was hard . . . considering.

"Lady Derby, may I have the honor of calling on you . . . later this day?" He raked back his hair in a habitual way. "When we debark, that is to say." He paused. "Are you teasing me or not?"

She really should take pity on him. His head must feel like a burned cauldron. She hoped it felt worse. She relaxed her face into a smile. "I suppose I should say I'm sorry, but I find it nearly impossible to resist the opportunity when it presents itself so perfectly."

"Thank you," he replied, a small smile finally appearing at the corners of his lips. "Forewarned and forearmed. By the by, I've arranged to repay you for a small portion of your, um, kindness."

The roots of her hair felt on fire and she was

sure she would go up in cinders from embarrassment. "I beg your pardon. I will not accept anything from you, sir."

He could have carried it off had it not been for the twinkle in his eye. "Pardon me. I merely asked the captain about accommodations on the isle. He will secure a chamber for you at the better of the two lodgings before the others fight tooth and nail over the limited quarters there." He paused. "I like to tease too."

"Fair enough." Her heated emotion retreated, only to be replaced by a sensibility unknown to her. She stared at him. She was very used to arranging and securing everything she needed for herself. She preferred it that way. She did not want or need to depend on anyone. She swallowed. "Then I guess it is I who must thank you."

He smiled again and it annoyed her for some ridiculous reason. He must know the effect he had on ladies with that look. Indeed, the Duke of Norwich was renowned for his magnetism. But the matchmaking mothers in Town had long since despaired of ever bringing him to heel. He was a rare catch, for he was not known to be in general circulation even if he did spend most of the year in Town. From her seated perch next to the potted palms on the sidelines of the battlefields, or rather ballrooms, in town, Esme had observed him and his ducal cohorts as they refused to allow anyone to pierce the tight, high-flying circle known as the royal entourage.

Her perverse nature took hold when he offered his arm to her and she accepted it. They walked toward the gangplank now that the rest of the passengers had debarked.

"I'm embarrassed to ask," he continued, "but had we been introduced before last night?"

She smiled. "I shall give you an awkward moment. Yes. We were introduced years ago at Lord Bartholomew's ball."

He exhaled. "Yes, I thought I recognized you."

"And then we met again at Miss Chapman's soiree a twelvemonth ago when you escorted your sister."

"Of course," he said with a hint of uncertainty. "I remember the event very well."

"And then again, there was the Hastings' house party three months ago. During the fortnight, we were occasionally seated near each other at table."

"It was a very large party as I remember," he defended, the space between his brows bunching in two worry lines.

"Yes, eight is a very large party." She assumed the owlish expression on her face that her family had always deplored.

His eyes widened. "I say, there were at least

three doz— . . . You're doing it again," he said, a smile breaking through finally.

"I beg your pardon?"

"Mocking me. I distinctly remember there were nearly more people than chambers, and I escaped two days after delivering my mother and sister."

"Yes," she continued. "Very easy to get lost in that sort of a crowd."

He would not continue the banter—or defend himself. He was staring at her as if she had a spot on her nose.

"Ummmm, why are you staring at me?"

"I've just realized that the only way to win at your game is to stop playing." He broke into another wide smile.

"Stop doing that," she retorted.

"I beg your—"

"No you don't. You don't beg anything of anyone."

"I'm begging you now." He scratched his jaw. "Everyone else has debarked, and I think you know how I feel about being on this floating wreck." He offered his arm again.

There was something entirely unnerving about this man. His magnetic appeal made her feel like a thousand eyes were peering at her. She refused to be drawn in. Like last night. It was far too dangerous a game for someone like her.

Esme March, the Countess of Derby, turned on her heel and marched toward the gangway. She heard his voice float toward her back.

"No worries. I shall have your trunks taken to the inn."

Roman Montagu glanced at his pocket watch, which he had set on the simple bureau in the best room of the Horse & Hound Inn. He glanced out the window. There was not a single horse or hound to be seen. And for the first time ever, he could not rein in the thoughts in his usually ordered mind.

That overly tall countess really was a most unusual female. Her face was undeniably feminine and aristocratic but not at all in the fashion of the fresh-faced milk-and-water misses decorating the ballrooms of London. Her brow showed intellect, and he thought he had made out tiny indentations near the bridge of her nose, which indicated reading spectacles. Her nose was aquiline and a bit long. Her teeth were even but her smile was uneven and charming when she chose to show it. But there were two things she possessed that trumped all. And he would wager his last farthing that he was one of only two people to have had a glimpse.

Her long, long legs . . . her calves . . . her thighs . . . and most likely even her feet were beautiful. Dear God, just the thought of the combination made his heart stutter.

And then there was the matter of her touch. Her fingers had felt like the finest velvet as they had traced his skin. He'd never experienced anything like it.

Roman shook his head in disbelief. Now was not the time to think about the amazing happenings last night. Indeed, he found it difficult to even believe such intimacy had occurred, or even existed on this temporal plane.

Well, then.

He forced his mind onto a new path. The captain had made good on his promise and had secured rooms at the inn on the west side of the small village. The captain, Roman, and Lady Derby were the lucky occupants, along with a plethora of visitors on the island. The rest of the ship's passengers had had to make do at the large, ill-kept rooming house on the opposite side of the village green, decorated with streamers for an upcoming summer fête.

He wondered what the countess was doing on the other side of the corridor separating their chambers. He was one part curious, two parts horrified that he'd taken advantage of a respectable lady, three parts dreading the proposal of marriage he was honor bound to offer her, and four parts (man that he was) fantasizing about the surreal night he had spent with her. He refused to consider the living hell the two of them would be forced to endure if she accepted his offer. But she would not. He was certain.

Well, he was almost certain.

As convinced as the fact that they were stuck on the Isle of Wight for as long as it took for another ship to sail into port and get them off of this damned isle. Then again, Roman wondered how he was going to screw up his courage to set foot on another ship.

A knock sounded at his door. Perhaps it was she. He looked down at his borrowed clothes and winced. The captain was a heavyset man. Roman tucked in the billowing cloud of shirt linen. At least he had left the last of the salt water in the copper tub in the corner.

"Come," he barked.

The captain appeared, his ruddy complexion speaking decades of raw weather.

"Your Grace? I would have a private word." The man of the sea glanced at the length of his form and his lips twitched.

"Thank you for the use of your linen, Captain. And what may I do for you?"

"Well, it is more what I must do for you, Your Grace."

"Whatever do you mean, sir?"

"I mean that I must carry out what your friend insisted at the point of his pistol."

Roman stared at the older man. "I beg your pardon?"

The captain chuckled. "When His Grace, the Duke of Kress, dragged you on board my ship, he paid me very handsomely to guard his vowels to give you if you survived the voyage."

Vague flickering of his closest friend, Alexander Barclay, the new Duke of Kress, racing hell for leather toward the docks, wandered just out of reach of Roman's mind. "Did he, now?"

"He did," the older gentleman replied, his merry eyes not matching his grave expression. "Had him escorted off *The Drake* when he began singing the French national anthem. It left a very foul taste in my mouth if I do say."

"I'm sure it did, bloody Frenchy that he is."

"Yes, well, there's more to it."

"Go on then. I am not too proud to admit that I was three sheets to the wind obviously."

"More like one hundred and three sheets in a gale force, Your Grace."

Roman sighed. "Go on."

"After he left, you promised me a thousand pounds if I tied you to the railing. You refused to take a cabin, but you were of sound enough mind to know you'd likely topple over the side given your state of, ahem, ill balance." He cleared his throat. "You couldn't form a sentence let alone a secure knot. I'm sorry to say that during the storm I was too preoccupied to come to your aid. But, I also knew my knot would hold."

"Of course, it would," Roman acknowledged. "And, of course, I shall honor my debt to you, sir."

"This will help, certainly." One corner of the captain's lips curled with humor. Roman was surprised the man was in such a good spirits given that his ship was nearly destroyed. Then again, the unexpected windfall from two dukes was most likely the reason.

The captain reached into his pocket and extracted a sheet of paper. In extraordinarily large and ill-written letters, Alexander Barclay, the half-French Duke of Kress, promised him his entire newly gained fortune if Roman completed a voyage of at least three days' duration. The amount was half the size of Roman's own family legacy. It was signed by both parties and noted the official wager had been written in White's famous betting book for good measure.

For Christsakes. He had to return to London as soon as he regained his nerve to rectify this abomination. Kress was one of only three gentlemen he trusted. He knew why his friend had done it. He could only imagine what had happened. But it had taken a new level of insanity for Kress to actually voice and wager his fortune against something that had haunted Roman for half his life. It was a subject that was not open for discussion. Unless, the drink of the devil was involved, apparently.

Unfortunately overindulgence was something that happened on a more frequent basis of late. Two, three, four nights a week, most members of the royal entourage gathered and bolstered themselves with spirits before making the mind-numbing rounds of soirees, and dinners, and balls, and *fêtes champêtres,* and coming outs, and going outs, and other such nonsense reserved for the rich and privileged set.

It was the way of it.

His current circumstances and whereabouts were not.

He stared at the captain, without really seeing him. How the hell was he going to get off this island? And when?

"Captain?"

"Yes, Your Grace?"

"Exactly how far are we off the coast?"

Chapter 3

Esme peered at herself one last time in the looking glass in the room she had been given at the charming inn. Fragrant bouquets of cottage roses rested on each end of the dressing table. She pinched her cheeks and tucked an errant wisp into the heavy coil pinned high on the back of her head before she let out an exaggerated sigh and abandoned her efforts. All of it was a waste of time.

Her maker had clearly had a sense of the absurd when he had imbued her with a talent to exalt and capture beauty in everything that surrounded her, yet had given her very little of the same if the image staring at her from the looking glass was any indication. Oh, she should be well used to it by now. It was just that tonight she had spent twice as long as usual to prepare for supper with Norwich and the captain, and the results were unoriginal.

She stuck out her tongue at her reflection and then laughed at herself. If she had just a bit less pride, she would have donned her plainest frock, rumpled her hair, and stuck one of her long, thin brushes in it as she was often inclined to do when she was alone and doing what she adored more than anything.

She would love to see Norwich's reaction. It would give her a measure of his true character. She wondered if he would still perform the requisite proposal of marriage, which she would be honor bound to refuse.

Esme wrapped a paisley summer shawl about her shoulders and descended to the Horse & Hound's elegant dining hall. A half dozen tables filled with diners graced the room. Her entrance caused only a handful of guests to take notice.

It took her but a moment to see why. Every female in the room was surreptitiously focused on the Duke of Norwich. And every gentleman, too. Then again, it wasn't all that surprising. Mystery and ill-fate had surrounded that family for the last two hundred years.

And her ancestor was to blame. She wondered if and when she should tell him. Oh, but she knew. She sincerely hoped he would not take leave of his senses when she informed him.

As she walked toward the table, for the first time in her life, Esme experienced the thrill of having the most sought after gentleman in the chamber stand up, nod a greeting, and smile at her. It was too bad it would likely be one of the last times.

Esme weaved past the other tables and eased into the chair the duke held out for her.

He leaned down as he arranged the chair closer to the table. "The trick is to look an inch above everyone's head. And to ignore them all if you can."

She bit her lip to keep from laughing. "But I like that they're watching. It's such a novelty."

"Ah," he said, "then by all means, enjoy it and stare right back at them," he replied with a warm smile as he regained his seat. "For my part, I shall forgo the pleasure."

The captain, dressed in impeccable officer's garb, glanced between the two of them and chuckled. He appeared far more interested in the fragrant trays of food the inn's servants carried to the surrounding tables.

"Good evening, sir." She nodded graciously at the officer.

"An honor, Lady Derby. And a delightful surprise. I daresay most of the other ladies are still abed, recovering from the shock of last eve's events. You are to be commended for your fortitude."

"Indeed," commented Norwich, with the hint of a smile.

Esme prayed a blush would not overtake her. "Not at all, Captain. I am only sorry about your beautiful ship. But you see, a storm would never dampen my spirits. I have waited a long time to see the world."

The duke cleared his throat. "And just what part of the world were we about to visit?" he asked gruffly.

"Well, if *The Drake* had held steady," the captain replied, while helping himself to a platter of roast pigeon and artichokes, "and we'd been fortunate enough to evade Frog warships, we would have docked on the northern Italian coast."

"How delightful," the duke said, looking very relieved that the trip had been aborted.

Esme pursed her lips together to keep from smiling. She accepted the spoon in the serving dish of potatoes a servant offered. She had to admit that now she wished the ladies at the surrounding table would stop staring. It made her feel as if she might drop the silverware and make a spectacle of herself. There was something to be said about the anonymity of being a wallflower.

The captain continued, "You were to tour northward to Vienna, were you not, Countess?"

"Yes, exactly. After we set anchor, I was for Prague and Vienna."

"Did you have any particular reason to see those two cities?" Norwich focused his eyes on her, and she felt the full force of his charm. She could not truly believe what had happened between them last night.

"Why, to drink in the beauty and magnificence of each. And to visit the museums, of course."

"Of course?" The duke looked at her quizzically.

"Lady Derby is an accomplished artist, Your Grace." The captain eyed the duke with surprise. "Did you not know?"

Esme immediately pushed off the subject. "Captain, you are to be commended again for seeing us through such danger."

" 'Twas nothing, madam, compared to the gales off the West Indies. Why, last night was but a mere gust of wind." The captain droned on and on about other storms in distant lands he and his crew had endured.

For the next half an hour Esme listened to the captain's stories of far-off lands and enjoyed the delectable fare placed in front of her, far more at ease as an observer than as the observed. Just as she relaxed and took a last large bite of berry fool, Norwich took advantage of the captain's obvious delight in the dessert and trained his attention on her.

"So you are an artist, Lady Derby? What medium do you favor?" His eyes studied her in the same fashion as last eve.

Esme swallowed too quickly, the effort causing

tears to spring to her eyes. What on earth was the matter with her? Oh, she knew. Those astonishing eyes of his were her undoing just as they had been all those years ago on the edge of a ballroom.

He handed her a glass of wine with concern. "Are you all right?"

"Perfect," she rasped behind her napkin.

Wait staff at table began the final remove.

"Have you never seen the West Indies, Your Grace?" The captain cocked his head at the duke.

"I do believe you already know the answer, sir, as someone who witnessed my, ahem, delight at unexpectedly finding myself at sea." Norwich's easy smile belied his determination. "But Lady Derby has not answered my question."

The captain's eyebrows, as dense and unruly as a hedgerow, rose. "And I wager she will not."

"My dear sir," Esme said, finally regaining her voice. "Why would you say such a thing?"

"Note how easily she turns the conversation," the captain inserted with a laugh. "I should know. I've been known to sketch a bit and tried to engage her in her methods before we set sail yesterday. All of it was to no avail."

Norwich looked at her thoughtfully.

"How provoking," she replied. "I've no notion of what you say, Captain. And I should like above all else the great honor of seeing your drawings."

"Then again, I should have known," the captain

continued. "Even when her work was shown at the Royal Gallery, an event no artist worth his weight in pigment would ever miss, Lady Derby declined to attend."

It was too much. She hated to talk about her painting. She didn't know how to explain what she did or why she loved to create, and she became entirely tongue-tied whenever asked to speak on it.

Both the captain and Norwich's full attention was on her.

"All," she finally blurted. "I like *all* mediums of art." How ridiculous. Could she not wax a bit more poetic when called on?

Those mesmerizing eyes of his did not move from her. There was no possible way she could expand on the topic.

She cleared her throat. "Captain, have you captured images from the storms you encountered?"

The captain opened his mouth to surely expound on his favorite subject when Norwich abruptly stood up, the heels of his chair scraping loudly against the floor. He bowed. "Come, Lady Derby. The captain, I am certain, will indulge me if I ask for a reprieve. I, for one, have endured enough talk of seawater for one meal."

The captain eyed the two of them shrewdly and then slowly rose. Esme had no choice but to follow suit and accept Norwich's arm. At least she had successfully evaded more questions.

She suddenly noticed that all the other occupants in the room were still seated. Not one person had dared to leave and miss the spectacle of a member of the royal entourage.

As they departed, she surreptitiously watched the way the duke surveyed the room just as he had advised her to do—in a polite but chilly manner to evade engagement. *Just as she had witnessed all those years ago when she had first seen his noble profile and his gaze had swept past her without taking note.*

"Perfect evening for a walkabout," the captain commented to no one in particular as he strolled toward the inn's main entrance. Esme and Norwich followed him. "I shall leave the two of you to your own devices, however." The former naval officer took advantage of a rustic bench on the expansive lawn of the inn. He retrieved a cheroot from his pocket and struck a match from his small flint box. Smoke swirled in the growing darkness.

She darted a glance in Norwich's direction and removed her hand from his arm. "I, for one, am for bed, I think."

"Shall we not take a bit of the night air, madam? I have something of importance to discuss, but I promise not to breathe a syllable concerning canvases or paint."

The captain slyly examined the both of them and had the extraordinary audacity to wink at her.

Esme was hard-pressed to think of a single

witty retort. It appeared the time had come for the requisite proposal of marriage to be endured.

"If you insist, Your Grace," she reluctantly agreed.

He offered his arm to her once again and she accepted it. The evening air was cool and calm; a breeze jostled the tree leaves in full summer splendor.

They walked in silence and she glanced from time to time out of the corners of her eyes to see his even profile, bowed forward in reflection.

It was painfully obvious he was finding it much more difficult than he had originally thought. He exhaled. At least he did not start pulling on his neckcloth.

"Go on then," she prompted, attempting an equal measure of good humor and dignity. "Have no fear, sir. We both know your question *and* my answer."

"I am trying to find the precise words that will leave you hanging on the fence, Lady Derby," he said with an honesty that surprised her. He finally looked at her fully and smiled.

"This should be interesting."

"Well, on the one hand, marrying me would be a good bargain for you. I will surely leave you a widow again at some point in the near future, with a fortune twice over."

Her lips parted slightly in surprise. "But I do not—"

"No. Allow me to continue." He raised his free hand. "But you see, the thing is, there is no guarantee precisely how long it will take. You might be stuck with me for longer than you'd like. But I could at least offer you a loftier station than you already occupy even if it does come with occasional mocking due to the unfortunate family history."

She was silent for a long while as they continued the march about the green, a full moon illuminating the lovely parish. He steered her toward the lane leading away from the village. The arc of a small stone bridge loomed not far away.

She stopped at the height of the arch and released his arm to look down at the running stream. "I suppose I should thank you for your offer but I cannot."

He started.

"You might reconsider your offer if you were better informed of my family, Your Grace."

"Please address me less formally."

"No."

"But we have shared—"

"No, we did not share. I freely gave myself. It is not something that can be repaid—even with marriage. You discredit me by thinking thusly."

"But I am asking for the honor of your hand in marriage." He continued with lowered voice. "Protocol demands it."

"Consider yourself off the hook," she said, forcing a smile to her lips. "I have no need of the honor you do me nor do I place much value in protocol. I have more than I need in life, and I've never sought a loftier station. I am the daughter of an earl, and the wife of a deceased earl, and I shall go to my grave as such."

He waited for her to continue. She did not. "Have I insulted you, Esme?" he asked.

"I did not give you leave to address me so intimately."

"Well, how should I address you in private? And I think it odd to address you in any other fashion given last night." He scratched his head. "I had thought you would have received my addresses with—"

"March."

"Pardon me?"

"You may address me as March."

"And who is March?"

"You would know if you had not drunk yourself to near oblivion."

He rolled his eyes. "Are you always this confounding?"

"I don't find it confusing at all. Gentlemen address each other by their family names or titles all the time. There. I have given you a hint as to why you may address me as March."

There was no recognition on his face. Not that she had thought there would be. March was her husband's family name, not her father's name, and certainly not her mother's maiden name—the one that would surely draw horror on the duke's face.

At that precise moment, the mournful if not oddly discordant sound of a duck's call echoed from above. Esme glanced skyward, but could not see the fowl in the darkness.

But it was a sign.

And Esme always paid attention to signs.

Her intention of telling him who she really was evaporated into the night air as quickly as all her ridiculously romantic dreams of old.

He shook his head. He'd never met a lady who wanted to be treated like a man. She stroked the rail of the tiny bridge and the hairs prickled at the base of his neck. He knew precisely why. He could not help but remember what those same fingers had done to his back the evening before.

"You will be happy to know you've achieved your goal," she said.

He could not make out her expression. "I don't understand." He sighed. "Again."

"I know you don't," she replied.

"What goal?" he insisted.

"That of leaving me on the fence. I cannot decide if I like you for your honesty and less-than-gentlemanly offer or if I dislike you for the same reason."

"I vote for liking me."

She turned fully to him and he had the unholy desire to take her hand in his. He resisted.

"So there is nothing I can offer you?" He paused. "March?"

Her large gray eyes stared at him. He could swear he saw a moment of sadness before one brow arched. "Well, now that you mention it, there is one thing."

"Anything," he breathed with relief now that marriage was off of his dish.

"You can promise on your honor never to drink a drop of spirits again."

"I beg your pardon?"

A gurgle of laughter rolled through the night air. "This is not going in your favor, you know. You're making it too obvious that the idea of marriage to me is more offensive to you than the trial of living your life without wine and whiskey. Or absinthe."

He scratched the back of head. It always itched at the hairline when he was hot. "That is absolutely not true." But he was afraid it absolutely was true.

"How about if you just make the promise and then all will be forgiven and forgotten."

"But why on earth would you ask this of me? It's absurd."

"You asked for a way to thank me. This is how."

"You sound like a governess, March."

"Good," she replied. "Perhaps you need governing."

"That's just the sort of thing to say to a man who you want to scare off." He shook his head and chuckled.

"Perhaps I want to scare you off, Your Grace," she said so quietly he had to lean in to hear the tail end.

"If I must address you as March, then you must address me as Montagu," he said. "Actually, it will be a refreshing change from my cursed title."

"All right," she said. "Montagu."

He took up one of her hands and kissed the back of it impulsively, before leaning in toward her startled, wide eyes. In that instant, she distinctively had the look of a lady who wanted desperately to be kissed. He knew that look very well. And he was happy to oblige since—

A rustle of footsteps and low conversation interrupted them. Roman turned his head slightly only to see a small group of people strolling toward them from the village green. He stepped away from Lady Derby.

"Hey ho," a deep voice boomed.

Good God, it was that boorish gossip, King. Roman raised a hand in greeting.

"What luck," Mr. King said, drawing near with a lady on each arm. Two gentlemen and another lady drew abreast. "Your Grace, I have been meaning to find you. And good evening to you too, Lady Derby. Oh dear, I hope I have not interrupted anything." He wore a smile that pretended to know everything when he actually knew not a whit.

"Your servant, Mr. King," Roman replied, annoyed. He refused to offer up an excuse. It would sound damning to the idiot in front of him.

The stout, tall man stopped and turned to look first at Lady Derby for a long moment and then to Roman. "Hmmm. Well, you still have not told us how you came to be aboard *The Drake*."

"Why do you ask, sir?"

"Out of concern, of course."

"Of course," Roman echoed smoothly.

Mr. King eyed him like a hungry boa constrictor regretting the impossibility of a sleeping tiger. "So?"

"So?" Roman replied.

"The reason you were not on the manifest, Your Grace?"

"The reason?" Roman dissembled.

"Yes."

"I see," he evaded. "Lady Shelby, how lovely you are tonight, my dear. And how is Lord Shelby?"

The lady on Mr. King's arm smiled. "Shelby is very fine. Shooting all the ducks he can find at the Abbey, in fact. He never stops until the frost drives him from his blinds. He—"

One of the gentlemen cleared his throat and she

stumbled to a stop. "I apologize, Your Grace, I did not mean to . . ."

"Of course, you did not, madam."

"And what finds you here with His Grace, Lady Derby?" Mr. King's smile showed all of his teeth. "I see you managed to find accommodations very well, just as you said you would. One wonders how you accomplished it."

"Mr. King, I find myself here the same way as you—with my own two feet. And I thank you for your compliment. It is good to see you recovered from your fright." She was cagey dodging the "Grand Inquisitor," as Mr. King was known in the privacy of most aristocrats' salons.

King's eyes darkened in the night shade of the silver birch nearby. Clearly, he did not like to be cast in the role of a coward. "I see neither you, my dear, nor His Grace is willing to be candid among friends. This typically speaks of curious goings-on, if anyone were to ask me."

Lady Shelby tittered, she of the very orange-colored hair, and one of the gentlemen cleared his throat again.

"Mr. King, there is a fascinating hedge on the other side of this bridge. May I have the privilege of showing it to you?" Roman spoke with a certain tone. It was the bored voice he employed when something unpleasant had to be done.

"Of course," Mr. King said, his smile widening.

Roman strode away while Mr. King waddled as fast as his overflowing girth would permit.

And then Roman allowed himself the pleasure all of the ton would have killed to enjoy. He hoisted the man onto his tiptoes by wrenching his knotted neckcloth with one fist. "Now see here, King. Let us agree on this one point. It matters not how much I detest those who feed on other's privacy, and how much you relish it. If I hear one breath of gossip regarding me attributable to you, I shall tell the world of your cowardly behavior last night. It is very simple, no?"

"I don't know what you're talking about, Your Grace," he gasped. "My intention was not to insult."

"Of course not. And by the by, you are not to say a word about Lady Derby either."

"I cannot imagine why I—"

"I can," Roman interrupted dryly and released the man. "Good night, sir."

He crossed back to the group of people who were not even trying to appear disinterested. He bowed to them with hauteur and turned on his heel without a word. Roman grasped Esme's hand and placed it on his arm, nearly tugging her to walk back to the inn. "Why pray tell," he ground out, determined to change the topic, "were you going to Vienna?"

"I refuse to reply until you answer my request."

"And which request was that?" He had a bad feeling in the pit of his gut.

"The one which you will stop drinking all spirits as a measure of your gratitude to me for saving your hide last night and for allowing you to escape parson's mousetrap, Your Grace."

"Montagu, damn it."

"Do you always blaspheme in front of ladies?"

"Do you always make unreasonable demands?"

"It was not a demand. It was a request."

"A bloody absurd one."

"The best ones are, Montagu."

"What has this to do with last night?"

"It has everything to do with it if you think about it. Did you not find yourself on a ship in the middle of a storm because of an obscene amount of spirits?"

"I meant what has this to do with what happened between us?"

She paused and looked into his eyes. "It is important to me."

He sighed and scratched the back of his neck again. "Fine. Whatever pleases you, March."

"Do I have your word, Montagu?"

What in hell?

"Between gentlemen, their word is law," she reminded him.

"This is not between gentlemen. This is between you and me. Two people who confided in each other on the eve of near death."

"So are you proposing that we remain confidants?" She smiled.

He shook his head. He would never, ever, ever, understand the female mind. "It would seem there is little choice in the matter, March."

Roman realized later, much later, when he was alone in his chamber that if she wanted to be a confidant, why hadn't she confided more about herself to him? What in hell was really so important to her in Vienna? Was there any reason to leave the epicenter of the world—London?

And why did he even care? He would give his eyeteeth right now for a glass of his finest brandy. Hell, he would give them for fine wine, or even swill. His head ached again. A pox on all females who wanted to be treated as gentlemen.

Esme was certain she would sleep like the dead after so many eventful hours. It was not to be. She tossed and turned, dreaming fitfully of a shadowed figure on a ship, swinging about a mast and hitting his head. And of her not being able to reach him in time before he was dragged to the side of the ship only to slip over the railing and be swallowed by the sea. And then Lionel was in her arms and making love to her as he had always done, so slowly, so kindly, so lovingly, and so often drunkenly. But then his dazed eyes changed from brown to piercing sky blue and she pulled away only to find she was in the Duke of Norwich's arms and he was taking her with such force while terror colored his face.

The next morning she dragged her weary bones from the twisted sheets and gratefully accepted the ministrations of the inn's maid. She knew exactly what she was going to do today to restore her balance.

She nearly skipped out the front entrance of the Horse & Hound, bypassing the dining room and any chance of seeing the duke who had dogged her dreams.

Esme set her easel high atop a sea cliff, facing the chalk-white crags jutting into the sea in the distance. She set her watercolor paints on top of a stump and splashed water from her large flask into a cup. She carefully unfolded her spectacles and perched them on the end of her nose.

She sat motionless before the beauty of the scene in front of her and studied the play of sunlight on the water and the texture of the rocky ledges. It was not Italy, to be sure, but it was a delight to have new scenery to paint.

This was always how she had maintained her calm when the murky waters of sadness had threatened to overcome her in the past. Oh, no one had ever known when she had felt that way. No, that was not true. Lionel had known even when she had tried to hide it. And he had felt so guilty and made so many promises, always with a wincing grin, as he tried to cover the aftereffects in the morning.

She dabbed her largest brush in the water and washed a pale hue of sky over the parchment. There was not a single cloud.

Two hours later she swirled her smallest brush in the muddied water, tapped it gently, and carefully applied a hue of brown, gray and green shades to the bristles for the minutest touches to the greenery on top of the cliffs. Esme jarred her hand at the worst possible moment when she caught a glimpse out of the corner of her eye of someone walking toward her.

"Oh pish," she exhaled, when she saw that she had ruined the painting. She quickly dabbed at the brush stroke with a cloth.

It was he. The one who had plagued her thoughts all morning. She took him straight on.

"Good morning, Montagu." She reordered her brushes in the tall jar.

He completed the last few steps to her side. "And good day to you, March."

It pleased her that he used the name she had requested. She looked down only to find her apron was smeared a thousand shades of brown, the result of so many hours before an easel. She felt the sting of a blush rise from her bodice. She knew she didn't look her best, but she refused to care. It was hot under the sun.

"May I see?" he asked.

"No, it's ruined."

"Hmmm," he said in that infuriating tone people use when they would instantly disagree without even examining the issue.

She sighed and moved a little for him to see her work.

For long moments he studied her painting, until the silence became so loud, she felt the need to end it. She opened her mouth but he stopped her by raising his hand in the air.

"You are a great artist."

"It's my dream," she replied. "But not something that I can truly call myself."

"So you insist I call you March for no good reason and yet you refuse to acknowledge your talent." He sighed. "Makes perfect sense."

"A true artist is one who earns commissions on the strength of their talent. I have yet to do so. But art is my passion, and since the day I discovered paints at the age of five, no one has been able to remove a brush from my fingers."

He examined her and she had the worst feeling that he found her very ugly with her spectacles. She struggled against the urge to remove them.

She would not try to appear more alluring. There was not an alluring bone in her body.

"You will be heralded as one of the best painters of our generation," he said. "I am certain of it."

She bit back the urge to deflect praise. "Thank you. Do you paint too?"

"Of course not."

"Why do you say that?"

"Do I seem to you to be the sort of man who could be a dabbler or dilettante?"

"I'm a dilettante," she stated without hesitation.

"No, you're not," he replied. "Although what is that in the right upper corner? Birds?" He turned the full force of his blue eyes on her and smiled.

She hoped he couldn't see her nervousness at his proximity. "It's what happens when you don't take care and you get flustered by someone's approach."

He chuckled with that voice that was so deep and masculine that its effect surprised her.

"Maybe you could fix it."

He turned his gaze back to the painting and Esme noticed his extreme squint. She grinned.

"And what is so amusing?"

She removed her spectacles, which she only used for reading and painting, cleaned the lens with a cloth and handed them to him.

He stared at them aghast. "Why are you offering those?"

"Because you need them."

"Me? Why I've never needed spectacles in my life."

She smiled. "Are you too vain to try them?" She knew how to goad with the best of them.

"How ridiculous. Norwiches are not vain. Arrogant, to be sure. And perhaps a bit too much puffery on their hunting prowess—at least earlier dukes than I. But vain? Never."

"Really? Then why won't you try these?" She offered again. "Or are you going to insist Norwiches are never farsighted, too?"

He rolled his eyes and snatched her small, delicate spectacles. He put them on with a deep sigh of annoyance. "See? Vanity's not an issue. Don't need 'em. That's all. By the by, your eyes are . . . lovely." He turned to her painting. "Perhaps you could turn those spatters into a flock of birds. See if you just elongate the dots and put a sweep of wings on them . . ."

Esme slipped a tiny brush in his hand. "Show me."

He was completely engaged in studying the artwork. All thoughts concerning her eyes were obviously gone. But his compliment, the first she'd ever received about her eyes, warmed a tiny chamber of her heart, a place that rarely received compliments on her appearance.

He drew down three colors onto the palate and dabbled the brush before delicately applying the paint to the paper.

She watched, fascinated by his natural, raw talent. Most people approached the easel with trepidation and fear. Especially with watercolors, which were difficult to correct. But his ease with the brush, his instant concentration, and sure hand was surprising. Within minutes, her brown speckles were transformed into a flock of birds.

He gazed at the scenery, lifted her ridiculously dainty spectacles from his eyes for a few moments before dropping them back in place and continuing to add touches here and there.

She said not a word. Finally he handed the brush back to her. "You see, not so complicated."

She squinted intently at the painting. "Are those ducks?"

"No, those are not ducks," he said sourly.

"But they're rather large to be anything else."

"They're seabirds."

"They're too dark to be seabirds."

"Seabirds on the Isle of Wight are darker than the ones on the mainland."

"Really?"

"How in hell should I know, March."

"Then why did you say—"

"To suggest what you should tell other people when they ask why the seabirds are too damn dark."

"So you're telling me to lie, Montagu?"

"Of course. For the sake of art."

"You forgot that vice in your list of family faults."

"Not at all, March." He smiled. "I just lied when I told you the list."

She laughed. "Are you always like this?"

"How?"

"You don't act very much like other dukes I know."

"I beg your pardon," he said, acting extraordinarily affronted.

"The two I know don't smile very often." She paused and squinted at him wearing her spectacles. "Do my eyes look that large when I wear those?"

He carefully removed them and handed them to her. "Twice as large, I assure you. Shall we take the air then?" He offered an arm, which she accepted.

"And why do you not paint since it so obviously gives you pleasure, Montagu?" She liked very much using his family name instead of his title.

He pulled her closer to the cliff and gazed at the grassy ledge as he spoke. "Producing art is a trifling effort best left to men who are dreamers, or far worse. Math and science are truth. They are the primary efforts that solve the world's problems."

"I should not like to be there if you decide to spout your ideas concerning artists in a museum." She stopped and darted a glance to see his cool expression. "Well," she continued, "you're allowed an opinion. But if you think being an artist is of so little importance, what about someone who fritters away their time going from amusement to diversion with a band of renegade dukes who drink day in and day out?"

"I do not go to amusements and drink all day." He paused before the smallest smile teased his mouth. "I only do that at night, and only on occasion."

"And during the day?"

His sky blue eyes bore into hers and his mysterious, intense expression added to the devastating image he presented. She wondered how many ladies had given their hearts to him.

"During the day I decide what diversions I will choose for that night," he replied in a way that spoke of the opposite.

"Why do you do that?"

"What?"

"Pretend to be a jaded rake."

"Perhaps I am a jaded rake."

"You're not," she insisted. "I know that animal very well."

"Really?" His eyebrows rose.

"Yes. For example, I would say the out and out bounder in the royal entourage is the Duke of Abshire, no?"

She noticed he had a funny habit of scratching the back of his head when he didn't want to answer a question.

"Well," he said slowly, "he is not an innocent. Are you well acquainted with Abshire?"

"Don't look so surprised. We are, of course, acquainted."

"How so?"

"I was raised in Derbyshire and so was he. And he was one of my husband's intimates for a time. A very short time, actually." She tried to keep the wistfulness out of her tone. "His ducal seat lies in the parish next to our manor, or rather the new Earl of Derby's manor."

"I don't recall well your husband, March. Was he a good man? Or are you glad to be rid of the nuisance of a husband ordering you about?"

She dropped her arm from his and stared at the sea from the path on the cliff. A strong wind buffeted her hair and she knew she would look like a washerwoman by the time they returned to the inn for supper. She really didn't care at all. "He was the best of men, Montagu." She paused and whispered the last, "And the worst."

Chapter 4

As Roman dressed for the revelry on the village green that early evening, his mind turned to the last words she had uttered before she had changed the subject and insisted they return to the Horse & Hound to prepare for the festivities.

It appeared the folk on Wight organized merriment on that day each year. And since there was nothing better in the offing, the majority of those who had been aboard the ship had decided to partake.

He ducked down and peered out the window of his small but very clean chamber. He racked his brain to try and remember what he knew about Lord Derby. For God sakes, he should be able to remember something about him. Then again, there were far too many earls—ninety *bloody* four if he remembered correctly—to keep track of in England, compared to dukes.

What had she meant when she had said he was the best of men and the worst? Sounded like a typical absurdity from a lady. No. He could not say that. March was not one of those flittering, giddy, empty-headed creatures who floated on silk and spouted nonsense while too busy examining the beauty of their person.

God, his head ached. He would have given a pretty penny for a gulp or three of whiskey. Or even gin. How sodding ridiculous. Since when did he remotely depend on spirits to rebound from a night of debauchery?

What exactly had happened that night? It seemed such a long time ago, but really, it had been less than forty-eight hours since the royal entourage had gathered at Prinny's Carleton House to mourn the impending loss of bachelorhood of one of their own. Candover, bless his premier ducal soul, had been the poor sodding fellow who had finally capitulated to the familial requirements of taking a bride to secure an heir and a spare. Didn't he know better? Roman had decided long ago that marriage was certainly not the answer—especially if one was saddled with a curse. Yes, a cursed duchy should be left to molder and rest in peace.

Roman's mother would shake her head if she

heard him. Then again, she shook her head at him most of the time. Not that he didn't love her. He loved her almost as much as he loved his sister Lily. But that was only half as much as he had loved his brother Vincent. And it was forty-seven times more than he had liked his father—the man who had sent him away to school at the age of six in a ruthless campaign to exorcise all but mathematics and science from Roman's mind. Oh, there had been an English, French, and history course now and again, but never any drivel as Roman's father had described all art, music, and even philosophy.

Roman watched a group of workmen setting out tables, and then the maids followed with platters of food and by God, yes, pitchers of ale. Ale . . . hmmm. They had not had such common stuff at Carlton House of course.

His very good friend, Alex Barclay, the brand-spanking-new Duke of Kress (the duchy could not have devolved to a better fellow, really) had been the purveyor of the first round . . . and the second and maybe third round of spirits in the prince's apartments. It was that wretched, Frenchified licorice-smelling stuff that had done him in. None of them had ever tried it before. Just the thought of it made him want to retch.

Roman remembered vague flashes of events thereafter. He could swear some of them had gone swimming, which was ridiculous. And, of course, he was certain he hadn't partaken of that tomfoolery. But he could remember a huge swan squawking, and chasing him, trying to take a beak full of Roman's bloody arse. He sort of remembered a pistol trading hands in the night, and he recalled riding a huge gray horse over cobblestones—even though he didn't own a gray. The clattering had been nearly deafening. He shook his head. That was all he could remember. Nothing about the ship. Nothing about the—

A knock on the door sounded and he answered it himself. There was something very novel about having to do things for oneself. For as long as he could remember, he had not answered a door.

"Are you ready?" March's gray eyes held much merriment, the captain's less. The reality of his damaged vessel was most likely finally sinking in.

Roman bowed very slightly. Dukes were taught to bow in the fashion of almost a nod. "For anything, Lady Derby. Good evening, Captain."

"How fare thee, Your Grace?"

"I shall be better as soon as I figure out a way off this island without climbing onto another ship, sir, if I may be so bold."

The older man chuckled. "If you learn how to walk on water, I should be glad to see it."

Roman motioned with his hand indicating they should depart, and then they were in the well-lit whitewashed hall, and making their way down the front stair, where one in three steps creaked, but in a charming kind of way—like the stairs to the attics of Norwich Hall.

Despite the ache in his head, Roman kept a pleasant enough countenance. It had been ingrained in him: dukes did not complain. Unfortunately, he would have preferred to complain all the time. "Lovely calm evening," he stated.

"It's always like this after a storm," the captain replied.

"And always like this before a storm, too," she said pertly.

"Right you are, Lady Derby," the captain said chuckling. "Have you always liked sailing, then, madam?"

Roman nodded to the inn's footman to open the door. "I would wager she likes it better than anything."

"And why would you say that?" She eyed him from beneath her lashes. On any other woman it would have been coquettish. On her it seemed natural.

"You like it enough to go off alone. You didn't depart London with a single other acquaintance, if I understood it correctly." He paused. "Almost like you were running away."

The night air was cool, still, and very clear.

"Of course not," she said. "I do not like to bore

others and I'm determined to do exactly what I would like to do on this trip. And I would rather someone else not bore me for the same reason."

The captain looked between them as Roman and Lady Derby examined each other. "Pardon me, but I must have a word with Jem. Must find out how the repair is coming along."

Neither said a word as the captain departed until finally she turned to face him. "How very lowering. I obviously bored the man to pieces. Like I said, it's why I am traveling alone. Was it something I said?"

"Yes," he answered instantly. "It was precisely what you said."

"What did I say?"

"Well, if you can't remember, March, I shan't tell you. Why suffer embarrassment twice when we can just ignore the whole thing and keep walking. Toward the table."

"What's on the table that's so fascinating?"

"Ummm, the spiked eel looks very good, no?"

She made a face. "No."

"The filet of goat, then?"

"Ugh." She wore an insufferably smug smile. "You're looking at the ale."

"Of course it's the ale. I'm bloody thirsty."

She turned serious. "But you promised."

"I promised not to drink spirits, for some insane reason. I must have been rummy to the gills to make such a promise. But that is just ale—not spirits at all." He nodded toward the tankards. "I must have been truly foxed to agree to something like that."

"No. Just suffering the regret of the night before," she replied.

He tugged at her arm. She willingly followed him to the relative privacy of the willow tree near the line of tables.

She examined him. "Tell me. Do you crave it?"

"I beg your pardon."

"Do you think about it all the time? My husband did, I think."

He stood very still. Finally, he would know who Derby was. "And what happened to him?" he asked carefully.

"You did not know him? Hmmm. I would have thought you might have."

He wished he had. It would allow him to know her better. "I'm not sure I did. The name is very familiar though."

She blushed for some odd reason. "I'm not surprised." She shrugged her shoulders. "But most of his friends deserted him in the end."

"Why, that is deplorable. What did he do to deserve such treatment?" he encouraged.

"Surely you can guess." She tilted her chin up. "He drank himself to death."

It was hard to think of a response to such brutal honesty. He slowly replied, "I am sorry to hear it."

"And I am not certain if I made his life better or worse. You see, I helped keep him alive. The doctor said he would not have lasted as long if I hadn't been there," she said, without pride. "I merely extended his misery."

Or yours, he thought to himself.

She quickly changed the subject. "It's the hair of the dog, right? You really would like some."

"No, no. I'd like just to quench my thirst. It was overly warm today, don't you think, March?"

She smiled that enchanting way and he thanked God those spectacles of hers were nowhere to be found.

"Drunken Derby . . ." she said quietly with a pleasant enough expression.

"Sorry?"

"My husband, Lionel. They used to call him *Drunken Derby* behind his back. They didn't think I heard them."

A thousand and one sticks in the house of his brain fell into place. Oh, for Christsakes. *He* was her husband. Or rather, *had been* her husband. The saddest yet most entertaining spectacle in Town—*Drunken Derby.* A gentleman who one never saw sober and who rarely remained standing throughout a night. He was ruined with a capital R.

No wonder she was hell-bent on reforming him. Well, Roman would set her right, straightaway. "I am not like your husband."

"Of course you're not. I would never insult you, Your Gr—"

"I told you to call me Montagu."

"—Montagu. But I want you to know that Lionel was not like others knew him. He was very kind, very jovial."

In truth, Derby had managed to do and say things so jovial and *offensive,* Roman remembered, that three quarters of the ballroom doors had been closed to him when he died a year or so ago.

Roman eyed the ale. Even though he was parched, he just didn't have it in him to reach for a tall tankard of the pale golden brew. Her assumptions were ridiculous, of course, of that he held not a single doubt.

"It's all right," she said. "I never expected you to keep your word."

Instead, he reached for the lemonade on the other side of the table and handed her a glass before taking one for himself. He eyed it with distrust.

She smiled and then took a sip. A dainty sip.

He gulped it down before the god-awful tartness nearly gagged him. "Delicious," he said, his taste buds revolting at the bitterness.

"Agreed," she replied. "Very good."

"If you are partial to lemons that is."

"Oh, take the bloody ale," she retorted.

"Not if my life depended on it."

"Well!"

"Well," he replied. "Shall we participate in lawn bowling?"

"Oh, yes," she said, eyes shining. "Oh, but I do not have my spectacles."

"Thank God," he muttered.

"That wasn't very flattering."

He liked it when she bristled. Females never dared bristle in his presence. They were either too much in awe or they were determined to catch the matrimonial prize of the decade by fawning in earnest. "You misunderstood. I meant that I am glad you forgot your spectacles so that I would have a better chance at besting you."

"Well, I shall just go back and retrieve them."

He held her back. "No. I'm actually famished. Let's eat."

"Are you always this grumpy and impolite?"

He almost choked with laughter. She was an original. "Grumpy? I've never been grumpy in my life. And I'll have you know that I'm in an excellent mood."

"Really?"

"Really."

"Well, I think you are just suffering the effects of being foxed like a skunk, Montagu."

"It takes a brave female to call me a skunk,

March." He made an exasperated sound as he picked up another glass of lemonade. This was utterly ridiculous. Just because her husband had been a blindingly mad drunk did not make him a fool when he enjoyed a pint of ale.

"Thank you, Montagu," she murmured sweetly.

Blast it all. That damned smile of hers made him almost want to drink the rest of the vile stuff he held in his hand. Almost, but not quite.

She was surprised he didn't just reach for the ale. She had never teased anyone the way she had just goaded the Duke of Norwich. She should not be so forward and provoking. It bordered on impolite—something she had never been in the past. She just wasn't sure why she couldn't stop herself.

Oh, she had a very good idea. It was the past. Her husband had chosen whiskey over a long life with her. And yet he had not been able to help it and so she couldn't blame him even if she secretly did. And that irritated her more than anything for he had seen the good in her when no one else had. And he had married her when no one else would. She had been a wallflower of the first order. He had rescued her from entrenched spinsterhood, and a lifelong sentence of uncompromised virginity. And then he had taught her all about pleasure, and about love, before he had fallen into the grips of a passion stronger than his with her.

The duke was leading her to one of the long tables, and the common folk made a space for the two of them. They sat side by side instead of across from each other. It was too bad the villagers were so in awe of him that there was not a chance of anonymity. They were surrounded by avid listeners.

He seemed to be able to read her mind and so they ate in relative silence. He consumed more food than she had ever witnessed someone eat in her life. Chicken and cabbage, lamb pudding with raisins, and even the beef with boiled potatoes. He did, however, push aside the breast of duck.

His table manners were flawless. He held his fork and knife as if they were artist's tools and the food was the medium. She watched as he quickly and deftly removed the skin of a pear without once touching the fruit with his fingers. And then she remembered what those same fingers had done to her.

Not for the first time did Esme remember what had happened between them not so very long ago—but what seemed almost a lifetime ago. He was so very handsome, like a prince—no, a king—come to life. But she was no princess. She was more the coach that turned into a pumpkin at midnight. And she was certain the events of that night would never be repeated. She wasn't even certain she would want them to be repeated. The intensity of it had been unnerving.

Eventually a small group of musicians gathered and began tuning their assorted instruments. "Shall we?"

"Are you certain you want to?"

"Why I love to dance, March. I like it almost as much as I like gambling and drinking and carousing."

"Of course you do."

He was trying to tease her.

"And besides, March, you won't need your spectacles to dance." He stretched out his palm and she placed her own in his and he led her to the center of the square. The shadows of the trees and the lanterns within them created an eerie yet romantic atmosphere. Surprisingly, in this rustic setting, the musicians began a waltz.

He grasped her waist in one hand and her fingers in the other, exerting complete control of their movements—just like he had at the end of the surreal, intimate act in the ship's cabin. It was a minute or two before he chanced to speak.

"So what was he really like, March?"

"Who?"

"Your husband of course."

"Why do you ask?"

"Because I refuse to talk of the weather. And . . ."

"And?"

"And I refuse to talk about me."

"But all dukes like to talk about themselves."

He smiled. "Not always. I rather remember your husband now. He was a, ahem, jovial sort as you said."

"That is putting it kindly," she said. "He was a desperate case."

"And yet, you loved him."

She started. "That's a very private matter."

He examined her face closely and she wanted to look away. "Yes," he continued gently, "you loved him and I suspect he loved you."

She swallowed. "And how would you know these things?" Her voice was a bit too high-pitched to her own ears.

"I am good at guessing."

She didn't know how to respond. She didn't want to respond. She had not spoken of this to anyone.

"Perhaps you're correct," she finally admitted. "It was a very good match even if it was officially an arranged marriage. My father was his father's best friend in the world and we had known each other most of our lives." She didn't want to tell the whole story. But for some odd reason she felt compelled to speak. "Something grew of it. He was very gentle and kind to me. He encouraged me. In the end, I do believe he liked me very much. And I him."

"He loved you," he stated again.

She stared at him and said nothing.

"And so you are in mourning."

"No. It has been a year since he died. A year and four months."

The waltz came to an end and he eased his grip on her waist. She was sorry he released her and led her back to the serving tables now filled with custard and fruit pies. His appetite was unimaginable.

"May I ask how he actually died?" He gathered two plates full of desserts and found a table where all the occupants had departed.

"Oh, the doctor would tell you all manner of complicated terms. Does it matter?"

"It explains your request."

"You cannot say it's a surprise. But now that you know, I am letting you off the hook again, Montagu. You have done your duty. You may go ahead and drink that ale you long for."

He looked at her with those unnerving pale blue eyes of his and did not move. "Thank you. I think I shall." He paused but did not move to pour a drop. "A bit later perhaps." His eyes had become quite serious.

A trumpet sounded and the voices of the revelers dimmed again as the haphazard orchestra struck the notes of a country dance. Sets were forming in the middle of the green and the Duke of Norwich raised one eyebrow and again offered his hand without a word.

She grasped it. "Oh, thank you. I suppose I

should warn you that I make it a point never to refuse the opportunity to dance." The wallflower within her had never wilted. She would have to have one foot in the grave before she would refuse to dance with anyone. She had spent too many years on the edges of too many ballrooms, a smile plastered to her face, as every other lady was asked to dance except her.

He smiled. "I only am asking you to dance to show you there is nothing wrong with living solely for diversions and entertainments."

She felt deflated.

He tilted up her face with a finger under her chin. "Ahem. I suppose I should now warn you that I sometimes say the opposite of what I mean in jest."

A warm feeling, very much like her favorite plum pudding hot off the fire, invaded her heart.

He didn't know why he kept up this front with her. She was a kindhearted lady and there was no reason for him to try and charm her. It was just that he had always assumed different façades for different people for so long that he didn't know how to be himself. Unless he was alone. There was only one thing he was serious about, and it wasn't diversions. It was physics and geometry and mathematics. There was nothing humorous about absolutes. And he loved the beauty of solving concrete problems without any remaining gray areas clouding the resolution.

There were only three people who knew a few details—a very few—of his life and interests and they were Kress, Abshire, and Candover, all members of the exclusive royal entourage. It was just a shame that the three of them did not get on. Abshire and Candover positively loathed each other. And Candover considered Kress a half-baked Englishman with French revolution on his mind, while Kress considered Candover a priggish bore devoted solely to duty and without an ounce of humor. They were both correct in their assumptions. Abshire and Kress's friendship showed promise but was still in the making.

Roman accepted Esme's gloved hand in his and led her to the set that was forming. He had never bowed to dairymaids, or do-si-do'd with innkeepers, but there was always a first time. He followed the pattern of the simple dance and enjoyed the effort. There was none of the jaded elegance of the amusements in town. There was only much laughter and boisterousness. And these simple folk sweated and didn't try to hide their enthusiasm.

Roman kept an eye on March. She was enjoying the dance too. There was a sparkle in her gray eyes and a lightness to her step. The way she held her head and the arch of her back was lithe and graceful. She might not be a ravishing beauty but there was something about her that intrigued him. If she were not a gently bred lady he would have enjoyed taking her to his bed again and making love to her. And he would kill to see and touch and stroke those legs of hers again.

But there was something else about her that stopped him. She had this untouchable air to her. She had dignity and he couldn't bring himself to suggest a liaison. It was ridiculous, really. Widows were his prime favorites in town. But he worried her heart might become engaged, and he would not hurt her after all she had done for him.

The only question was why had this intelligent lady loved her husband. And while she had loved him, it had been obvious he had loved spirits more than he had loved anything else.

Yes, Lord and Lady Derby were just one more example of what was wrong with marriage. And there was a lot that was wrong with marriage. His parents' cold, dutiful, typical ton union was a prime example.

And he was the result.

Chapter 5

What was that confounded sound? Roman opened one eye to find that his chamber at the small inn was still dark.

Birds. It was birds chirping. Oh, for God sakes. This was the reason he preferred Town. No bloody birds to wake one up. The clattering of hooves on cobblestones, yes. Birds, no.

He tried to settle back into the cocoon of the bed and could not. He finally groaned and got out of the great yawn of a mattress which took up more than three quarters of the quaint room not fit for a duke.

And he was exhausted. Country hours were for the birds. Quite literally. He grimaced.

The scent of oil was about; he sniffed to be certain. She was at it again in the room adjacent to his.

Painting. Forever painting. He crossed to the window and opened the sash for fresh air.

Her industriousness was astounding. Since he loved his own work, he understood her devotion, but it was unusual for a female. As he watched a maid pumping water from the well on the green, his fingers itched to find paper and a ruler to further his designs.

He was torn about his immediate concerns. On the one hand he needed to be in Town; on the other, his mind froze at the thought of stepping onto a gangplank again. But his ideas were in delicate balance right now. He had to go back. His desire to find a permanent solution to supply all of London with clean water had flaws.

It was beyond ridiculous that the center of Christendom had seven private companies who refused to provide water more than two hours each day. He would find a solution or die trying.

Indeed, before that fateful night with Candover, Kress, and the others in the entourage, he had been certain he was on the verge of solving the pump problem plaguing the huge design.

His evenings were spent thusly—lost at his drafting table, except when forced to play the part of draconian brother while his beautiful sister Lily selected a husband. This at least served to occupy his mother so she wouldn't harass him to find a bride to continue the bloody, cursed Norwich line. One would think his mother would know better than to urge further creation of Norwich dukes. Why, he found it bordering on premeditated murder during his more lighthearted moments.

Well. He was just going to have to screw up his courage and take the next ship back.

He would just have to drink until he fell into a stupor and then have someone carry him onto the ship. After, he would never set foot on anything that floated again. He would remain forever in the lovely peace of England, where—

A sound snagged his attention and he chanced to see the captain crossing the village green toward the Horse & Hound. Roman was glad the rest of the passengers from the fateful voyage had sailed from Wight yesterday afternoon. Only he and March had remained. He from his fear; she from her desire to complete a painting. Or so she said. He had the ridiculous notion that she might have stayed behind to coddle him when he regained the nerve to cross the sea back to London. It was lowering to be considered the coward that he was. He didn't know why it mattered so much what she might think of him. The rest of the passengers—indeed, humanity—he could care less about.

The last time he had seen that sodding Mr. King, as well as Lady Shelby and her friends, Roman had had the distinct feeling they were all of them enjoying quite the tittle-tattle about his refusal to go with them. He knew they all laughed about his family's history, just as most everyone else in Town.

He sighed when the captain suddenly looked up and made a motion toward him.

"Hey ho, Your Grace. Have something you will want to see." The rotund man waved a newspaper in the air.

He had no desire to go downstairs. Roman would much rather crawl back under the covers, request a coffee, and close his eyes so he could become lost in the diagrams that were constantly filling his mind.

Instead, he scratched the back of his head, yawned, and pulled on his discarded, borrowed clothes. At least the shirt he now wore fit him better than the captain's. Thank God there had been a retired admiral on the isle who had been willing to come to his aid, and was much the same size.

Roman didn't even bother to shave. He dashed cold water on his face and dried it before descending below. While the deprivations of life without servants at every corner were inconvenient, there was something to be said for the expediency of doing for oneself.

He caught the attention of the parlor maid and asked for coffee and breakfast to be delivered to the salon in which the captain waited on him.

"Good morning, Captain." Roman nodded.

The captain chuckled as he always seemed wont to do. "You might want to reconsider that idea after you've had a look-see at this."

The balding man removed his hat, shoved it under his arm and placed the newspaper on the edge of a low-slung table between two well-padded brown leather armchairs in front of a small fire, attempting to chase the chill of the morning.

Roman took his seat. "Do join me, sir."

"Of course. Actually, I am more than a mite curious to know if the report is true."

"What report?"

"Front page, center. I should tell you I asked the footman to fetch Lady Derby as well. There is a ship just arrived and since it is the last scheduled to depart for London for at least a week, she might very well want to prepare to depart. It's too bad there are no ships bound for Prague or Vienna for her to continue on, but one can't expect that. She will just have to return to—" The captain stopped. "Well, are you going to read the article or not?"

"It's a bit rude since you're speaking."

"Balderdash," the captain said. "Go on, then. What I really want to know is did you really do it?"

"Do what?"

"Swim with the king's swans in the Serpentine." The captain ended with his signature chuckle that rumbled like an approaching storm.

"I beg your pardon?" That feminine voice

Roman was beginning to know very well interrupted them both. He glanced at the doorway to find Esme March standing there, as cool and collected as he was not. Early risers always had that air about them. The one of having bathed and gotten half the day done before the rest of humanity had had a rasher of bacon, several eggs and a loaf of toast to see them through dinner, which was a distant four or five long hours hence. If one got out of bed when Roman did, that is.

The captain pointed at the newspaper still lying on the table. "News from London, Lady Derby. Fairly interesting actually." He glanced at Roman. "I've always found swans to be vicious, Your Grace. What say you?"

Roman wanted to close his eyes desperately. A wisp of a memory of the swan that had chased him floated past. God. It was in the newspaper? He reached for it at the same moment the countess did.

Only the politeness that had been drilled into him from the moment of his birth allowed him to relinquish his grip to her lighter one.

At least she wasn't wearing a reproving expression on her face like his mother usually did. Then again, this lady had been married to the most dissolute aristocrat in all of England. What would she care about a simple midnight run-in with royal fowl?

She began to read to herself and her gray eyes bugged out most unattractively as her spectacles made her peepers twice as large.

He sighed. "One can hope you are not going to keep the rest of us in suspense for too long."

The captain interrupted. "Not a worry, Lady Derby, I've already read it."

Roman harrumphed. "Well I haven't and it's all about me, according to you." He glared with hauteur at the seaman.

Her eyes were glued to the page, her lips moving slightly. She held up her hand. "It's very bad. Do you want to read it yourself?"

A maid delivered a tray brimming with delicious fare. He delicately picked up the rasher of bacon and tucked into it. He waved his hand. "No, no. Go on, have your laugh and read it to me."

Reluctantly, she returned her bespectacled gaze to the top of the sheet. "It's dated the morning after we departed Town." She shook her head and began. " 'In a continuation of the regular obscene excesses of the Prince Regent and his *royal entourage,* not one of the party made an appearance at St. George's earlier this morning, with the exception of our Princess Caroline, darling little Princess Charlotte, and Her Grace, the young Duchess of March. His Majesty's absence and that of the groom and groomsmen caused all four hundred guests to assume the worst. And indeed, this columnist has it on the very best authority, partially one's own eyewitness account, that not only the august bridegroom, His Grace, the Duke of Candover, but also seven other dukes, one archbishop, and the Prince Regent himself, were seen cavorting about all of London last eve on an outrageous regal rampage. Midnight duels, swimming amok with the swans in the Serpentine, a stream of scantily clad females in tow, lawn bowling in unmentionables, horse races in utter darkness, wild, uproarious boasting, and jesting, and wagering abounded. Indeed, this author took it upon himself to retrieve and return to White's Club their infamous betting book, which one of the royal entourage had had the audacity to remove without even a by-your-leave. In this fashion we have learned that the Duke of Kress lost the *entire* fortune he so recently acquired with the title, although the winner's name was illegible. Even the Queen's jewels were spotted on one duke as he paraded down Rotten Row. Yes, my fellow countrymen, it appears the English monarchy has learned nothing from our French neighbor's lessons concerning aristocratic overindulgence. As the loyal scribe of the Fashionable Column for two decades, you have it on my honor that all this occurred and worse. I can no longer remain silent on these reoccurring grievous, licentious activities, and so shall be the first plain-speaking, brave soul to utter these treasonous words: I no longer support or condone a monarchy such as this.'"

The Countess of Derby halted. The normally bustling inn was so quiet, Roman had the distinct impression every last occupant in the residence was listening beyond the door.

He could not move from the shock of it. It was worse than he could have ever dreamed possible. Candover had stood up his bride? It had been billed as the marriage of the decade. And Roman's closest friend, Kress? *Ruined*. Roman uttered an oath no lady had probably ever heard in her life. He looked at her and she stared back at him unwaveringly.

He immediately rose and the rasher of bacon fell to the floor, in an act of inelegance which would have horrified him in normal circumstances. Would anything in his life ever be normal again?

He was going to *swim* to London if there was no vessel to take him. Within seconds he had a plan. "Captain, a handsome sum is yours if you secure a berth within that ship you mentioned."

"Wait. There's more," the captain said, with something like a damned twinkle in his faded blue eyes.

"More," Roman replied indignantly. "How could there possibly be something worse?"

The other man pulled another thin copy of the *Morning Post* from his waistcoat. "I snagged this from the captain of the ship which left port yesterday."

Roman snatched it while Esme March kneeled down to retrieve the fallen food.

"Leave it," Roman barked.

"I will not," she retorted. "The drippings will stain the nice carpet and I know you'll not want a servant in here while you read. You might say or do something you regret."

The captain nodded. "Aye, he will. Especially when he gets to the part where—"

"Enough," Roman nearly shouted. He waved them away and scanned the print. He refused to read it aloud.

Hell.

This columnist is delighted to inform that His Majesty has had *words* with his intimate royal entourage following the grave debauchery and bungled wedding of the Duke of Candover earlier this week. What words did he have? Why the words of a monarch, pretending he had no part in the high flown antics of these privileged dukes of the realm. Word has it in Carleton House that Prinny had the audacity to chastise his cohorts while it was obvious his royal nob was half shaven and he was still green about the gills like the rest of them.

And his orders to his favorites? Reform, cast

away all idea of sin (especially all mistresses), marry according to their station, produce heirs, and allow not one hint of scandal to touch them further.

I suppose the prince does not care for the rotting vegetables that he is forced to endure each time he attempts to leave the glittering prism that is known as Carleton House.

According to an intimate in the matter, Kress is to be the first on the marital chopping block. The duke has been sent south to molder in Cornwall until a gaggle of suitable candidates for marriage and their various chaperones and parents can be sent to surround him. Other sacrificial dukes are to follow.

The one duke, however, who is not to go, is the Duke of Norwich, *who cannot be found.*

Let it not be said that this columnist is not willing to do his utmost to help find this duke gone awry. May I be so bold as to beg everyone who chances to read this column to search high and low for this important peer, known as Seventeen to his cohorts in crime. And if you do not start by searching every last place where a duck or a cousin to a duck may be found, why, this columnist will think you a simpleton. Even if it is far too soon to plant yet another Duke of Duck, I would wager my last column that the curse has had her way with him. And by the by if you take this matter to heart, the art of duke hunting is simple: plan a grand entertainment, send invitations, and lure him in with plenty of spirits and deviltry.

Long live the king!

The next king. After the Prince Regent is sent packing.

The paper fell from his fingers. March was good enough not to immediately retrieve it.

Roman opened his mouth like a carp and then shut it when no words would come out.

"Oh, come, come, Your Grace. 'Tis not that bad." When Roman remained silent and motionless, the captain changed tactics. "Do you want me to find a ship sailing to some port far, far away? You could hide until the worst of it blows over. That's what I would do."

The countess casually reached down and finally retrieved the paper. He did not want to be in the same room with her when she read it.

"Captain, I shall triple the amount of coin that found its way into your pockets from taking on passengers on your last voyage if you get me the hell off this bloody isle *today*."

Without missing a beat, the captain retorted. "Understood. And is Lady Derby departing as well?"

Roman looked at her and she nodded without a word as she finished reading the last of the column. Her face was as white as the underbelly of a royal swan.

The captain nodded and took his leave of them both. An awkward silence invaded the room.

"Go ahead and say it," he insisted raggedly.

She paused before responding. "It's never been my way to beat a man when he's facedown in the muck."

"And why is that?"

"No one needs someone else to tell them they are a fool. Most are capable of figuring it out all by themselves."

He could not bring himself to look at her.

"What"—she continued—"are you going to do when you arrive in Town?"

"First things first. Let's see if I survive the voyage." He finally met her gaze. She was still holding the rasher of bacon. For the first time in his life, he had lost his appetite. He grasped the now cold food and placed it on the tray. Covering it with a napkin, he continued. "You might want to reconsider your decision to travel on the same ship as I. You know it's not safe to rub feathers with the Duke of Duck." The last he said with all the distaste he could muster.

"You know," she said. "I like you."

He swiveled his head toward her. "Yes, well, your taste in gentlemen is . . . oh hell. Forget it. I can't be trusted to say or do a bloody honorable thing right now."

She ignored him. "I like you because you don't shy away from the truth and you don't offer up excuses." She turned on her heel, her head high, and her back straight. Without looking at him again, she left him alone.

Roman was not proud of what he did. But a man had to do the only thing he could do to accomplish an end result. In this case it was the last thing the Countess of Derby would have liked. This would take her respect for him down a peg or two.

He had not a doubt that the captain of *The Drake* would secure a berth in the ship to take him to Town. He was so certain that within a quarter of an hour he had accomplished two key tasks. The first was to make Jem, the captain's doltish, coltish, and trustworthyish cabin boy an offer that would leave the young man crying in gratitude. The second was to offer the innkeeper the same amount for an entirely different reason. Both sums were to ensure that they kept their word upon striking hands on the bargain, and more important, that they kept their mouths shut. The men were eager to comply.

The innkeeper supplied Roman with the finest whiskey the Isle of Wight possessed, with a few bottles of fine wine thrown in. Once they were on the vessel, Jem watched Roman as he steadily plowed through the bottles. The cabin boy knew the second part of his job was to stand guard over him all the way to the London docks, and then deliver him to the massive townhouse in Wyndam Square.

If they made it.

It was a large if.

A large percentage of the list of Jem's duties also included keeping the Countess of Derby away from him. Roman wanted no part of any of the solutions she might offer—even if they included a repeat performance of the last time they were stuck in a cabin together. He didn't need a managing female now. He needed complete and total oblivion. And short of having Jem punch his lights out, this—this glass of whiskey he held in his hand—was the only sensible solution.

The only problem was that it was not doing the job. No matter how much he consumed, he remained stone cold sober. He was methodical in his efforts. He could not drink too quickly as he would become ill. He could not drink too slowly for then there would be no effect. And he could not offer a drop to Jem to act as a drinking companion for then he would not be able to carry through with the rest of the damn plans.

"Yer Majesty," the young man said with deference befitting a crowned head of Europe. "Does you wants me to open the wine?"

"Perhaps that will finish me off. Have at it, Jem." He watched with amusement as the boy attacked the cork with vigor. But his gut clenched as he felt the pitch and sway of the ship as they departed the harbor.

For the third time in an hour a knock sounded at the door. A muffled female voice seeped into the room. "Montagu. I would have a word with you." Silence. "Don't think I don't know you're in there. And I know what you're doing. Let me in." More silence. He was sure he heard an exasperated sigh. "You owe me, remember?"

Of course she would throw that in.

"I have the key and I'm not afraid to use it," she finally said, her voice very clear.

"Lean against the door," Roman whispered and pointed to the threshold. The first threads of silken oblivion were finally taking hold.

"But—" Jem began.

"Do it," Roman insisted.

The young deckhand shook his head and mumbled something but did as he was bid.

The sound of a key being inserted in the lock was quite clear. Jem leaned against the door and rolled his eyes.

A moment later Jem was flat on his bottom, the door open. "I tried to tell yew, Yer Majesty. Them doors here open outwards."

"I don't think you told me that precisely Jem. But that's all right. Never been able to keep a lady away when she had her heart set on finding me." He slurred the last two words. "Well, now that you're here, my dear, make yourself useful, will you? Would you like to go on as we did before or would you prefer to uncork the wine?"

"Jem," she directed to the young man, "you may take your leave. I'll call you if we need you."

"Well, I like that, undermining my *authority* with the *shervants* now, are you?" he said it with as much dignity as a man about to pass out could muster.

Jem knew when he was outgunned. He did the right thing by tucking his tail between his legs and getting the hell out of the way. "I'll be right outside the door, Yer Majesty." He backed out of the cabin, in the manner of a commoner taking his leave of his sovereign.

"You should be ashamed of yourself," she said quietly as she turned to lock the door and slid the key into her half boot.

"Is that the best you can do?" he asked, pleased he did not slur. "A goddamned platitude?"

"At least it's far more polite than you can manage in this state."

"And you don't even *possessesss* (why were there so many bloody esses in that word?) the, the originality to hide the key in a different place than the last time, do you?"

"You want originality?" She said it so softly it masked the anger in her voice. "I'll show you bloody originality if you don't apologize."

"For what?" His head was spinning as he ground out the words.

"For suggesting I would ever offer to you again what I was kind enough to share with you once."

He would have apologized. Really he would have. It was just that the entire bottle of whiskey chose at that precise moment to alter the delicate alchemy of his brainbox and he passed out cold on the bunk beside him.

Chapter 6

Esme wondered under which star she had been born to anoint her the Patron Saint of All Drunkards. At least this time, she did not have to talk, or cajole, or even comfort.

In this tiny cabin on some ship the name of which she was not even certain, there would be no repeat performance of the events on *The Drake*. The Duke of Norwich was so deep in his cups that his lips were resting on the bottom of the glass, or bunk as it were. She sat beside his prone form.

Well, after this voyage, she would never see him again. It was a promise she made to herself here and now. She forced away all her old romantic dreams she had formed the first time she had seen him in that ballroom all those years ago. No man would haunt her dreams ever again. Her only passion would be her art.

The voyage wasn't long. And so she sat watching him the entire journey, after she had dismissed Jem from his post with the promise that she would not breathe a word to His Grace.

When they docked, she watched Jem put him in a common hack carriage and give directions to his famed townhouse.

Esme turned from the sight and allowed one of the ship's officers to hail another hack for her. She was going to the lovely Derby townhouse in a less prominent address in Mayfair. Oh, it was still very fashionable, but it was not Number 1, Wyndam Square. The new earl was a kindly relation who always welcomed her and, indeed, had invited her to reside at any of his estates at any time she wished. Peter March was of the mind that dowager cottages were frightful things and he would brook every argument on her side to remove from Derby residences to live with her mother, the Dowager Countess of Gilchrist. And so Esme had chosen to reside on Derby property. There was the added benefit that her mother often came to stay for long visits.

When Esme laid her head on a pillow at Derby Hall after a surprised yet delighted greeting by the new earl that night, a list formed in her head of all the things she had to accomplish on the morrow to resume as soon as possible her trip to see the vast, marbled art museums in Prague and Vienna. Never in her wildest imaginings would she have guessed that she would wake only a few short hours later to meet her future husband.

It began with a discreet royal summons. An anomaly if ever there was one. A royal summons was usually accomplished with much fanfare. Not that she knew much about royal summonses, but she could imagine them. Peter March, dressed in proper nightclothes since it was three o'clock in the morning when they were awakened, was vastly impressed, though left stuttering by the request that she should wait on the Prince Regent that instant. He wanted to accompany her, but the summons clearly stated that she was to come alone. Reassuring Peter with a promise to return or send a note, she took her leave, with haste.

Bewigged coachmen in light blue satin livery nearly threw down a roll of carpeting as they escorted her into the gold dipped carriage fit for a queen. Indeed, it looked very much like the Queen's favorite barouche, if Esme was to hazard a guess.

The only problem was that Esme looked nothing like a queen. She feared she looked very much like a dairymaid. The Prince Regent's messenger had insisted they depart without a minute to spare. Esme had been roused from her bed, her hair in rolling rags no less, with nothing more than a thin, pale lavender robe covering her fine lawn nightclothes. There was nary a scrap of lace or ruffle in sight. Not even Betsy, her very young maid, was allowed to accompany her wherever they were taking her.

Within a quarter hour they drew into the mews of Carleton House, and Esme's spirits sank. She supposed she had known the minute she had seen the coat of arms on the side of the carriage what might be the cause of Prinny's demand.

A dozen servants hurried her through the vast, elegant tunnels to His Majesty's chambers; their footsteps echoed off the walls, magnificently decorated with portraits of eight hundred years of royalty.

She was pushed over the threshold of the royal chambers and a light click proved a lock had been engaged behind her. There were three people there—and only two did she know.

Roman inhaled sharply when he saw her and stepped back. A man dressed in the ways of the church stayed rooted to his spot but gazed skyward as if asking for a miracle.

She could have told him it was a useless cause. She had been praying for various miracles for nearly two decades without a single response. First she had prayed that beauty would creep up on her in her second decade. In her next decade she prayed that she possessed the sort of raw talent necessary to succeed at the highest levels of her craft. In her—

"Good evening, Lady Derby," the Prince Regent said, his fat hands beckoning her forward.

"Sire," she said, curtsying deeply. "Please excuse my appearance. I was told there was not a moment to lose and that it did not matter how I was garbed. I would never—"

"Never mind that, my dear," Prinny said. "I will see to it that you are gowned befitting your station shortly. Now then, please do stand next to your good friend Norwich, will you?"

"Of course, Your Majesty." She walked to Roman and nodded to him under her lashes.

He appeared dead on his feet, but he did not sway.

"Hello, again," he said simply.

"Hello, to you, too."

The prince clapped his hands. "You see, I knew it. You both will do very well together I am certain. You even speak to each other like an old married couple. You are to be—"

Esme's mind stuttered. Yes, her mind. And she did the unpardonable. She interrupted the ruler of Christendom. "I beg your pardon? Did Your Majesty just suggest we will do well together? In what fashion could you mean, sire?"

The prince gestured wildly with his hands, but said not a word. Roman spoke clearly. "You heard correctly. He means to marry us off." He paused. *"To each other."*

A chill down her spine chased away the heat from her nerves. "What?" She whispered much louder than she had meant to do. People did not interrupt the Prince Regent nor did they exclude him from the conversation. "I-I don't understand." She was dreaming. Having a nightmare.

"You understood, March." Roman scratched the back of his head restlessly. "It's that bloody Mr. King's doing. He came to His Majesty straightaway yesterday with a host of half-cooked suggestions and innuendos."

Prinny cleared his throat. "Are you two finished? Did not your parents teach you it is unforgivable to interrupt your sovereign and then continue the conversation in a manner that speaks of indifference to my being right before you?" The older man's wig slipped and a half-shaved head was revealed.

Esme bit her tongue to keep from laughing.

"Now, then. You are to be married in an hour's time."

She bit her tongue harder so she would not start to cry.

The prince's voice turned sour. "And I'm certain that vulgar little columnist, whoever he may be—and I fear it's a very rude woman, I do—will eventually report your marriage with great pride, which will be a balm for our nation. Of course I will choose the best moment to impart the news as we are all of us balancing—balancing, I tell you—on a very, very high bundle of twigs which could collapse at any time given the gravity of the moment."

Esme didn't bother to try to dissuade the Prince Regent from his silly ideas. She knew when a man was at his maximum limit, unable to see anything clearly. She knew the best course was to say not a word.

"Your Highness," Roman said rubbing his forehead with one hand. "This is impossible. I am certainly not the man for Lady Derby. And she does not want to marry me."

"And what does it matter what anyone wants these days? Do you think I want rotten potatoes thrown at my head every single morning? Do you think I want talk of revolution spreading through the country like a wildfire on a summer afternoon? You are to be married, I say. Right this blooming moment, sod it all."

Esme's heart was pounding so hard she could swear she could see it beating on her breastbone. She looked up to see the prince staring at her.

"Have you nothing to say about this, Countess?"

"May I be so bold as to ask if there is any other possible recourse? May I ask what happened precisely?" She tried to remain cool despite the fact that it was the first time she had spoken directly to the future king.

"Of course, my dear. Our dear Mr. King fancies himself the keeper of the moral code in Christendom. And . . ." He studied her with hooded eyes.

"And?" she urged.

Roman took over the topic. "And Mr. King will tell the world that we had a liaison and that he saw us touching hands and worse on that bridge on Wight."

"But we did nothing scandalous there. What did he suggest exactly?"

"He said we were carrying on in an infamous fashion, as he put it—despite His Majesty's threats and . . ." He looked at his sovereign.

"Oh, might as well tell her. Even my bribes these heat-riddled days appear to be far less enticing than in the past. When one is out of favor with the populous, one is truly out of favor. And that idiot of a man is poised to tell everyone and their dog about your, ahem, affair. Not that I would dream to suggest that either of you engaged in—in . . ." The prince looked at first one then the other of them.

Esme prayed that her face would not give her away. She tried to imagine herself as stone. The prince leaned forward and peered closer.

She blinked.

"Well." The Prince Regent shook his head slowly. "That is certainly a letdown. So you must look at it

this way, my dear—while your last husband's reputation was in shreds by the time he died, yours is unblemished. In fact I am not sure I have ever heard of you before now, if you will forgive me for saying."

Would anyone ever remember her except for Mr. King?

"You will both make a splendid match. The people of London will rejoice on the day I impart the good news. And I, for one, could not be more delighted. The thing of it is this. While Mr. King has promised not to say a word, I am willing to wager he will be able to glue his fleshy lips together for only so long. Maybe six weeks at the utmost?"

"How ridiculous," she muttered. "Please . . . please help me. I was planning on departing the country for at least a year in any case. This really isn't necessary. If you do not want me to depart, Your Majesty, I could instead take a carriage to my former residence, the Earl of Derby's manor in Derbyshire. I could remain there for a decade. Or two. And what should I care for what is said of me in London? But, surely there is no need to—"

"Oh surely there is, my dear," the prince repeated. "Now you, Lady Derby, are to follow Madame Cooper, a delightful émigré, who is waiting for you right outside these chambers. She will see to you and dress you properly. You shall adore her, I assure you."

"Pardon me?" She could not understand what the prince was saying.

Roman cut in. "He wants us to be married by the bishop"—he nodded to the thin man standing slightly behind him—"within the hour."

"But I couldn't possibly—"

"Oh you can and you will, my dear," the Prince Regent interrupted in a mollifying tone. "Indeed, I *command* it. Think of it this way. You will be doing me a favor. And I reward those who do me favors. And there is also the fact that you, ahem, made your own bed."

She pinned Montagu with a glare, which he returned balefully.

She could not think of a single argument. But she could run. Yes. She would smile, agree to anything and everything and then she would run. All the way to Prague and Vienna if needed. She was not the sort to be told what to do.

She curtsied without a word and backed out of her sovereign's chambers. Unfortunately, there were so many royal footmen lining the hallways she had not one chance for escape.

"I do not like to be kept waiting, Lady Derby," the prince called out to her. "I expect you to return within a half hour's time."

Esme choked on a retort. And she dragged her heels every moment to avoid the inevitable. The lady's maid assigned to her had other ideas. In an astonishingly short period of time Esme was stuffed, trussed, and plucked. She rubbed a spot between her eyes. "Why are you doing that?"

"It is attractive to have fewer hairs between your eyebrows, my lady," Jacqueline Cooper insisted.

"I don't care if there is a jungle growing between my brows. Stop that."

The royal lady's maid ignored her and kept plucking. And that was the least painful part of the skilled torturer's plans to transform her in twenty-odd minutes. The lady was ruthless. She tore out the rags in her locks and brushed her hair until it crackled. The maid said two or three little French curses while she curled Esme's light brown hair into a style that added twice as much volume as Esme had ever seen on her head. Her hair was actually the only feature she had that she liked. It now looked . . . quite beautiful.

Esme was so stunned at the vision staring back at her in the looking glass that she couldn't find the words to stop the woman from applying rouge to her cheeks and lips followed by some sort of charcoal to her lashes.

My God.

She looked like a *tart*.

Well, perhaps not exactly like a tart. Maybe more like a well-preserved pie. She giggled once. It was the absurdity of the entire hellish nightmare. Here she was at a quarter to four o'clock in the morning at Carleton House preparing to wed one of the most famous dukes in England.

It was going to be a disaster. And all her dreams of travel? Of painting in cities all across Europe? Of following through with all the plans arranged during the last year? Well . . .

As the maid corseted her with a force that rivaled a prizefighter, Esme remembered one thing. Important ton unions were very unlike the marriage she had had. They were like two countries forming an alliance but with distinct and separate borders, and completely independent of one another. Who said she could not follow through with her original ideas?

She would just have a word or two with Mon—

After an insistent knock, two footman appeared and in their impatience, nearly dragged her back to Prinny's chambers. When she re-entered, the future monarch was snoring on his throne. All the servants removed.

Roman started when he saw her.

"Don't you dare say a word," she hissed. "If you tell me I look pretty it will only confirm that you found me plain until now—something I am very well aware of, I assure you."

He raised the level of his chin. "I was simply going to say that I liked you better in your night rail."

"Oh, stop it," she ground out. "And by the by, I

want your solemn promise that this will change nothing between us. I will marry you because I have to but that does not mean I will alter my plans to travel and paint."

"Look, March, you could at least act as if you are charmed by the idea of snagging a duke. Most ladies would."

"Well, I am not most ladies."

The bishop cleared his throat.

"Not yet," they both said to the poor man at the same time.

"Do I have your vow, Montagu?" Esme insisted. "Do I have your vow that you will leave me in peace to do as I please? Not to insist I accompany you on your trips?"

She paused, discomforted by what had to be said. "You will never embarrass me by rubbing mistresses in my face, will you?"

He appeared very offended.

She parted her rouged lips to apologize but he cut her off.

"I shall only ask in return that you never bear another man's child during our union."

She felt the heat of a blush at her low neckline as she nodded in agreement. She was so hurt, she could not stop herself from declaring something she did not want—a passionless marriage. "Our union will be in name only."

He appeared relieved. "Good."

And now she had only regret for allowing her pride to have its say.

He nodded curtly and cast his gaze upon the bishop. "We're ready."

The wisp of a man examined his fingernails, looked as if he wanted to sermonize and then thought the better of it. "We're waiting for the witnesses."

"Witnesses?" She addressed the bishop.

He did not answer. Roman replied, "Candover and Abshire."

She widened her eyes. "My cousin is here?"

Roman started but before he could speak the prince awoke.

"Oh, I say"—Prinny glanced in her direction—"you're very fetching, Lady Derby. Are you certain we have never conversed before tonight? No, no, don't answer. And where are the others?"

"In the adjoining chamber, Your Majesty," the bishop indicated with a wave of his hand.

"Well, bring them in. Let's see if they are both still alive, shall we? I, myself, would not wager on it."

The bishop did as he was bade and the two dukes, Abshire followed by Candover, entered, the first with a derisive mocking smile, and the other, Esme's lofty cousin, looking at the former with more disdain and scorn than Esme thought it possible to exhibit on his otherwise handsome face.

Her cousin, the premier duke, immediately crossed the royal chamber to greet Norwich with a hint of a smile. It was the most teeth Esme had ever seen her cousin show.

Candover turned to her and embraced her in a rare show of affection. Over his shoulder, she saw Norwich's shocked expression. He obviously had not known they were related. It only proved once again how he had never bothered to notice her in all the years they attended the same ton events.

Candover pulled away to address her. "My dear cousin, I cannot tell you how relieved I was to receive Derby's note that you were returned to us. That storm took the lives of all those aboard a ship that sailed not two hours before *The Drake*."

"I'm so sorry to have worried everyone."

"Esme?" That low rasping baritone quivered up one side of her and rolled off the other like a warm wave of danger.

She tilted her head to spy the Duke of Abshire. "Your Grace." She curtsied.

"Oh, come come, Esme. You break my heart with your reserve. Never say you wish me to address my finest fishing companion as Lady Derby?"

"That was when we were in leading strings as I remember."

He hooded his eyes. "That's not how I remember it a' tall, my dear."

Candover's expression grew very dark. "Am I

to endure yet another indication of your never-ending interference with my family, Abshire?" he spat out without endeavoring to regard the man he had detested for as long as Esme could remember. No one knew the precise event that had led to their estrangement but it appeared that they had become even further strained if that was possible. Esme would even go so far as to hazard that her cousin would have bashed the other's head into the royal hearth if he could have done it without raising the prince's ire.

"Enough," Prinny commanded. "I'll not waste another moment listening to either of you. We shall get on with this so I may get my beauty sleep. I for one fear I need it."

"Majesty," Candover stepped forward, "may I beg a small moment alone with my cousin?"

The prince shook his head and sighed. "You are trying my patience, Candover. One moment and only one moment."

"Don't worry, Majesty, according to the ladies I know, he only ever takes a moment," Abshire inserted. "What? Oh, all right. I'll stop. Do hold him tightly, Seventeen. I've got better things to do than to bruise my knuckles tonight."

Her cousin appeared ready to explode. It was to his credit that he merely narrowed his eyes, shrugged off Norwich's grasp and offered his arm to Esme. He escorted her to a shadowed corner of the chamber. "My dear, shall I put a stop to this? I'm not certain I'd be able to actually, given the horror that has overtaken London recently. But I won't have you unhappy again. Norwich is a decent enough fellow—one of the best truly. How came you to be in this pickle?"

"Did not the prince explain it?"

"Yes, but I could not make heads or tails of it to be honest."

She knew he did not mean to insult her, but it was obvious no one would understand why the Duke of Norwich would have even noticed her. "I cannot make heads or tails of it either, but really I have no choice given the situation." She attempted a smile. "Everyone will be very impressed, especially my mother. I'm coming up in the world, am I not, Cousin?"

He regarded her carefully. She wished he would fight for her—or at least not assume she would be grateful for this opportunity to wed again. And to a duke no less.

Roman approached and tilted his head toward their sovereign. "Prinny awaits."

Candover studied first Roman and then her. And then Roman again. "While I consider you a fine enough man, Norwich, if I ever, ever I say, receive one complaint from my cousin about your conduct toward her, you will be held accountable by me."

"I'm shaking in my boots," Norwich stated impassively. "And if I have complaints?"

Esme finally felt a stirring of amusement in this absurd evening.

"You will keep them to yourself and still be held accountable," Candover replied. "And no, I do not want to know what happened on Wight. There is not a single doubt in my mind that you are both blameless and that we have that contemptible Mr. King to thank for this evening's farce of a union. I am sorry for you, Esme. Congratulations on your happy future, Seventeen. You could not have found a better bride."

Norwich leaned in to whisper something into Candover's ear. Esme heard something about the Duke of Kress and the fortune lost.

"What are you saying?" The Prince Regent boomed. "I'll not have another word between you. Come along then."

Out of the corner of her eye, Esme saw her cousin shake his head in response to Norwich's request.

"I'm sorry, I cannot," Candover murmured.

"You never liked Kress. You know, you must begin to try to like some people sometime." Roman sighed.

"I like you well enough, Seventeen," Candover ground out. "Enough to allow you to marry my cousin."

"That's different," Roman replied with a grin. "You have no choice in the matter."

"Excuse me," Esme said with hauteur, "but in case both your eyes are failing, and in Norwich's case there is a distinct possibility, I am standing right here. I shall always choose my own husbands, Cousin."

"As you should, my dear. As you should," Candover said with something resembling a smile on his lean face.

As there was no more to be said, there was nothing left to do but perform the unthinkable. And with astonishing speed they were wed.

When Esme echoed the promises the man of the cloth put forth, she had to hold back the tears that were threatening to spill down her cheeks. She wasn't sure why her sensibilities were so involved. She wasn't even sure what she was feeling. This was not how it had gone when she had first wed. Then, she had been suffused with a quiet happiness. It had been a lovely little country wedding complete with a lovely little wedding breakfast after.

She looked at the man promising to love her, to cherish her, to care for her in sickness and in health and realized she had not a notion if his family members lived with him. She wondered if she would live with his mother and also his sister, a beautiful lady named Lily Montagu who was surrounded by peers at every entertainment Esme had ever attended. And she would now be sisters with the pretty creature. It was unfathomable.

Her thoughts were interrupted by the bishop. "Your signature is required here, Your Grace." He extended a large official-looking book toward her.

It took a moment before she realized the man was referring to her. *Her Grace.* For the rest of her life she would be addressed as such. Esme only wished her mother was here to hear it. She would laugh so hard she would cry . . . with good-natured amusement. The wallflower of the era marrying a dyed-in-the-wool duke and an overly handsome one at that.

The bishop nodded toward the ledger pointedly. She took his cue and signed the necessary document, Roman following the same course a moment later.

Candover came forward silently and embraced her tenderly again. She had always felt he considered her as much a sister as his five actual sisters. He had actually been far kinder toward her than the others.

Abshire was clapping Roman on the back and saying something that caused her husband—*her husband!*—to grin.

Prinny steepled his beringed fingers together. "Delighted for you both. Norwich, I would arrange a celebration for you but we must delay. You must first go on an extended secret honeymoon. I insist."

"Honeymoon," they both said simultaneously.

Unnerved, Esme eyed her cousin. He shook his head and rolled his eyes.

"Yes. Far north, I think. Would you like to visit the Queen's castle in Littleshire? I shall order fires in every grate. Then again, you shall have each other to keep warm. Yes, that is a far more preferable plan. There shall be no fires, then."

Abshire chuckled discreetly.

The prince's lewd wit was far too well known to cause shock. His jowls flapped again when he laughed with the dark duke.

"But I must go to Cornwall, Your Majesty," Roman said. "I shall first see Kress and return his fortune. I did not earn it and the matter must be resolved."

"Oh no, no, no, no no," Prinny said with a wag of his finger. "We cannot have that. It's as I told you. You are ordered to leave the matter to me. I shall inform Kress of the good news of your return when I choose. There is not a moment to waste. And Candover and Abshire? You are not to breathe a word of any of tonight's goings-on until I allow it. Understood?"

The two dukes agreed.

"But I don't understand, Your Majesty," Esme inserted. "Whyever can we not remain in London?"

"Because that is not what newly married peers of the realm do," he said, his lips twitching. "Now

I will hear no argument on this. It will also serve to silence Mr. King once and forever when I inform him but swear him to secrecy. We must be very careful with our timing, you see."

Esme had heard the Prince Regent could be very odd at times. The gossipmongers had the right of it. But who would ever dare question their sovereign? She had the notion this had something to do with Kress.

"Yes," the future king continued, delighted beyond measure. "No one will listen to that ridiculous man's silly gossip after they eventually hear you are marvelously married and happy. You shall leave straightaway. Your affairs will follow but a few hours behind you. And have no fear, I shall inform all those family members or friends you have seen today, and swear them to secrecy."

"But . . . but—" She tried to gain time.

"But, what?" Roman asked, exasperated.

His tone brought her back to the scene. Lord. She had married him. He was her husband. "I want to meet your family."

"My family?" Roman looked at her with surprise.

"No, that will not do," the prince inserted. "That joy will have to wait until after you return. Besides, no one takes their in-laws on their honeymoon. Not even the most unhappy of couples, such as myself. By God, if I endured a honeymoon, you two can too."

"Well, could we at least stay at Derby Manor in Derbyshire, Your Majesty," Esme requested, editing out pertinent information concerning the dwelling's current residents.

"Your former husband's estate?" Roman asked, annoyed.

"No, the current earl's estate," she replied peevishly. She couldn't believe she was peevish on her wedding day. Then again she still couldn't fathom that it was again her wedding day.

"Perfect," the prince said. "It's even further from London. And the last place anyone would look for Norwich."

And with that, the entire absurd matter was put out of its misery. And she didn't even care that she was mixing clichés in her thoughts.

This entire business was irregular. It followed that the departure would be irregular too. At sixes and sevens they were hurried into one of two plain black barouches, the curtains fully unfurled.

They sat there in silence for nearly a half hour, leaving each to their own thoughts. She was decided she would not say a word to the man who had thrown a proverbial dash of cold water over all her long-held, well-laid plans. He would have to—

"Well, he can't command us to have intercourse," Roman muttered under his breath.

Chapter 7

Roman repeated it as if he hadn't realized he'd already said it once aloud. "No, he can't command us to have intercourse." He paused. "At least after the marriage is consummated."

Something fluttered in her stomach. Good Lord. She would not let his comment affect her. He hadn't meant it the way she heard it. Oh, but her sensibilities were ruffled. She had at least thought he had enjoyed sexual congress with her, even if he had been terrified of the storm. Now she was too hurt to say a word. And the idea of consummating the marriage now held little appeal. It was absurd. Oh, perhaps she was being overly sensitive, but she couldn't help herself. Her self-doubt concerning her plain appearance ran too deep for her to second-guess.

Well, she would have two days to consider her options. Surely he would not suggest that they consummate the marriage straightaway. Why, it would take them at least two days to reach Derbyshire—and that was only if they traveled with no delay, stopping only at posting houses to change horses.

She watched him remove a flask from his waistcoat. And perhaps for the first time in her life, Esme understood the desire for oblivion.

He paused, the flask half lifted toward his lips. He glanced sideways at her. Without a word, he offered it to her.

She looked away.

"Suit yourself," he replied and then drank long and deep.

"I suppose now would be the time to tell you that we will not be alone at Derby Manor," she said coolly.

"Since I understood Lord Derby is in Town, I suppose you are referring to the new earl's servants," he replied.

"Not precisely."

Perversely, he irritated her further by dropping the subject. He apparently did not have any curiosity whatsoever about the people who would witness their honeymoon gone to hell.

Well, all the better to surprise him.

* * *

Roman wasn't sure what irked him more—his aching head, or the suddenly mysterious woman beside him.

His wife.

He had never thought he would live to say those two words together. They sounded every bit as ridiculous as he would have imagined.

But if he had to take a duchess, there was some small shriveled part of him that was rather pleased it was she.

It was not that she was *suddenly* and *mysteriously* possessed of a certain type of aristocratic mien, nor was it her odd mood, one he was willing to overlook considering the extraordinary circumstances. But there was something more to it. If he had bothered to brush away the myriad complicated mathematical notations clogging his brainbox, he might have seen what it was about her that he valued.

It was her heart.

She was a giver. In a world of takers, she was the opposite.

But what he was unwilling to part with was his own heart.

The rest of the long journey was accomplished in peace after that first discomforting hour. It was done quite easily for the new duchess made a slight adjustment in the travel arrangements. At the first posting house, she descended to attend to her needs, taking forever and a day. She then never ascended back into the carriage wherein Roman sat in deep contemplation.

No. Instead, he was told by the coachman that Her Grace, the Duchess of Norwich had chosen to sit in the second carriage, where her new maid, sent along by His Majesty, resided. It annoyed him to think that his sire had not thought to send at the very least a valet for his use. He refused to consider that what really irritated him was that March had decided to sit with a stranger instead of him.

And so Roman brooded alone. He brooded alone for one day and then for a second day. After the first hour of that second day, he pulled out his plans for the city's waterworks and gained much ground in solving several problems. But in the back of his mind, he really contemplated only three things:

1. How he was going to consummate the marriage.
2. When he would consummate the marriage.
3. And who in hell would be residing at Derby Manor while they consummated the marriage. She had made it sound quite ominous.

After two days of solid work and reflection, which followed the week he had discovered absinthe—the hellish drink of the devil, become shipwrecked, and been forced to marry, he was absolutely, positively certain in his godforsaken life that he was no longer cursed.

He was *damned.*

And he was damned for seventeen reasons.

Reasons one through seventeen were variations on a theme. The Esme-March-now-Montagu theme.

She might very well place one of his lifelong goals in jeopardy. He had decided long ago that he would put an end to the damned curse by being the very last Norwich in Christendom.

He would have no cursed heir—damn it all. He would not. And he was in a position to see it through. There were no more male cousins removed or otherwise. He was the last bloody one. And when he died the duchy would devolve back to the monarchy.

His mother and sister would have not a single worry with which to contend. There were more unentailed gold guineas to his name than to half the dukes in the royal entourage.

And so he would take every precaution to ensure his goal was met. It would be a simple matter.

He would not hurt Esme March for the world. While he could have done without her unfounded fear concerning consumption of spirits and the resulting looks sent his way, she had only ever been kind to him. But he was going to have to ensure there was no heir. And he would do it by wishing her bon voyage at the end of the six weeks. He would see her to a ship bound for all the art museums she could possibly want and then he would find his way to Cornwall to put Alex Barclay out of his misery no matter what Prinny had warned.

Most important, he would go on living his life. Avoiding ducks, rubbing shoulders with the others in the entourage, and plugging away at his designs. Of course, every now and again he would see his wife to ensure that no tongues wagged behind her back to embarrass her. He had the strongest urge to protect her, to guard her sensibilities from unkind gossip. And so he would make an effort to see her between her travels and her painting. He wanted her to be happy. He did.

What he did not expect, was to be happy himself.

Of course, it would take a long while, a very long while before he could accept that fact.

The royal forward rider did his duty and informed the inhabitants of Derby Manor of their impending arrival and then returned to report the fact to Roman. That there was another person who could have been considered an occupant, due to the amount of time he spent at the estate, was another matter.

Roman was not sure if he should be pleased or uneasy to learn that Esme's *mother* resided at the manor. On the one hand, the Countess of Gilchrist would be the perfect confidante for Esme. If his new bride was like most ladies he knew, she could not survive without a confidante. He paused in thought. For some reason, he wasn't certain Esme was like other ladies he knew. Perhaps she didn't need a confidante. But nonetheless, she obviously liked her mother or else she would not have suggested they retreat to this place. On the other hand, Roman knew a thing or seventeen about mothers. His own was a very reserved female with only three things on her mind: how soon she could marry him off (oh, she would consider her life's work almost complete if she knew he was married—although sad for not being witness to it), how soon she could locate the perfect husband for his sister Lily (who had so far refused more than a dozen offers of marriage over the last six seasons), and how soon she could retire to a villa she had summered in many years ago. Then, she would be happy, in quiet raptures over the knowledge that she had done her duty. Of course, there was a fourth thing she also spoke of, thank the Lord, only rarely. Something Roman endured with great fortitude. It concerned an heir. He forced his mind away from the thought as he always had quite successfully.

As he traveled alone up the allée toward the large, pleasantly situated white stone manor house, Roman gazed out the window. Sheep dotted the green, green pastureland, and a pheasant darted across the path. He prayed pheasants were not related to ducks.

The crunch of footfalls on pea gravel alerted him to the approach of footmen.

The coachman opened the door and let down the stair. Roman ignored him and leaped from the barouche, happy to stretch his aching legs.

A lady daintily descended the five marble steps fronting the manor and curtsied in front of him. She was no doubt Esme's mother, but her features were different. *Different but the same.* She was a little smaller, and her limbs were more delicate and petite than Esme's. Her lovely gray eyes were similar, yet her mouth was not as wide and her nose was not as long as her daughter's. The mother's unlined face was heart-shaped instead of Esme's oval visage. And where Esme's expression radiated intelligence and kindness, her elegant mother had something else entirely. He feared there was more than a soupcon of wit or shrewdness hiding behind that serene mask of hers. Most likely both.

Quite properly, the lady waited for him to introduce himself. "Delighted to make your acquaintance, ma'am," he said as he bowed. "Norwich. I am your servant."

She eyed him carefully and smiled the same smile he had seen on Esme. "Lady Gilchrist," she said with a proper curtsy. "Where is my daughter? What have you done with her?" She glanced about him and looked at the open door of the barouche.

"I'm right here, Mother." She descended from the second carriage. Her new maid followed discreetly behind and faded toward the servants' entrance to the rear.

"There you are, darling. Oh, you are wearing that divine Parisian hat William Topher arranged for your birthday."

"Yes," Esme said with a grin. "Although, why we mimic the French when we are trying to kill them at the same time has never made any sense to me at all if I do say so."

"Well, I for one am willing to admit they have something over us when it comes to fashion, and food, and elegance. What say you, Norwich?"

"Who is William Topher?"

Mother and daughter were now in each other's arms, and he gazed at two pairs of matching eyes.

"William?" Her mother glanced at Esme before continuing. "Why, have you not told your husband yet about Mr. Topher? He is my daughter's teacher and mentor, sir."

He looked at his wife.

She finally picked up the thread. "He is more than a teacher, Montagu. He is a very good friend of the family. He's resided with us for many, many years. You shall like him very much. Everyone does." She smiled her widest grin, the one that was hard to resist returning.

"Dearest," the countess said, taking her daughter's chin between her fingers, "I see marriage agrees with you. I like the way your hair is dressed, and there is a certain sparkle in your eye. Did Norwich put it there?"

"Mother—" She shook her head. "You must give the duke a chance to get used to the goings-on here before you tease . . ."

The countess sighed. "Oh pish. There are no goings-on here. The neighborhood is positively empty of anything entertaining. Everyone has gone to Brighton or Bath. Now come along then inside, I must see to a tea tray. I'm certain you are both parched. That will give enough time for the maids and footmen to arrange your baths after such a long, dirty journey. Tell me, Esme, did you chance to see any of Verity's sisters? She's quite anxious for news."

He suddenly had a very bad feeling in his gut. *Verity* . . . "Verity, who?" he asked most inelegantly.

"Why Lady Verity Fitzroy, one of the Duke of Candover's sisters. You must know them very well, no? You are an intimate of Candover, are you not?"

"Yes," he replied, a proper expression glued to his face.

"I'm sure Verity will come tomorrow when we send her news of your arrival."

In some very tiny path, not well traveled in his mind, he had known Candover's ridiculously large country seat was in Derbyshire. He had just been too concerned with his own travails and had not made the connection. "And just how many of Candover's sisters are at home at the moment?"

"Only one of the five. Come, let's go inside. It's too hot to stand about."

In his mind he retorted *no*. He would rather climb in that carriage and retreat all the way back to his study in London where more important plans occupied his mind. Instead, he replied, "Of course."

His mother-in-law smiled radiantly and Esme followed suit. Tea was served within the confines of a picturesque and carefully designed room filled with Frenchified decorations. There was one addition to their small party.

Esme's teacher, the one who had apparently taught her everything there was to know about anything concerning art, as he arrogantly suggested, was lounging by the mantel, one booted foot crossed over the other, his little finger extended in a dainty manner as he held the delicate rose-patterned porcelain teacup. A Mr. William Topher. A gentleman whose years in his dish were hard to decipher. He was most likely a mere five years Esme's senior. What was not hard to decipher was his effect on females. The gentleman was far too handsome and far too sure of his excellent opinion of himself.

Instantly, Roman took a dislike of him. And no matter how much he tried to converse politely with this Mr. Topher, there was something that was not quite up to snuff about the character.

"Your Grace," Topher said, "while I live and breathe, I would have never guessed I would have the great honor of meeting you in the flesh, here at Derby Manor. Is it not the grandest place? I am very fortunate to have earned the patronage of Lord Derby while he was still with us, poor, dear man that he was. Did you know him?" The man looked at him expectantly.

Roman had never heard anyone string together so many words so quickly. "No." His economy of words would make up for the other's cornucopia of verbiage.

Mr. Topher laughed. "There you see. Once again my fault rises to the fore. I must warn you, Your Grace, that I have the unfortunate habit of speaking too much when I am overly awed by someone. Then again, I am easily overawed, so you are forewarned. Does it strike you as odd that I am revealing so much to you so quickly, sir? Yes, by your look it does. I do apologize, Your Grace. And I would stop if I could."

Esme burst out laughing. "Oh, William, I see you have not lost any of your wit. I have missed you."

The ridiculously handsome man's sorrowful brown eyes filled with emotion. "And I have missed you too, my dear. But how shocking. You went away to paint and acquire a painting or two and you come back far less than a fortnight later with a *husband*? The Fitzroy ladies will be very jealous, don't you know? I say, may I be permitted to take my leave to pay a visit to Lady Verity Fitzroy?"

He was the strangest, most annoying man Roman had ever met. And while Roman was solidly built, Topher was a tall wisp of a man. His limbs were thin, yet he wore his dark, elegant clothes with great flare. A Beau Dandy of the first order, Mr. William Topher was. It remained to be seen if he had as much talent teaching art as he had making ladies lust after him. Not less than three serving maids took pains to offer him foodstuffs from the tea tray.

Esme brought a biscuit to her lips and took a bite. "You may not gossip to our friends, William. But, I'll allow you to announce the news to Verity when we see her next. Will that suffice? By the by, I am going to paint a landscape tomorrow even if it means I will miss my cousin's call."

Roman desired to enter the conversation. "Where?"

"Oh," her mouth made a little *O*. "Would you like to join me, Montagu? I know you don't fully enjoy art or the process, but you are very welcome."

"I haven't the faintest idea what you are talking about, March. I esteem artists. I married one, did I not?" He smiled his widest smile in the hopes of disarming them all as he stretched the truth far past any recognition.

"I shall join you and we shall work together as always. I am so glad you are taking my advice and concentrating on landscapes versus portraits, Esme," Mr. Topher inserted. "And there's absolutely no need to bother your husband with our endeavors, my dearest girl."

"You shall address my wife as 'Your Grace' from this day forward, sir."

Mr. Topher's face fell. "Of course, Your Grace."

Lady Gilchrist smoothed over the awkwardness of the moment. "May I ask why you address each other as March and Montagu? It's quite novel."

"Are you certain I may not address you as March too, Your Grace?" Topher was addressing Esme, but he then quickly turned to him. "Oh, I do beg your pardon, Your Grace. I was addressing Her Grace, not Your Grace. I just wanted to clarify as it is a bit confusing when you are both to be addressed as 'Your Grace.'"

Topher was asking for it.

For some absurd reason, Roman wanted nothing more than to punch this sodding fellow's handsome lights out.

Instead, Roman addressed his mother-in-law. "It's a habit."

"William," Esme replied to Mr. Topher, "Don't be ridiculous. I will always be Esme to you. Why, you've known me for over a decade."

"I most certainly will address you as Your Grace if you prefer," Topher said with a fake glint of humility in his eye.

"Oh, botheration," she replied. "William, do stop."

It was very hot in the salon and Roman had had enough of the stupidities. It was why he preferred to avoid wasting his time with social calls of absolutely no importance. He returned his teacup to the side table and stood up to cross to one of the windows to examine the view when Topher continued to fawn over Esme.

"Shall we not get started on a new work straightaway?" Topher was gleeful. "I should like to show you a new technique for painting tree leaves rustling in the wind that I've developed recently."

Roman stilled to hear her answer.

"If you do not mind, William, shall we not begin tomorrow? Mother?" She said with some degree of seriousness as she turned to Lady Gilchrist. "I should like to take a little lie-down if I may. The trip was a bit tiring."

"Of course, my darling. I asked Mrs. Jenkins to make up the nursery for you and His Grace as I thought it would not be in good taste to return you to the small chambers you chose when the new earl's affairs were placed in the master chambers."

Nursery? Why on earth would they be put in a bloody—

"Mother, let us have no lies. I know you've taken up residence in my chambers as I suggested before I departed. And you are correct. Those rooms will not do. The apartments of the nursery are far and away the largest and most beautiful rooms in any case." She paused.

Roman knew she said these things to reassure him. He said not a word and continued looking at the view.

"So it is agreed. I shall stay in the nursery proper. But we shall all stop referring to those apartments thusly. It is ridiculous. They are no longer fitted out as such. Mother, where shall His Grace's affairs be placed?"

"Why in the *nanny's* room, of course, my darling." Her not-so-darling mother replied without a hint of sport in her voice.

He turned to look at the two ladies still seated with their teacups perched on their knees. Mr. Topher had a smirk on his face.

"With any luck there will be an actual infant sleeping in those apartments one day soon." Her mother had the audacity to wink.

"Mother," Esme said quietly but firmly.

A chill ran down Roman's spine and then raced down his legs, singeing him to the spot. Good God. They were actually talking of babies? He had entered a madhouse. Yes, that was it. Was there so little respect left in England for a goddamned duke? *The nanny's room?*

Then again, his own mother and sister acted remarkably like this pair. He was damned twice over to be forever surrounded by a horde of females. And now the added insanity of a hangdog of a teacher, who was clearly bent on following her around every chance he had. Roman wanted nothing more than to retreat to a study, order a tea tray of whiskey with a side order of drafting paper and pencils, and then lock the door and throw away the key.

Instead, he crossed the room toward the door. "I shall take my leave of all of you."

"Oh," Esme said, "allow me to show you to our apartments."

"No, thank you," he replied, walking to the threshold.

"But where are you going, my son?" Her mother's voice was less gleeful.

My son? "To take the air."

"Shall I go with you?" Esme asked.

"I should like to go alone." He really didn't give a fig if he was impolite.

The silence in the room was as deafening as morning prayers in a monastery.

He departed the manor house without noticing what direction he took. He walked past the rear gardens, passed the well-maintained kitchen garden, barely took note of the handsome stables, and ignored the smell of the cows, sheep, and pigs in his wake. He plowed up the hill and walked quickly past the dale. He kept going so far and so fast that he knew not if he would be able to find his way back easily.

Babies?

At the sight of an enormous lake, he stopped, breathing hard. He leaned over, squeezed his eyes shut, and let the dizzy sensations subside. He swallowed the bile that had risen to the back of his throat and clenched his hands on his knees.

He finally straightened after a few long moments and made his way southward to a stand of birch. He would have liked nothing more than to continue walking all the way back to London.

There would be no goddamned baby.

Instead he laid his head on a mossy spot at the base of one of the trees and rather than remember the rest of the vile conversation in the salon with the people who would surround him for the next several weeks, he promptly fell fast asleep.

It would be the rest he would need to see him through that night.

Chapter 8

"Mother," Esme began, "you have scared him off. And you, too, William."

William Topher was doffing his hat, and hooking the handle of the cane he did not use over his wrist. He kissed her on both cheeks and took his leave. "He is a very powerful-looking man, Esme. A touch too serious of course, but I wish you very happy, my dearest girl, or shall I say Your Grace?"

She gave William a look.

"If you change your mind and need something to divert your attention from the spectacular alteration in your life, just trot down to the dower house and we can resume painting, Esme. I do hope you will not let this new husband of yours interfere with your aspirations, my dear girl," William stated. "It would be a shame. We all know your father, bless his artistic soul, had great plans for you. Plans I was to guide you toward. I do hope your second husband does not go on like . . . well, then. I shall say not another word."

The countess shook her head. "Nonsense, William. I can tell Norwich is a very good man."

"Mother," Esme said, "You know very little about him."

Her mother did not respond. Instead she looked pointedly toward William Topher. "Good day, William. You will join us for dinner tonight?"

"Of course."

William Topher bowed and departed. Once out of sight, Esme heard him whistling softly as was his way.

"Mother, you have never been so familiar with someone you did not know before. Nor do you usually put on airs, except of course in Town when everyone puts on airs. Please do not make this more difficult than it is." Esme poured the last drops of tea from the teapot into her mother's cup.

"Well I shall put on airs when a duke is in residence. It is important to get off on the right foot with an adversary, don't you think?"

"Adversary? I assure you that Roman Montagu is not an adversary."

"Of course he is. He did not come to your marriage willingly. Now, after your lie-down, you must tell me what happened, in private. The forward rider gave me your letter, but really, my darling, I had so little time to digest it before you were arrived."

"I'm sorry I could not send news earlier."

"Of course you could not, my darling. But I am glad, actually, for I would have worried dreadfully if I had known a storm had nearly sunk *The Drake*. And I am so sorry the trip you planned so meticulously was ruined."

"It is not a tragedy, Mother. I will just plan it again."

Her mother studied her for a long moment. "Of course you will. It is too bad the Prince Regent would not allow you and His Grace to set off for Vienna for your honeymoon instead of here."

Esme refused to tell her mother of Roman's terror of ships.

"But I suppose I understand. Of course, we saw the astounding columns in the *Morning Post*. And any of the royal entourage stupid enough to remain in London would be the target of the lower classes' ire, as the prince endures every day, I understand. But . . ."

"Yes?"

"I don't understand why your marriage could not be announced properly in the newspapers. It would help the Prince Regent's effort to show the public that his entourage is reforming its outrageous ways."

"Mother, I can only tell you that His Majesty ordered us here, and demanded that we not publicly announce our wedding until he decides it is the correct time."

"Well, he could not have sent you to a more remote area. News travels about as slowly as a slug in winter here," she said distastefully. "Dearest, I shan't hold you any longer. I've kept you too long from your lie-down. We shall continue after." Her mother studied her face with a knowing eye. "And then you will tell me if you've informed His Grace that you are a descendant of Esmeralda Mannon."

"I have not," Esme replied quickly. "Nor do I intend to do it. I do not want to over worry him."

Her mother gave her a look. "If this is a marriage of convenience, and clearly it is, I would suggest you tell him as soon as possible, my love."

Esme sighed. She really did want to rest. But her mother would not leave off without an answer. "I don't want him to treat me differently—and he will if he knows."

Her mother raised her eyebrows. "Perhaps it would be better if he treats you differently." Fluffing out the skirt of her gown, Esme's mother continued. "Your happiness is all I care about, Esme. I will not have another Norwich ruin the future of another Mannon. You are my one and only daughter and I promised myself and your father that I would do everything possible for you to reach your full potential."

Esme rose to take her leave. "Please do not worry, Mother. I know I was gifted with only one talent. And I have never thought I would find happiness with another husband. But I must make the best of what has happened. And you must trust me to muddle my way through this as well as I can."

As she climbed up the last stair to the nursery, Esme was grateful to her parents. Her father for nurturing their shared passion for art and her mother for loving them both. And her mother had always taken the correct course of action where Esme's, ahem, lack of charms were concerned. Her mother never falsely praised her. If anyone knew she had been born with few admirable physical attributes, it was Esme.

A long time ago she had decided not to care about her lack of beauty. One could not concentrate on flaws one could not fix. She would never have allure. But she could paint. And the more she painted, the more she liked what she put on the canvas. It was the one thing she could count on to bring her a measure of joy. That and caring for the people she loved.

The Duke of Norwich would never love her the way she knew in her heart that she could love him. It was ridiculous, really. But that fateful evening she had first seen him in that London ballroom, she had felt the shiver of fate. He had quite obviously never felt it. But perhaps they would treat each other with kindness, and mutually respect each other in their day-to-day lives.

Esme wondered if she would be lucky enough to have a baby. Oh, she knew they had both agreed to remain childless, but one could never guarantee it. No matter how careful they might be, one could become with child.

She tried not to let hope flourish. She had had two disappointments. Twice she had found herself with child and twice she had lost the infant within a month's time. She had not told anyone of her delicate condition either time. Esme had wanted it that way as she knew her mother would be heartbroken if she learned of the two losses.

Esme gazed at the lovely large chamber on the second floor of the manor, facing the side tiered garden, where a large oak tree proved a shaded retreat near one of the windows. Esme had sat in the rocking chair near that window many months after losing the second infant. It was where she had taken the decision to put away her desire for a child and concentrate on her art instead. There was no point pining for something one could not have.

As she sat there now, she forced back the longing she had. She would not put herself through it again. If her mother brought it up she would take her aside and tell her of her failures and ask that they never speak of it ever again.

And her mother would do it. She could be counted on when the going was rough.

After Lionel had died, her mother had come and had brought her breakfast and dinner in bed for many days, cajoling her to eat every bite. Esme bowed her head. It was her art that had seen her through in the end. And it would do so again. She rose and smoothed out the wrinkles in her gown.

She was no longer tired. She would go and paint. She would take the half-finished painting of the mill and complete it. Maybe even start a new work.

Esme struggled to climb the hills and navigate the dales with her easel, canvases and painting gear. She was crossing the last rise before the mill, when she spied someone under the weeping willow in the pasture. She changed directions and stopped just short of his boots.

He was such a very handsome man. His chin jutted out, the hint of a snore whispering from his lips while she watched him. He looked far more at peace now than the last few days. She understood why. He had consumed too much drink, endured far too many ships, and one too many weddings. His own.

Her heart softened. Barely a week ago he had not even known of her existence. Yet, he had married her to save her reputation by order of the

Prince Regent. All in all, he was a true gentleman. Perhaps a reluctant one, but at least he possessed good character.

She nudged his foot.

He awoke mid snore. "Whatzfuget?" His eyes snapped open.

"I just wanted to tell you something," she said. "Then you can go back to sleep."

He sat up awkwardly. "What is it?"

"I just wanted to say that I am sorry about the strange welcome you received. My mother and William were merely surprised by our arrival and all the news. They had not had time to fully understand what had happened. They are not usually so ridiculous." She smiled. "At least they are not so ridiculous until they know someone better and they take a liking to the person."

"So they have taken a liking to me?"

She bit her lip. "I only ask that you give them time to adjust—especially William. I shall make them keenly aware that we have a marriage of convenience only. I don't want you to think that I expect, or anyone else will expect, anything more than that."

"Pardon me?" He rubbed the back of his neck.

"Since love is not involved, I only have one request."

His eyes were glazed over. "Yes?"

"I would only ask if we could endeavor to always

be very civil, polite and respectful of one another, especially in front of others. I would hate to be one of those couples who argue and spite one another."

"Have I ever been impolite and disrespectful?" he asked.

"Not very much, no."

"When?" he asked gently.

"When what?"

"When have I been impolite and disrespectful?"

She studied her fingertips. "When you said Prinny could not force us to consummate our marriage."

"I did not say it to hurt you."

"I know. But it did."

"If you think I said it because I do not want to be with you as we were that one time, then you misunderstood."

"Then what did you mean by it?"

"I said it because I was tired of Prinny telling both of us what to do."

"I see."

"And I will try never to be unkind or impolite or disrespectful to you. Ever, March. I am sorry if I hurt your sensibilities."

She stared at him. She swallowed her pride. She was very good at doing it usually. This time was harder than other times.

"March?"

She could not meet his gaze. "Yes?"

"Will you put your easel down and the other things?"

"Why? I had planned to paint at the mill."

"Please?"

She carefully laid everything at his feet and stood in front of him very still.

"Will you not join me under this tree? It's quite peaceful here."

"I don't want to disturb your solitude."

"You are not disturbing it—at least not since your boot nudged my boot."

She tried to hide a smile. She sat next to him, about a foot away.

He scooted next to her and very gently put his arm about her shoulders. He leaned forward and gently kissed her cheek.

"You don't have to do that," she said quietly. A breeze ruffled the leaves, and the long tangles of weeping branches swirled.

"I know," he said.

"Then why did you do it?"

"I'm trying to tell you that I really am very sorry for hurting your sensibilities. I do want to consummate our marriage, March. And I thank you for agreeing to become my wife."

"I'm sorry you were forced into it. We shall have to try and make the best of it."

"And the way to make the best of it," he said, "is to remember the importance of each other's independence and freedom. I will not be like other husbands. You must travel and paint and do what you love just as I will do the same. I will never stand in your way. In fact, I will encourage it. I will always remain in England and attend to my own affairs, and I will insist you follow your own path no matter where it takes you."

She pondered what he said. There was kindness in his words but also a sting. He had made it clear that he wanted her to live apart from him—never to have to see her. He wanted to share not an inch of her life. She could not form a reply.

He continued. "As you know, marriage changes people. It brings out the worst in most of them. My parents were a prime example of how to live miserably together. We will not have to worry about this since we will not be in each other's pockets, will we, except for on very rare occasions? Say Michaelmas and other annual celebrations?"

She brushed a wisp of her lovely new maid's elaborate hairstyle out of her eyes and took the opportunity to move a little away from him. He really did not want to commit to share any part of her life. "I understand."

"Do you?" He appeared very relieved.

"Oh, yes. More than you think." She stood up. "I shall just go on to the mill then, before the afternoon light fades. I want to capture it."

"Shall I come with you?"

"Oh, there is no need. I am very capable of doing things for myself and I know you must be very tired. I'm sorry to have disturbed you when you were resting so comfortably."

"You did not disturb me, March."

"I'm glad." She turned on her heel and began to walk away.

He said something and it drifted toward her. "Then, I shall see you at supper? And shall we adjourn to your chamber after?"

She clenched her hands but did not trust herself to speak. She nodded her head but did not turn. She kept on walking.

She ruined the painting of the mill. It took her four hours to do it but she did an excellent job of making a mess of it. After, she felt much better. She felt better still after walking around the lake three times, missing supper, and watching the moon rise.

He could not understand what had detained her. He had thought he had made it perfectly clear. He had apologized, reassured her, and assumed they would endure dinner with her mother and William Topher, who spoke of nothing but oil paints and Esme. And the more the other man spoke, the more Roman was convinced William Topher was besotted with his wife.

Oddly, both the dowager countess and Topher

were not the least bit concerned that Esme had not joined them at table.

"Oh, my daughter is incorrigible," the countess said with a smile. "Once she has a brush in her hand, she forgets all time. Her father had the same fault. You would do well to accept it as I did when I was first married. She is probably contemplating the shades of moonlight."

Roman refused to listen to what Topher had to say on the matter. He was quickly becoming the most boring man in all of Creation to Roman's way of thinking.

He did not linger at table. Indeed, as soon as the dessert was removed, he stood up, the back legs of his chair squealing. "I shall take my brandy, say good night to you both if you will excuse me. It has been an exhausting day—week."

The countess nodded. "I shall send my dear Esme up to you when she returns. Fear not, she always returns at some point. And I shall have a chat to remind her that husbands do not like to be kept waiting."

"I would ask that you do nothing of the sort, madam. Your daughter and I have already discussed how we will go about our marriage."

Topher was looking at him with extreme curiosity. At least he had the good sense not to say another single word.

Roman mounted the stairs, but paused on the

floor of the nursery. He really wasn't at all sure where he would go. It was odd to go into a chamber to wait for her, but in the end that is what he did. And then he took a new decision and went in search of a servant to remove his affairs into another apartment farther down the hall.

He then pressed into service the footman as valet. After dragging out his evening ablutions for as long as possible, Roman returned to the blasted nursery, began a book he had selected from Derby's library, and waited for his wife. When the shadows grew too long in the chamber, he finally closed the book, eased back the covers of the large bed, and lay in the growing darkness.

For a long time.

Esme mounted the stairs to the nursery on tiptoe. She knew she was being extraordinarily juvenile about this. It was just that he had made her feel like she was just one more thing on his list of Things That Must Be Done, or People I Must Attend to with as Little Effort as Possible.

Oh, he was a loner. Of that there was no question. He wanted his freedom. He wanted his independence. He had made it very clear. And she knew that feeling.

She just could not understand why he continued to harp on the subject. It was not as if she was clinging to him in any fashion whatsoever. Had she not just provided him with enough freedom as possible the last two days by traveling with the maid?

She undressed in a guest chamber she had occasionally used, and donned her night rail. As Esme stood before the nursery room door, she hoped he would not be inside.

Tonight, she just didn't have the spirit necessary to consummate the marriage. It was going to require a supreme force to pretend that everything was all right.

She hated that this would be done without love. Aside from the one evening on *The Drake,* when she had purely given of herself in his terror, now she was going to have to give of herself to him in duty only. And it would most likely be the one and only time this would happen. He had made it obvious he wanted to be a husband in name only. There would be no children unless a small miracle occurred tonight and she very much doubted this.

She swallowed, and gently eased open the door, holding her breath.

Yes, he was there. His feet tented the sheet.

Esme tried very hard not to wake him as she eased on the right side of the bed. Her body dipped the bed slightly as she got in and she held her breath for a few long seconds. Thank the Lord he did not awaken. She lay on her side but within moments he turned toward her and was spooning her, drawing his strong forearm around her middle and pulling her close to him. He was so much warmer than she.

"Where have you been?" he asked in a groggy whisper—not unkindly, only curious.

"Sorry. I lost track of time. Sleep, please. So sorry to have disturbed."

He did not reply. Instead his hands became restless and turned her to face him, and she was suddenly transported back in time to the evening on board the ship. He was touching her the same way. It would be so easy to believe he truly wanted her for herself.

But he did not love her and he was not seeking comfort. He only needed her body to sink into, this one time and then they could truthfully admit to consummating the marriage. She concentrated on regulating her breathing. She was proud of herself for remaining calm.

"Esme?" he whispered behind one ear.

"Yes?"

"Shall we?"

She did not pretend not to understand. "Whatever you like."

"I think we should," he said gently.

"All right."

He began to gently touch her breasts through her thin night rail, and she was embarrassed to feel herself respond. She did not want to react. She just wanted to dispassionately consummate their forced marriage, be civil to one another for the next few weeks, and then go back to her way of life when he returned to London, and she attempted to depart on her trip again. She could not let her heart become engaged.

When she returned from her travels, she would live here, apart from him in London. It would all be *very convenient*—as if they were not married at all.

He was tugging at her gown, and he wanted her to lift up her bottom so he could remove it. She just could not do this.

But she had to. And so she allowed him to lift the night rail to her waist, but not over her head.

And suddenly, he pushed the bed covers off the bed, and she was lying there, by the light of the nearly full moon flooding through the open window.

"You are lovely, March," he whispered.

She wasn't sure what she felt, but she did not feel beautiful.

She stared at the shadows on his face as he removed his nightshirt and eased over her. He was aroused, she could see. And then she felt the hot length of him on her thigh.

For a few moments, he rested his forehead against hers as if he was unsure how to go on. She heard him exhale, and then gently reach between her legs. She was slightly moist; she could feel it from the friction of his fingertips.

He removed his hand, placed his arousal against her opening, and slowly pushed himself inside of her.

He rose onto his forearms and worked just the merest edges of her for many minutes before deepening the penetration. It was the only part of his body that touched her.

She turned her face to the side and saw the moon out the window. This was as unlike their first union as it could possibly be, except for the fact that he was very aroused, and she was not fully ready to receive him. She was becoming sore.

And then he was finally completely seated within her depths and as hard as could be. It felt like an invasion. An invasion that would officially bind him to her.

He suddenly stopped. "Esme?"

"Yes?"

"Are you all right?" Strain and concern laced his words.

"Oh, yes. I am perfectly fine."

"Are you certain?"

"Certain."

"Will you tell me what I can do to help you find your completion?"

Completion? She just wanted this entire episode finished. And then she would be able to cry in peace. "I don't want to find completion," she said, truthfully.

He stilled. "Please, Esme."

He so rarely used her true name. It nearly undid her. But she had to guard her heart. It would just be too painful otherwise. She could not reply for the life of her.

He rested his forehead against hers and closed his eyes. "I am sorry, my dear. I am so sorry."

"I am too," she ground out. She wasn't even sure what she was sorry for, but it seemed the best thing to say.

He finally raised his head, and took her face between his hands. He had a look of such innocence in that moment. And of wanting to give her anything she wanted.

But she knew he would never be able to give her what she truly wanted: his love.

He brushed his lips against her cheek, and finally thrust into her several times. And just as she guessed he was reaching his peak, he pulled outside of her as he had done on the ship. He emptied himself on the sheets.

She was chilled to the bone.

She had never felt so unwanted in her life. He did not even want to finish inside of her? They were married. And this was a chance, very likely the only one, for conceiving a child. She was so confused she could not form one syllable. She refused to remember that they had agreed to remain childless.

"I am sorry if I hurt you, March. I shall leave you in peace so you may sleep," he said gently. "I asked a footman to remove my affairs to another chamber as I am a restless sleeper and do not want to disturb you."

Never once in her life had she ever felt so alone, as she did right now. She remained silent as she heard the rustling sounds of him gathering his clothes in the darkness.

A moment later he was gone, leaving only his faint, unforgettable scent on the pillow.

Esme moved to the other side of the bed and wrapped her arms around the bolster. A few moments later she sat up and violently threw the pillow he had used across the chamber. She fell back onto the bed and allowed tears to course down her cheeks and pool in her ears. Oh, how ridiculous she was being. How childish. She was a fully grown woman. She was not an innocent. She knew she was not pretty and had never been sought after by gentlemen, but she was well educated, had goals in life, was adept at conversation, and tried very hard to be the best she could be. She was very good at friendships, and she was a female of worth.

But for the first time in her life, she doubted herself. No matter how kind he was to her, he clearly found her unworthy of being his wife.

And that was the exact moment hope died. She

folded all her most cherished dreams of finding love one day, and of children, and of growing a family, and she tucked it away in the most secure chamber of her heart.

She refused to feel sorry for herself. She had found love once—a flawed love, of course—but a love nonetheless. There were many who did not ever find love. But she could not be lucky twice. And so she would live her life alone, with her mother, William, and all her friends in the neighborhood. And she would travel and paint. She had an excellent life. She just did not have a husband who could be counted on for anything other than financial support—something she would never need considering the adequate fortune she already possessed.

In truth, she didn't need anything from anyone. She brushed away her tears, lit a candle, and retrieved her spectacles. She opened her drawing book to a blank page and began to sketch her father's face, something that always brought her great comfort.

A half hour later, she set aside the half-drawn face in despair. The image looked far more like Roman Montagu than her beloved father.

And she wondered how long it would take before she would be able to begin to forget him.

Chapter 9

Well, Roman thought, that had gone spectacularly poorly. He had no idea what had happened.

He had showered her with assurances that he would not try to change her life or her dreams. He had given her, essentially, permission to live her life however she chose. He would gladly pay for anything she needed or wanted, just as he did for his mother and sister. Was that not an action of affection? He was and always would be her protector and provider until one of them stopped breathing.

And yet, gone was the extraordinary caring and kindness he had felt when they had lain together on that damn ship. He didn't require care or kindness, but he had thought he would at least receive a measure of warmth from her. Yes, he had caused this mess, and he had apologized and taken the ultimate responsibility by marrying her to preserve her reputation.

And now? Well, now he was tied to a woman who might not even like him. Indeed, the only thing she seemed to care about was her bloody painting—something in which he had no interest whatsoever. In fact, he loathed art. He would never tell her that, but it was a trial to be surrounded by drying canvases, and the smell of pigments and oils in half the manor. It had not always been that way. He had spent hours sketching and painting in his youth until his father had put a stop to it.

Had not his father ever and always insisted that artists were an untrustworthy breed of gypsy not to be borne? His father might have been an unpleasant, stern taskmaster, but he had always taken on responsibilities no matter what the consequences. Well, no matter, Roman would be gone within a few weeks. He wasn't sure he could wait out a full six weeks.

He decided right then and there in the privacy of his small chamber three doors down from hers, that he would leave within the month.

He would leave for Cornwall to see Kress—His Majesty be damned. Period.

His decision taken, he closed his eyes, and with the maddening ability of a man who was able to regulate his mind and sensibilities at will, fell into a deep, deep sleep.

The next morning, Roman awoke once again to hear birds chirping.

While he would have liked nothing better than to call the carriage and depart for Cornwall, he pulled the chamber cord, requested breakfast delivered to the chamber, and dressed himself, without waiting for the servant assigned to him.

Within a half hour, he was riding one of the manor's horses about the property. It was a lovely estate, and he had to give Esme's deceased husband credit where it was due for maintaining the land so well. The tenant cottages were solidly constructed, the farming land in use, the animals in excellent condition, and every single last tenant and groundskeeper appeared contented and well fed. He even spied a group of children carrying lunch pails heading toward a school in the village when he arrived there. The former Lord Derby might have been a drunk, but he also had been an excellent caretaker of the parish.

After surveying the village, he turned the gray gelding in the direction of the manor.

Lost in thought about his project, he came upon a mill on the edge of the property. He stopped to watch the water wheel turning in a majestic arc.

And just like that, the first glimmer of the answer he thought would forever evade him shone brightly in a corner of his mind. He had been trying so hard to find a solution in one direction, when all along there had been a grander scheme with a far simpler device to see it through.

A thousand possibilities flowed through his mind. He needed something on which to draw.

A fluttering object caught the corner of his eye and he spotted Esme's easel propped against a birch tree, but she was nowhere in sight.

He urged the horse into a canter but slowed soon after to jump off near the tree. He grabbed a piece of sketching paper and some charcoal from her small box. Lost in thought, he began to draw geometric diagrams so quickly that he soon had five pieces of paper before him, every inch covered with figures and arcs, and numeric equations. He reached for another piece of paper and realized he had used it all.

"Do you need more? I would be happy to fetch some for you."

He looked up only to see Esme resting against the side of the millhouse, nearly invisible in the deep shade of the tree nearby. He had been so lost in thought, and she so quiet, he had not seen her. "How long have you been sitting there?"

"Not long."

"And you said not a word."

"Why would I? You were obviously doing something very important to you."

He shook his head in disbelief. The females he knew would have interrupted him within a half minute of seeing him.

She repeated her offer. "Shall I fetch more paper for you?"

"You would do that?"

"Of course."

He let the silence hang in the air, along with the rustling of the leaves in the hedge and trees nearby. She did not ask the obvious. Why did she not barrage him with a thousand questions about what he was doing? "That would be more than kind of you."

She stood up, laid down her own sketch on a nearby stump, and placed a book on top of it to keep it in place. "I shall take Dobby and be back in a trace."

He said not another word. As he waited, a ball of sadness rose to his throat. She truly was an extraordinary female. Generous, kindhearted, and possessed with great talent. She gave of herself. And what had he done? He had done nothing but take from her.

He stared at the mill again, and the relationship between the wheel and the water. One could say the water was the energy, the giver, and the mill was the taker, making a product.

He crossed to the stump where she had left a stack of her own drawings. Moving the stone weight, he examined her efforts.

He was transfixed by the images. She was a master. Image after image it was proven to him. He could not figure out why he had not fully recognized it when he had seen her painting on the Isle of Wight.

He studied more closely the drawings. He finally understood. While her landscapes were lovely, it was her ability to capture people that set her apart.

He shook his head. Had not William Topher told her the opposite? He should refrain from saying anything. Roman was by no means an expert, nor did he want to complicate or question her vocation.

He stared at her drawings until he saw her in the distance.

He quickly rearranged her sketches, placed the weight on them once again and thanked her for the new supply of sketching paper. March returned to her place in the shade.

For another two solid hours they worked together but apart. It was an amazing sensation. He had always worked alone. Every five to ten minutes, he would look up from his computations to see if she was still there.

He finally saw her rise from her perch, gather her artist supplies and turn to face him. "I'm for home," she said. "By the way, Lady Verity Fitzroy is coming to dine with us tonight. Will you join us?"

He jumped up to do the right and proper. "Of

course I will join you. But you should take the horse. May I escort you?"

"Oh no. I like to walk after sitting so long." She was near him now. "I had the impression that you disliked art."

"This is not art."

She angled herself for a better view.

He was certain she would not understand. It was better that way. No one understood his work or the mathematical machinations of his mind.

"Hmmm. I always loved geometry," she said. "But the computations are . . . complicated. This has something to do with water?"

"How did you guess?"

"Well, it is not the equations. It's just that you were staring very hard at the mill wheel for so long. What is this for?"

"I shall tell you, but you must not relay it to anyone else." He did not stop to think if it was wise to trust her. "I do not want to rush this. I've been secretly working on a water delivery method so that clean water could be pumped through all the boroughs in London every hour of the day."

"You mean no one would have to rely on private well water? Or wait for the two-hour allotment?" Her eyebrows rose. "So many are sick from the water in Town."

"Exactly."

Her eyes lit up. "When will it be ready?"

"I do not know. The problem lies with the pumps. They require too much space and are very complicated."

"Who knows you're working on this?"

"No one."

"Why on earth not?"

"As I said. I do not want to be rushed. It's complex."

She looked at him. "You're absolutely right. I hate to be hurried."

"Did I rush you last night, March?" he asked, looking deep into her gray eyes.

She looked away, embarrassed. "No."

"Are you sure?"

"Yes . . . I mean, no, you did not rush me."

"I did," he insisted. "I should have prepared you. Taken my time. I am very sorry, March."

She shuffled the sheets of sketching paper in front of her.

"Do you . . ." He paused, unsure of what he had been about to suggest. "Pardon me, March. But will you allow me to try again?" He wanted desperately to do right by her. She was everything kind and good and he had been the opposite.

She appeared very embarrassed by his words, and her face was still averted. Then all at once, those piercing gray eyes met his.

"No, thank you."

Chapter 10

She could not believe she had had the audacity to turn down her new husband's gentle request to "try again." Oh, she knew why she had refused him. First, she was angry at him for deeming her unworthy of being a wife and mother by spilling his seed on the sheets. Second, she couldn't lie with him again. She just could not. The first time with him had been an act of reassurance and comfort. The last time had been an abomination and had left her feeling empty and worse.

Perhaps he respected her well enough, but that was all. He did not love her and never would.

He stood in front of her with his coiled virility taunting her spinsterish demeanor. He had expected her to demur to his suggestion, but she could not.

The idea of once again having intimate relations with someone who did not love her, and would never love her, left her feeling cold.

"And is this all the answer I am to receive?" he asked slowly.

"Yes."

"Have I hurt you in any way, March?"

She examined his face. "I am perfectly fine physically."

"And your sensibilities?"

A flush wound its way up her body and settled on her face. "Why did you spill your seed on the sheets?"

He paused. "Because I do not want to get you with child."

Well, at least he was honest.

"March, I know you want to travel, and paint. You will not be able to do that if you become with child."

"That was the only reason?" she asked, hope stirring in her breast.

"All except one," he replied slowly.

"And that one would be?"

"Something I don't care to discuss." His face was now as cynical and hard as the marble busts in the Prince Regent's apartments.

"Please tell me. I am willing for both of us to have private lives apart from one another but this is too important." Lord, this was the most embarrassing thing in the world. "What was the other reason?" She could see in his eyes that something was not quite right. "It's all right. Just tell me."

"I do not want a child. It has nothing to do with you," he said quietly. "I ask you not to bring up the subject again."

"All right," she said, "but tell me why. As your wife, even if it is not a real marriage, I deserve to know. But I promise never to say a word to anyone."

His sky blue eyes searched her face.

"Please," she added.

He looked away. "I do not desire a continuation of the Norwich duchy. It will revert to the Crown upon my death. But I want you to know that I shall settle my affairs, leaving you a significant portion of unentailed wealth when I die. It will be far more than you could possibly need, but I never want you to be in fear of straightened circumstances."

She should tell him about her ancestry. But for some inexplicable reason she could not find the words to do so. She just did not want to ever doubt his intentions toward her.

"How kind," she said with an odd note in her voice that she could not hide. "So to reiterate, you want to have relations again. You do not want us to nurture a child. You want both of us to live apart and have complete freedom to do as we choose. And the duchy is to be dissolved all because of a ridiculous curse involving ducks?"

He did not look in the least bit put out. She fingered the edge of her painting apron.

"Exactly."

"I see," she said, not seeing anything whatsoever. "And why do you want to lie with me again?"

"Because, it is as I told you. I was not gentle. And . . . and it's *you,* March. It was not well done."

"I told you I was fine." But something had gone soft inside of her when he'd said, *"And it's you, March."* "But I shall not turn you away if you choose to come to my room at some point." She suddenly felt very warm, and very shy. Then her sliver of pride, which she carried with her and displayed at only times of extreme stress—pushed up inside of her. "But, I must tell you it will have to be the very last time we lie together. I do not really enjoy such intimacy unless both share a deep love for each other."

He studied her without a word.

She could not stay another moment. Esme turned on her heel and strode away.

That evening, she felt equally ill at ease when she was near him or had to speak to him. He was such a solid and handsome man, with his aristocratic mien. His premature gray hair was combed back from his noble profile. His large forehead and prominent nose spoke of innate intelligence. He was too handsome for his own good, sitting there at the opposite end of the long, formal table, she thought wryly.

Her best friend, Verity Fitzroy, obviously thought so too, for she kept nudging Esme under the table and raising her eyebrows pointedly.

"Stop it," she hissed. Her friend finally halted her ridiculous behavior until she invited Esme outside to take a short stroll in the night air, away from the prying eyes and ears of Esme's husband, mother, and teacher.

"I'm sorry I was so silly at table. I think I'm losing my manners and I'm beginning to act like a child, so little have I been allowed to mingle with others," Verity said, with a lilt in her voice that belied the sadness in her eyes. "How can I be counted on to act content when my brother has had the audacity to lock me away at Boxwood?"

"Are you ever going to tell me what you did to deserve such archaic treatment?" Esme arched a brow. "Well, you aren't truly locked away. You're here now after all."

"I'm confined to Derbyshire and I'm not to go with my sisters to Town for the Season. But enough about me. How on earth came you to be wed to Norwich? I thought I would explode with curiosity when your mother came to call to invite me tonight."

"I suppose she explained everything to you?"

"Not a single word. She looked like a beautiful

Persian cat who had swallowed the most delicious canary but she would not spit out a single feather. It was most annoying."

Esme laughed. "That is what I adore about my mother. She will always surprise you. I did not know if she would be able to keep such a secret. But have no fear, my dearest cousin, for you are the one and only person I shall tell the whole of it to. Every last embarrassing, terrible, scandalous detail."

During a half hour of lightning-fast conversation, Verity was apprised of the outrageous goings-on of the past weeks. Indeed, her friend looked ready to swoon at several points. She even extracted her smelling salts from her reticule. Then again, Verity loved to pull out her smelling salts at every possible occasion as she believed life was one long slog of boredom and she loved dramatics in any form.

After Verity had examined and exhausted every single last possible question surrounding Esme's rushed marriage, she stopped under a lantern in the tiered gardens.

"He is very handsome," her cousin said gently. "Do you love him? It would be hard not to fall in love with a man like that."

"No. I do not love him."

"But you like him. You *esteem* him."

"I esteem him, but I have just enough pride to

refuse to love someone who does not love me."

Verity's brown eyes were dark and huge in her face. "Tell me he does not love you. I shall bring James's dueling pistol case, load each weapon and discharge both at his derriere to make sure he understands what an idiot he is. He should instantly love you after all you did for him on that ship."

"Oh, he likes me, I suppose. He *esteems* me, I am sure. *Like* and *esteem* are the words one uses to express the most boring sentiments in the world." She paused and cast her gaze at the moon. "But he will never *love* me. There is something in his expression that makes me think he does not want to love anyone. So I am trying not to take it personally."

"I would take it personally." Verity reached for Esme's hand and urged her to sit on the cold earth at the base of the tree. The lantern light shone on their faces.

"Dearest, I have told you everything there is to tell. Now it is my turn to hear what you've done to deserve your brother's ire," Esme insisted with a smile she forced to her face.

"I cannot."

"I beg your pardon?" Esme was shocked. They shared absolutely everything between them. They were as close as any two sisters if not more so as they had chosen to be each other's only confidant and they were cousins.

"It's only because my brother forbids me to speak of it to anyone. He has never asked that of me and what happened is so awful—even worse in some ways than the events on that ship you spoke of—that I cannot speak of it. While I always tell you everything, this I cannot."

A long silence erupted. Esme tried not to feel hurt. She had, after all, spilled everything to her dearest cousin.

Verity finally spoke. She lifted her eyebrow. "But I suppose I can give you a few *hints*. James did not precisely say I could not hint to my best friend in the world." Verity smiled. "It occurred that awful night before my brother was to be wed in Town. This is really all his fault, although he will never admit it. That night of infamy led you to your predicament and it has led to mine. And the whole of England knows my brother and the rest of the dukes of the royal entourage behave abominably. They deserve every inch of the punishment Prinny metes out."

Esme said not a word. She could see Verity's mind working on a way to reveal more. Her cousin did not disappoint.

Verity picked up a dead leaf that had fallen from the gnarled knuckles of the plain trees above, whose branches had grown and knotted together through the decades. She feathered her other hand with the curled, dried brown leaf. "While I cannot tell you who, I can tell you that one of the members of the royal entourage was indeed secretly wed that awful night."

"Dear Lord," Esme murmured.

"And I arranged it." Verity appeared a tad pleased with herself. "There is really only one problem."

"Yes?"

A look of consternation and worry appeared in Verity's brown eyes. "He doesn't know."

"Who doesn't know!?"

"I told you I cannot reveal names," Verity said crossly.

"Will you at least tell me if it is Norwich?"

"How absurd," Verity said. "Of course it isn't Norwich. I would have told you if it was!"

Esme breathed a sigh of relief. "Is it Abshire?"

"No, of course it is not Abshire!"

"Kress?" Esme knew it had to be Kress. He was the one who had been sent to Cornwall in disgrace.

"I refuse to answer!"

"Hmmmm," Esme murmured. "Or is it Sussex? No, don't answer. I see I've tested the limits of your patience and I can't have you angry with me. I need your friendship now more than ever before."

"Thank you, Esme." Her cousin looked away. "By the by, have you heard that Abshire has been in the neighborhood of late?"

Esme smiled inwardly. Everyone knew the

Duke of Abshire, who lived in the adjacent parish, and the Duke of Candover, Verity's brother, absolutely despised each other. No one knew why. It was a topic that was off-limits by both families but much discussed behind their backs—by everyone except Esme. She loved her cousins too much, and respected Abshire's family too. And everyone knew Abshire was an exceedingly jaded rake, but he was witty in an odd sort of way, and the few times Esme had been in his company, he had always noticed her and had had one or two kind or humorous words to say in her direction—such as on her wedding day. She had never felt like a wallflower when she was about this grand duke.

Esme looked at her cousin. "He was in London."

"Not for very long," Verity said, not quite meeting her eyes. "He was in Town with the rest of the royal entourage the evening before James left his bride cooling her heels at the altar."

Esme smiled at Verity. "Is it not odd how sometimes one's fondest wishes come true during the worst of circumstances?"

Verity burst out laughing. "You said it very politely."

"Well, have you and your sisters been quietly celebrating?"

"Of course. I cannot tell you how relieved we were when the grand event became the grand finale of five years of—of . . ."

"Oh, go ahead and say it."

"Of hell," Verity whispered.

Esme pulled the decimated leaf from her cousin's hand. All that remained was the skeletal main veins of the leaf. "She was not a nice person, Verity. Everyone knew it. I am so glad she will not be your sister, even if I am sorry she was forced to endure such embarrassment."

"I know. No one deserves to suffer as she did," Verity returned.

"Well, I am not so kind as you. The day she had the audacity to hint that she would send you and all your sisters packing after she married your brother, I wanted to find your brother's dueling pistols too."

"Well, there are a lot of us." Verity giggled. "It was the part about suggesting we would all do very well in a religious order that stunned the imagination. Just because we are all of us uniformly ugly does not mean we are pious."

Esme bit her lips to keep from grinning. "We are not going to have this conversation again, are we? Where we compare our physical attributes and the merits of our great characters? You know I always win this debate."

Verity picked up another tree leaf and began to pick it apart. Her dark brown eyes and hair appeared black in the moonlight.

Esme took the leaf from her favorite cousin and

forced her back to the right track. "You mentioned Abshire was in London the night before James was to wed too."

"Yes."

"And?"

Verity inhaled long and slow. "Something happened. But it was nothing. I promise you. It was just the stupidest, most abominable mistake and misunderstanding. Nothing happened at all. And James knows that. He believes me. But it concerns Abshire and you know how much they detest each other. And once James takes a decision, no matter how idiotic, he is as immovable as a tomb. Abshire refuses to consider my idea. Actually, no one cares what I have to say about the matter." Verity stopped after such a long explanation. "Promise me you will not ask me to clarify anything. The only other thing I can add is that I have refused to obey James's order."

"I won't ask what Abshire's role is in all this. And even though I sense he is a gentleman under all his ridiculous layers of worldly reserve, I know enough to know he would not like to accede to anything James would ask of him even if it was to his benefit. But is there any other path that you've considered that will release you from your brother's order?" Esme stared at her friend's profile in the darkness.

"I will stay here until I am old and gray before I

take a decision that will so wholly disappoint me."

Esme asked her dear friend gently, "Do you love him?" There was no need to say Abshire's name.

"Of course not." Verity said too quickly. "And what has love to do with anything? Are you in love with Norwich? No, don't answer. I know you are not. We are talking about honor and reputation—which is what makes this so ridiculous since there is not a single hint of damage to my saintly reputation." She paused. "And I have another thing weighing heavily on my mind."

"And what is that?"

"I'm so ridiculous." She paused on the gravel path between the climbing roses. "I should not have said a word."

"Of course you should have. Am I not your confidante? Did you not help me when I was at my bleakest?" Esme reminded her.

"You look even worse now."

Esme gave her a look. "And that is why we get on so well. You never censure your thoughts."

"Well, to be honest, I was just trying to change the topic. It's the reverse, in truth. You appear far lovelier than I've ever seen you. Are you willing to share the talents of that lady's maid the Prince Regent sent here to tend you?"

"Jacqueline Cooper?"

"Do you think you could spare her tomorrow to

help me look half as pretty as you do right now?"

"And what is so important about tomorrow?"

Verity looked away. "Abshire is to visit."

"Now that is interesting. Did not James say he would shoot him if he ever dared to set foot on Candover property again? Although, obviously an exception must be made for some reason you will not say. Still, does James know Abshire is paying a call? And did I tell you, James was my witness during the secret wedding?"

Verity smiled. "It's your eyes."

"My eyes?" Esme bit her bottom lip. "What have my eyes to do with Abshire or my ridiculous, hushed-up marriage?"

"They are more beautiful than ever, but they are haunted. No, it is your eyes that ruin the effect Madame Cooper created. What has happened, Esme? Is the marriage that difficult? He seems very kind."

"No. It is everything right," she contradicted. "He values independence and freedom and he's vowed to allow me both. He says he wants me to do what I love, to travel and paint. We are not to be in each other's pockets. It is to be a dream of a marriage. It will be so perfect and easy that we will not even have to lay eyes on each other except perhaps on Easter Day and perhaps Michaelmas, when we will attend church together to keep the tongues from wagging. The rest of the time he will be in London, and I," she paused, "anywhere except London."

Verity's velvet brown eyes were huge in her face. "He said that? In those very words?" she breathed.

Esme nodded. "Except the part about Easter Day and Michaelmas."

"Why it sounds perfect!" Verity chuckled. "You are the most independent creature, are you not? And you will be able to paint to your heart's content. No one will bother you. I wish I were you. I would like nothing better than to never again be under a brother or a future husband's thumb."

Esme looked away. "I know," she said slowly. "I am happy."

Verity grabbed her friend's chin between two fingers and drew her face back toward her. "Now, you listen to me, Esme Mannon Morgan March Montagu . . . My, you have a lot of M's in your name. Listen to—"

"Yes?"

"Your problems are very simple compared to mine."

"I know. They always are."

"Stop agreeing with me."

"No."

"Why not?"

"You just told me to stop agreeing with you so I did. Make up your mind."

"Oh, Esme. I've missed you. Can you not steal me away when you depart? I am certain I will find a solution to my awful predicament if you allow me to hide in your trunks along with my abigail."

"Your abigail? And how is the fair Amelia?"

"As beautiful as always. And just as outspoken. But then that is why I adore her, as you know."

"Won't Amelia be hurt if you ask Madame Cooper to attend to you and even do your hair?"

"I don't care about my hair. There is very little one can do with hair as straight as a stick. But . . . what did she do to your eyes? They are very different."

Esme harrumphed. "'Tis not my eyes. She plucked half my brows. Can you not tell?"

"Well, now I can since you mention it. Your eyes look farther apart, and larger. They are the most important part of your face now. I should attempt to take a likeness of you. I'd like nothing better than one of your canvases right at this moment."

Esme looked at her and they both dissolved into a gale of giggles.

Verity mopped her face. "Oh, all right. I won't. I do owe you far too many canvases than I can afford now that my brother has cut my quarterly pin money to a third of the usual."

Esme took both her cousin's hands in her own and really looked at her. "Will you not tell me what Abshire did or said to you? Why is he coming to call?" She desperately hoped it would lead to her cousin's happiness.

Verity stared at her. For a very long time—until Esme squirmed.

"Oh, all right, cousin. Don't tell me. But it is highly unfair. I tell you everything and you are like a tomb."

"Actually it appears as if this moment is long overdue. Usually—no—*always*, the reverse has been the case. Perhaps now you will see how unpleasant the sensation is." Verity examined her fingernails. "By the by, will you please come to Boxwood tomorrow for dinner? For propriety, I will not see Abshire without others present," Verity said very properly.

Esme sighed. "I suppose the invitation includes Norwich as well as my mother and William?"

"Absolutely, Your Grace," Verity smiled in the moonlight. "You have no idea how much I adore addressing you as such. And by the by, have you told Norwich about your bewitching ancestor?"

Esme sighed. Why had she thought her cousin could be counted on not to remind her of the one thing she wished she could ignore?

Chapter 11

Roman Montagu would never understand females. Oh, he tried with the best of men, but failed right alongside the hordes of comrades left dazed and confused.

After their long afternoon at the mill, her comforting, silent presence, and his attempt to ease the tension between them after the disastrous moments in her bedchamber, he had thought they might find their ease with each other.

Yes. He had.

Instead, he, like all the many fools before him, was pacing the floor of his chamber, trying to decipher the best course of action to please a mysterious female.

Should he or should he not go to her bedchamber? Would she welcome him? Or would she throw a slipper at his head? Would she be insulted if he did not go? Or would it be more insulting if he went to her?

Lord, he needed a glass of brandy. It was the best idea he'd had the last hour. Enrobed in his dressing gown, he descended the front stair, as quiet as you please.

Roman opened the door to the room he presumed was the absent earl's study, and found four heavy crystal decanters as empty as his brain, concerning ideas for how to please a woman. And damn it all, she was his wife! This should be easy, should it not?

He refused to search for spirits in another chamber. It was downright lowering. She had very likely emptied the manor of all spirits the day her husband had died.

Roman marched out the door, and headed off to bed sans brandy. At least he had taken his decision. Tonight was not the correct moment to seek out Her Grace, the Duchess of Norwich.

Said duchess, seated in the half-curtained window seat in the far corner of the study, silently watched Roman Montagu as he examined the empty decanters, and didn't know whether to laugh or cry.

She wanted to laugh because she suddenly remembered the intricate etching of geese or ducks in tall grasses that decorated the decanters. Had he noticed?

She wanted to cry because this window seat was one of her favorite places in the beautiful stone manor, and she had spent many an evening right here, sketching or reading. In the past, she had at least had the comfort of knowing that she was loved by her husband.

But now? The one man she wished most could one day come to love her—never would.

Esme eased from her perch, retrieved the book William Topher had lent to her, and mounted the stairs to find her bed.

If ever she needed another sign that her marriage was a complete disaster in the making, this was it.

Esme opened the book to try to lose herself in the beauty of centuries of art in Vienna. Between the lines, she tried to forget all about Roman Montagu and concentrate on the trip she would take by the end of the season. Away from England, and Roman, she would finally be free to immerse herself in the only thing that was guaranteed to make her forget all about the Duke of Norwich.

Early in the afternoon of the following day, the entire household descended on Boxwood, the Fitzroy family seat, per the formal invitation sent by Lady Verity Fitzroy. Rory Lennox, the Duke of

Abshire, arrived within the hour. Candover was in Cornwall, most likely turning the wedding screws on Kress, who Roman was hamstrung to help.

Nevertheless, the day would be a diversion in Roman's world, which had gone to hell in the same fashion as the world of every other duke he called a friend. Well, at least he could converse with Abshire. Indeed, there was nothing quite like a private chat with another member of the royal entourage to make one remember the natural order of things.

Abshire sat in what was presumably his archenemy Candover's ducal chair before a tiny fire in the grate of a great yawn of a fireplace in one of countless salons. The ladies and Topher had left the two dukes in peace and were either taking the air, skipping down pebbled walkways, or frolicking in the lake for all either of them knew.

And so Roman let down his guard and allowed himself to be drawn into a topic that was one they all tried to avoid at every opportunity. The infamous evening before Candover's nuptials had only served to make the matter even more unbearable.

"Marriage, my dear fellow, is nothing but a black hole of despair as Prinny's own union is ample evidence," Rory advised. "It was created for two reasons only: the orderly procreation and raising of heirs and to place two otherwise sane individuals into a recipe for a complete and utter quagmire of bitter accusations and unhappiness or, if one is very lucky, simple and complete boredom."

Ah, Abshire was in fine form today. It was just what Roman needed.

"I am telling you, Seventeen, your best chance for success is to always keep an ocean between the two of you. My guess is that in the end you will let her go off on a ship, make her own way—which is the only solution really. Of course, you will have to attempt to look the other way when she takes a lover, which she should do since you do not want her. Oh, you'll hear news of every step of her travels. And she will outlive you and most likely be happier. They are not the weaker sex, don't you know?" He began to show a hint of a smile. "Then again, you will do many of the same things to sweet Esme—such as taking lovers whenever needed. It's the way of our age, thank God. Yes, this entire marriage business will be a disaster. You'll see."

"And just where," Roman replied, "did you obtain all these truths since you've never married? Not that they are not the most wise words I've yet to hear concerning the solid foundation on which to build a marriage."

Abshire snorted. "Build a marriage, eh? I'm a very tolerant man, and would never question another man's ideas unless, of course, he is speaking of marriage, a subject about which I know more than a fair amount."

"And yet, if memory serves, you were on the verge of wading into this unhappy quagmire at one point. No?" Roman hoped his friend would not challenge him to a duel with these words.

Abshire elegantly crossed one leg over the other while staring at the flickering flames. Only his eyes spoke of the level of anger he bore without a word. He changed the subject just as Roman knew the other duke would.

"I shall wager you a thousand quid that Kress refuses to marry anyone on Prinny's list of eligibles in Cornwall."

"I will not take the wager," Roman replied. "I saw the list in London and every last one of those females is impossible. But I will wager you the same amount that Kress will wed someone—anyone—within the year, if only to save the monarchy."

"Oh, all right," Abshire muttered, "I accept your wager if only because I am bored all to hell and back. Prinny was every bit as guilty as the rest of us that night. I, for one, blame the Prince Regent more than anyone. Except Kress, of course, and that damned, bloody absinthe he gave us all. He deserves to be the first to be leg-shackled. It's too bad we can't force Prinny to go through with it all over again."

"Oh come now, Prinny is merely terrified England will become the next France, where excess led to revolution."

Abshire slowly raked his face with a jaded, hard stare. "So, you never replied. How are you planning to conduct this sad union of yours?"

"No, you changed tack when I mentioned that you had almost waded into this same quagmire state—voluntarily, I might add—a long time ago."

Abshire leveled a stare at him. "Pass me my glass, will you?"

Roman silently handed his friend one of the two glasses of wine at his elbow. He knew then that Abshire would not say a single blasted word about his near brush with matrimony many years ago. But Roman could not leave off his curiosity about his new wife. "You do not think very highly of Esme, then, given your thoughts on leg shackling?"

"There you are wrong, my friend. Very wrong."—the dangerous eyes of the most cynical gentleman of Roman's acquaintance glazed over a bit—"She was always loyal to her husband, despite his descent into absolute dissipation. She is very well liked by all who know her, and she can be quite witty." Abshire paused. "But don't ever go fishing with her. The last time I did at the age of nine, I do believe I broke her pole in half after she caught twelve fish and I caught none."

Roman scratched the back of his head. "So, she likes to fish? That's unusual."

"But it's nothing compared to her devotion to her passion."

"Art," Roman said, resigned.

"Yes," Abshire mused. "She's quite talented, don't you think? It was too bad she did not have someone better to guide her, help her develop her gift."

"We're agreed on that point," Roman retorted. "The man is not to be borne."

Abshire cocked a brow and a half-smile decorated his face. "Who?"

"Who do you think?" Roman retorted. Abshire knew exactly of whom they spoke. *Topher.* Had not Rory opened the topic? There were times Roman understood Candover's dislike of Abshire, who could play the all-knowing bemused observer better than anyone Roman knew.

"Actually, I'm not certain," Abshire insisted. "I was referring to husband number one, old man."

For some blasted reason he could not name, Roman's neck itched. "And I was speaking of that idiot, Topher."

"Hmmm. Topher? Really?" In a rare mood, Abshire smiled. "I've had some enlightened discussions about art through the ages with the man. I do not consider him ill-informed a' tall."

"Well, he certainly is a poor mentor. I do not agree with the majority of his stream of drivel. Indeed, I believe he is consciously or unconsciously giving Esme very poor advice."

Abshire steepled his fingers and rested his chin against them. "Really?"

Roman exhaled in annoyance. "Is that the best you can do? Answer *really* to my every utterance?"

"Yes," Abshire immediately retorted. "Unless, of course, you would prefer for me to tell you what I really think, which might leave you feeling like the bloody idiot you claim Topher to be."

"Oh, go ahead," Roman ground out. "I've never seen you restrain yourself before."

Abshire chuckled. "Jealousy is such an uninspired and unamusing trait. You could at least try to inject a bit of originality in your experience with it, my dear."

"Absurd," Roman replied. "I merely said the man was . . ."

At that moment, the idiot of the hour, Mr. William Topher, himself, entered the chamber without a single knock of warning. The man was not only a fool, but a cheeky one to boot.

"Pardon me, Your Graces." Topher halted and bowed. "But have you seen Esme?"

"Why do you ask?" Roman made a good show of ignoring Abshire, who let out a cough to hide a vile snicker of amusement.

"We had a rendezvous to descend to the lake."

"I see," replied Roman, not seeing at all.

"She was to take my likeness again—this time in one of Boxwood's rowboats. She needs to refine capturing the essence of a subject in different settings." Topher accepted the silent invitation from Abshire to join them in front of the fireplace.

Again the man had nothing but nonsensical advice. Of course. In the stacks of paintings Roman had secretly seen in his wife's private salon, she had excellently captured all her subjects in their many settings. "In your bloody opinion," Roman muttered under his breath.

Abshire turned to Topher and recovered the moment. "You are a favorite subject of Her Grace, are you not?"

"Well, you know, I've guided Esme for the last ten years." Topher preened. "Naturally, she took my likeness many times over, and learned something each time. But her forte lies with landscapes, of course."

"I disagree," Roman immediately retorted. "Portraiture is where her talent is fully revealed. Any bloody person can see it."

A long silence settled into the salon, like a wet blanket. Abshire coughed again. It sounded remarkably like a choked bark of laughter to Roman's ears.

William bloody Topher was smart enough not to argue.

Abshire could not stop himself from goading further. "I say, Topher, I very much enjoyed our conversation about Renaissance art. I'm certain Norwich would vastly enjoy an afternoon spent discussing the finer points with you."

Topher's visage brightened before he allowed a moment of doubt to register. But before the handsome sod could say a thing, Roman gracefully rose to his full height.

"Of course, today would not be the time to discuss anything," Roman grit out so Topher would take the hint and leave them in peace.

Topher cleared his throat. "So sorry to intrude. I shall just keep looking for Esme, Your Graces. Do ask her to find me if you see her. I shall return to the lake to wait for her. She's not always good at following directions, don't you know."

When Topher disappeared, Abshire turned to Roman. "Perhaps you should go after her, too, my dear fellow."

"Says the man who just described marriage as a black hole of despair."

"Yes, but it would be an amusing and adventurous black hole if she is anything like she was when I was nine years old." Abshire studied him and narrowed his eyes. "But I warn you, Norwich, do not break her heart. There are few females in Derbyshire whom I would defend, but she is one."

Roman placed his empty glass on the side table and stretched. Yes, it was long past Abshire's turn to roast over the coals of the fire he had built. "Finally."

"Finally, what?"

"Finally, there is something you and Candover can agree on."

Abshire scowled, and a dark lock of his hair fell forward. "We agree on nothing."

"Then again," Roman said quietly, "it is not the first time you both agreed on the merits of a lady."

Abshire rose up, knocking his glass off the table. He blasphemed so blue and advanced toward him.

"If you say one more idiotic word, Norwich, I will consider you more contemptible than bloody Candover. Now get out of my sight and go find your wife instead of attempting to make me find an excuse to knock you senseless."

Roman gave a long look at Abshire, whose expression had gone white as a ghost. He should not have referred to the rumors that swirled over the enmity between Candover and Abshire. It only made matters worse. Roman just didn't want to discuss his own life and how it was contaminating the happiness of a woman who was blameless.

He left without another word.

An hour later, hot from the exertion of searching for her, he stopped in the shade of a stand of trees. Where in hell had she gone?

He wondered if Topher was lollygagging by the lake or if the idiot had forgotten all about Esme in favor of charming the other ladies present. The man was the most ardent sycophant in Creation.

Oh, he was being ridiculous. He knew from firsthand experience that Esme was a lady with only painting on her mind. And she was clearly somewhere with her easel, canvases, and paints. It annoyed him. For some odd reason, he had the strongest desire to see her. Not to speak with her, or distract her. But there was something so calming and peaceful when they were alone together.

How absurd. Alone *together*? Impossible.

He untied and unwound his damp neckcloth and removed his coat and waistcoat. Rolling up his long white linen sleeves, he cursed as pointedly as Abshire had done earlier.

He began the long walk to the estate's famed boxwood maze. What had changed?

At least Roman knew he possessed one positive trait. He was always bitterly honest with himself. He could admit Esme was everything Abshire and Candover had hinted. She had only and ever been fair, and kind, and honest with him. Yes, she had let pride rule her emotions when he had hurt her with his suggestion that they lie together again. But, her extraordinary giving nature, very evident the night she had comforted him in the most primal way possible, was everything.

God.

He was such a fool.

If he had to take the rest of his life to make it up to her he would. If he had to spend every waking moment smelling oil paints he would do it. He would do any bloody thing she wanted. But damn it, he would make her happy—because seeing her happy would make him happy. And he had to tell her. Tell her how important she had become to him. Tell her that he wanted to make her happy. Tell her there was something inexplicable that had formed between them.

And he had to find her and tell her all this right away. Before he lost his nerve.

He began to run. He ran and ran until he reached the top of the long hill to the north of the estate. Finally, he looked down, and saw the enormous maze in the distance.

There was something small and white caught on the tall branches near the center. It had to be something of hers. But he was too far away for her to hear him. The blasted maze had to be a half mile long on each of the sides of the hexagon.

Roman stopped and searched for a better vantage point. There were none. The thing was not meant to be easy. And so he studied it, memorizing as many features, turns, tricks he could see from this hill. He stood there, desperate to start, and desperate to stay and work it out.

The former won out in the end and he ran down the hill and entered the maze from the nearest opening.

At every turn in the tall hedge, he paused, placed

two fingers between his lips and whistled shrilly and then waited for a response.

Nothing.

God, it was hot. Hotter than Hades on midsummer's night eve. Given his innate fine sense of direction, he was confident that he was at least making progress toward the center and took care to check the location of the sun as he worked his way ever closer.

He didn't know why he was beginning to panic. It was absurd.

She might be thirsty, or tired, or worried, but she would not be hurt. No one could get hurt in a maze. They could only get lost.

An hour later, panic set in fully. There was something about the place that was downright eerie. The boxwood was too dense.

He remembered hearing Candover say something at some point about how he was going to ignore the entail and tear the whole bloody thing down, it was so dangerous.

Someone—was it a poacher?—had actually perished in here.

He stopped. Yes. Candover had actually said that. He whistled again.

Nothing.

Roman looked at the wall of evergreen before him and took a decision. He put on his gloves, searched the interior and found a medium-sized trunk. He tried to grab it and climb to the top. It was next to impossible. There were thorns on the branches. Since when did boxwood have thorns?

He refused to stop and continued to climb, despite the vicious jabs of the branches. Near the top, the trunk swayed and he lost his grip and half slid, half fell back to the ground.

He cursed and cursed. His gloves were in ribbons as were his clothes. Well. That was not going to work. He picked himself up, ignoring flashes of pain and finally began to seriously run down every possible lane and avenue, yelling her name.

Finally, blessedly, he heard something. He stopped and called again. A feeble voice said something unintelligible in the distance.

"Esme!" He shouted again. "Please, please keep talking. I will find you. Stay where you are!" He prayed she would do as he bid.

He kept shouting to her every few moments, and listened hard for any response. A wisp of her voice drifted back to him, but it was different and it filled him with unease.

Another half hour passed in utter frustration. He was terrified he was getting farther away from her instead of nearer. He stopped again and closed his eyes, trying to remember the elaborate geometric design he had viewed from the hill.

And then finally, he turned a corner and saw her lying on the ground.

Chapter 12

Roman dropped to his knees in gratitude. He half crawled, half ran to her. He grasped her hand in his and squeezed.

Her eyes barely slit open. What he saw made him ill. One of her eyes was very bloodshot, and that side of her face was scratched. Her gown was torn, and her arms marred by long scratches too.

"March!"

Her eyes opened more fully. "Montagu," she whispered.

He leaned down to hear her better.

"I'm so sorry," she whispered. "So sorry for everything."

He pulled out a flask he had tucked into the back of his breeches. He uncorked it, cradled her head, and dribbled a little brandy between her lips.

She coughed and then moaned.

"What is it?" He demanded hoarsely.

"I will never be able to thank you enough," she whispered. "It was so stupid of me. I know better than to come here."

"Stop it," he gritted out.

"You're bleeding," she said unevenly.

"Stop," he insisted. "Can you not walk?"

"I tried to climb there." She pointed to a place that showed almost no trace of her attempt. "But I stupidly fell. My foot . . . I don't know what's wrong with it."

He glanced down and moved to her feet. He felt beneath her torn stockings and one ankle was swollen.

When he squeezed slightly, she did not make a sound. "It might be sprained or even broken, my darling," he said with concern.

"I guessed as much," she whispered and lowered her head to the ground.

But she was far too listless. Something was off in her manner. "March, what is it? Something else is wrong. Tell me where it hurts."

She closed her eyes and he rushed back up to her face.

She said something but he could not make it out.

"Tell me. March, please. I beg of you."

Her eyes closed, she said, "Head . . . my . . ."

He gently felt her head beyond the tangle of her pretty light brown hair. His fingers came away sticky and wet; the back of her head was full of blood.

It was just like the night when his brother had . . .

He lost every button of his shirt as he immediately yanked it over his head and tore it into strips.

"March," he ordered brusquely. "Open your eyes and listen to me."

She murmured something.

"Just listen to me. Do not fall asleep. Do not. Stay here with me." He tried to be as gentle as he could as he bound her head with the linen strips, to stem the loss of blood.

Her eyes fully closed.

"March, open your eyes, I tell you."

They fluttered open.

"Do you remember the night of the storm? Do you remember when you told me to take your hand and told me you were there? I am ordering you to do the same, do you understand?" When she did not respond, he continued. "Squeeze my hand."

He felt a gentle pressure in his grip. "All right. Now, drink more of this." He held her head and poured a few more drops.

And then, with the meager amount of luck a cursed duke could count on, he heard voices.

He stood up and shouted as loudly as he could. And then he took off his boots.

For what seemed like hours, he tossed first one then the other as high as he could in the air, past the top of the tall wall of boxwoods. He took care to aim properly for if he lost the boots, there would be no way for them to be found.

Every two minutes, he would stop and drop to her side, to tell her he was there and to stay with him.

She would squeeze his hand.

And then she stopped squeezing his hand.

"Esme, my love, please . . . please try to stay here with me. I won't leave you. Truly I will not."

He closed his eyes and remembered all her tenderness, her wit, her desire to always please and bring a measure of happiness to everyone.

And what had he given her in return? He had protected her reputation, and he had promised her another fortune, which she did not need. And he had told her she should go live her life.

Alone.

He had wanted no bloody ties. He didn't want anyone to have an ounce of a reason to depend on him for anything except money.

He didn't want to depend on anyone for anything. Because to depend on anyone except yourself always led to unmitigated disaster. He would be born alone, and die alone. It was better to know it and live life that way. All the people who fluttered in and out of one's life were naught but other creatures caught in the same cycle of life. Most were under the grand illusion that they were tied to other people—that they were not alone.

But it was not true.

He did not, and could not, depend on anyone. Except . . .

He looked down at her bruised and bloodied form, and his heart broke. "March, damn it all, I love you. Come on. Don't go away. You cannot. I am"—his throat clogged—"I am *depending* on you. Please."

Her fingers fluttered like a small bird in his hand.

And just like that, they were found.

Esme lay in her bed, gazing at the shadowed scene she had painted so many years ago. Night had finally fallen, but ironically, she was too tired to sleep. She tried not to feel the pain that had been radiating from the back of her head and her ankle for the last day and a half.

She tried instead to remember what had happened when Roman Montagu had found her in the maze. Some of the moments were so clear. His warm, rumbling voice. The startling depths of his clear blue eyes filled with concern. She thought she might have seen him throwing something up in the air. But through it all, he had tended to her—in a way she had never experienced in her life. No man ever took care of her. She didn't like it, really. She preferred to be the one to give than the one to receive.

She had never seen Roman Montagu in this fashion. He had tried desperately to comfort her, and to ensure that she not drift toward unconsciousness. It would have been so easy. But would it have been dangerous? She didn't know, but apparently, he knew of such things.

She remembered nothing of the journey from the maze back to Derby Manor.

There was really only one thing she remembered with crystal clarity. Some of the words he had uttered as she had been about to let herself fall into darkness.

"March, damn it, I love you. Don't go. I am depending on you. Please . . ."

He was the last person in the world she could ever imagine saying those words. Had he said them in an all-out effort for her not to swoon away? Or had he truly meant them?

He couldn't really love her, could he? And what did love really mean anyway? He had made it very clear that he wanted the freedom and independence of a life apart from her. He did not seem to be the sort who would choose to actually depend on anyone.

There was a light tap at the door, and it opened with a small creak. It was he.

She tried to sit up.

He came forward. "No, don't move. I don't want to disturb your rest, Esme. But I brought you a little tea. Your mother told me you had very little to eat."

"I like it better when you call me March," she said.

"All right," he said with a smile, "March."

He placed the tray on the side table and re-arranged the pillows without any of the finesse of a true nurse. He then drew up a chair, placed the tray on his lap and plucked three lumps of sugar and plopped them into the dish of tea. It warmed her heart that he had obviously noticed how she liked her tea.

He waved away her hand and placed the cup to her lips. "Drink," he said simply.

The tea was cold, but she drank it all, slowly and in silence.

"Your easel, and paints, and canvases are all re-covered," he said.

She took the cup from his tense fingers and placed it on the saucer. "It wasn't worth it," she replied.

"What wasn't worth it?"

"My things. That maze is far too dangerous."

He didn't reply.

"You retrieved them, didn't you?" She examined his handsome face.

"It was not so very difficult when Verity gave me the map."

She closed her eyes. "I'm so sorry," she whispered. "I should have told someone where I was going."

"Where were you going?"

"Verity had told me once a long time ago that there was a lovely sculpture garden in the center of the maze. I wanted to see it and maybe paint it." She bowed her head. "But I detest dramatics. And I am so sorry to have caused everyone such worry."

"Ah," he said, with a small smile that revealed only the edges of his teeth. "Now you know precisely how I felt after that storm."

"Did you feel this embarrassed?"

"And much worse, I assure you. But you have nothing to be embarrassed about. You follow directions well, and you did not cry. I wish I could say the same."

She started to smile but it hurt her face.

"Are you ready to sleep a little?"

"Of course," she answered without meaning it.

He examined her face carefully. "You know, you are going to have to stop doing that with me."

"What do you mean?"

"You are going to have to stop agreeing to everything and causing the least amount of trouble for everyone."

She couldn't respond.

"You can do that to everyone else—especially your mother, who I never would have imagined could be so worried given her good humor. But with me, March, you are going to have to be yourself."

"How ridiculous," she murmured. "You are speaking of simple courtesy. One must show courtesy at all times or we are nothing but wild animals."

His eyes darkened. "Perhaps, I might like to see the wild animal from time to time. The one I saw the night we met."

She held his gaze, transfixed.

"But now is not the time," he said gently, once more. He stood up and placed the tray on the long table. "Would you like for me to read to you a bit?" He picked up the book about art in Vienna.

"Not really," she replied.

"Good," he said, moving next to her bed again. "What would you like, then?"

It was so hard to tell him. She forced herself to remember his words and hoped he had meant at least a small part of them at the time. She hated asking him or anyone for anything. "I should like it if you would sleep beside me."

"Ah," he murmured. "Very good. Not even one word suggesting that you would only like it if it did not inconvenience me. Which it very much does not by the way."

He crossed to the door and locked it, then returned to her, removing his watch and fob along the way. He placed them carefully beside the tray, and slowly, but in that efficient manner of his, removed his clothes with the exception of his unbuttoned, nearly translucent linen shirt.

He looked at her for a long moment before he pinched out the candle near her bed. In the darkened room, his deep voice comforted her. "Don't move, March. I'm going to crawl in on the other side."

His solid weight moved close to her in the darkness, and he pulled up the covers. He arranged the heavy weight of his body alongside hers and then, very gently gathered her into his arms, taking care with her head to place it in the cradle of his shoulder.

He was so warm, and he smelled of soap and exotic spices. "Are you all right, like that?" His voice rumbled through her.

"Yes. Perfect." She sighed.

"Good. Now let's sleep." He gently placed a kiss on her brow.

"All right," she replied. She knew better. There was not a chance of her being able to sleep.

He loosened his grasp a little, and within a few moments, she heard the hitch in his breathing that signaled he was falling into slumber's grasp.

She wanted to cry. She really did. But she worried the wetness of her tears would wake him. Instead she regulated her breathing and tried to sleep.

A moment later, his strong arms clasped her closer to him for a moment before relaxing again. "Are you all right, March?" he asked sleepily.

"Yes, thank you. Better than all right."

"Good," he said and drifted again toward sleep.

She wasn't sure if she could sleep in his arms. She had never slept in anyone's arms. Oh, she had always slept in her marital bed. On the left side. The indentations on each side of the bed were fairly deep. She had thought she enjoyed being sprawled out on her side of the bed. She snuggled closer to Roman.

"March," he asked with weariness.

"Yes," she whispered, surprised he was awake.

"I won't sleep unless you do."

"I'm not sure I can," she replied. "I've had too much rest, I think."

"Are you certain you're comfortable like this?"

She nodded as she couldn't speak.

"Good."

He waited a moment before he continued. "Then just rest, my love. I am here if you need anything. Anything at all."

"Thank you, Montagu," she whispered. He had called her *his love.* Again, when he had not been terrified for her safety. And it warmed a very small place in her heart that she did not know existed.

She joined him in slumber within moments.

For seven days and six nights, Esme's convalescence passed thusly. During the day, she was coddled by her mother, and Verity, who refused to discuss anything about Abshire.

The problem was that Verity was just as good as she at concealing her thoughts and sensibilities. Usually, Esme could wheedle it out of her given enough time, and energy. But, she was depleted of the latter, and her mother rarely left them alone.

William was allowed to visit for an hour each afternoon. He was very dutiful in his attentions, encouraging her more than ever to begin planning the revised trip. He was so very kind to her, even suggesting he would accompany her since she might need his physical support due to her ankle. Something kept her from agreeing to his suggestion.

Toward the end of the week, the doctor consented to her drawing as long as she remained in bed.

During the nights, Roman came to her, and held her all through the darkness. He never spoke of the day in the maze or what he had told her and she didn't dare raise the subject.

Instead, over the course of the week she gradually succumbed to the strong, silent comfort of his arms. After that first night, she slept solidly, and recovered more quickly than anyone could have predicted, most especially the doctor.

Esme was most surprised by the Duke of Abshire, who condescended to visit the last day she was confined to her room.

"I see you will live, then."

"If only to go fishing with you again, Your Grace."

"How absurd." A sly smile slid onto his face. "Is Norwich taking care of you?"

Esme could feel a blush overtake her.

"Oh, we'll have none of that," Abshire snorted. "Well, is he? Shall I thrash him if he is not?"

"Don't be ridiculous," she said, hiding her amusement. "He has been enormously kind."

He stared at her, and she could see an internal debate clouding his face.

"Is there something you want to say to me?" she asked.

"No. It's the opposite," he admitted. For the first time ever, she watched a rueful expression cross his features.

Amusement filled her. "How about this? I'll look the other way, and you can just spit it out and leave. Then we'll both pretend you never said anything."

He threw back his head and roared with laughter. She was so pleased he had actually made the effort to see her.

He winked. "Agreed. Turn the other way."

She did as he bade, and stared at the blank wall.

"Look, I'm telling you this because I like you, Esme. Norwich is another story. I've never been able to make heads or tails of the fellow, to be honest. Oh, he's a good enough sort to be sure." He stopped short.

"And?" she resolutely kept her face toward the wall.

"And you were forced to marry. And you will either live together or live apart. I wanted to warn you that he is the sort who will choose to live apart from you in the end. I tell you this so you will guard your heart. I once knew someone very like you and I do not want to see you hurt."

She swallowed.

"It has nothing whatsoever to do with you. You must, please, understand this. Even if he cares for you, he will choose a solitary life."

"Why?" she said, trying very hard to sound casual.

"I'm not certain. I am breaking every bloody rule between the sexes by what I've advised you. But, there is nothing wrong in reminding you of recent Norwich history if you are not aware of common knowledge." He paused for but a moment before continuing. "His elder brother, who would have been duke, died when the ship he and Norwich were sailing sunk off the coast more than a decade ago."

"I remember hearing a little about it," she acknowledged.

"Everyone admired the elder. The old duke adored his heir. The mother and sister doted on him, and the two brothers were inseparable. The elder was the golden one and when he perished, the family changed. The father never recovered. Roman and the old duke were . . . well, I will not go on. I'm beginning to sound like a scandalbroth-sipping magpie."

She turned to finally face him and caught sight of his sly smile and hooded eyes.

"But I'm willing to appear a sodding idiot for a quarter hour to warn the best fisherman this side of Christendom not to place her heart in his hands."

She pursed her lips. "Thank you. Thank you more than you know. But you see, I think it's rather too late."

Abshire shook his head. "I thought as much. Well, I've done my duty by you. It's really too bad you weren't born a man. I think we would have formed a fine friendship. Instead, we are forced to dance on far too many levels. And I hate to waltz unless there is something to be had after the ball." He winked again.

He really was the most entertaining man she knew. And she never would have guessed how kind he could be under all his many jaded levels of reserve. But now she would turn the tables on him.

"I feel it necessary to return the favor of concern. But to do so, I must first ask your intentions toward my very dear cousin Verity Fitz—"

A light tap sounded at the door. Esme felt like cursing as much as she was certain Abshire suddenly desired to escape.

"Yes?" she called out.

"May I?" Roman's deep voice returned.

Abshire jumped from the chair and strode to open the door.

The two eyed each other warily.

"Where is my wife's maid?" Roman asked, annoyed.

"Oh, shut up," Abshire replied. "It always comes down to a maid, doesn't it?" With that nonsensical remark, he walked past the door and slammed it behind him.

Esme had not the slightest idea what Abshire meant by his odd remark, but she would wager her last gold guinea that it had something to do with Verity Fitzroy. Or her maid—or rather, her abigail.

And Esme realized she had not once seen Verity's ever-present lovely Scottish abigail, Amelia, since arriving in Derbyshire.

Chapter 13

"Just tell me he didn't cause you any worry. I know the scoundrel only too well," Roman said coming toward her. "Shall I thrash him for you?"

Esme smiled. "I have the oddest notion you two are of the same mold. He offered to do the same to you, by the way."

He set the beeswax candle down on the table. "So, I must keep on my guard, then?"

She paused and remembered Abshire's advice. How on earth was she supposed to guard her heart when she was afraid the man standing in front of her might have already stolen a large part of it? She swallowed. "I don't think you have anything to worry about," she said softly.

"How is your head?" He sat on the edge of the

bed and she moved away to give him more room.

"Everyone keeps asking me but no one believes me so what is the point of a reply?" she said wryly.

"I shall believe you."

"I am perfectly fine. I might limp a bit, but my head is healed. I am leaving this bed at dawn and going outside. I cannot bear another day of coddling."

He was staring at her with an odd light in his blue eyes.

"Except, of course, when you indulge me," she said, her eyes unable to meet his. "It's ridiculous to admit, but I will never be able to thank you enough for coming to me each night. It is a great comfort."

"May I?" he asked, reaching toward the bandage on her head.

She nodded.

He unwound the small strip of linen and felt the injury on the back of her head. "The swelling is down. And the cut?"

"Is nearly healed. It's so silly. Everyone knows that there was so much blood because it was a head wound. But I am perfectly fine now. Please do not worry." Abshire's caution overshadowed the words Roman had told her in the maze. He was not a man who would be steadfast in the end. It would be better to try to stop her intense sentiments, if she could. "Really, I do not want you to feel any obligation to stay here tonight. If I need anything, I shall call my maid."

"Do you want me to leave?"

She couldn't bear to lie to him even if it hurt her more by telling the truth.

"No."

He removed his coat. She drank in the sight of him as he undid his waistcoat, and pulled one end of his neckcloth. He always undressed in the same elegant, efficient manner—as if he had deciphered long ago the most scientific means to an end.

She tried to memorize the way his eyes watched her as he undressed, and how he placed his clothes on the back of the chair. This was the last time she would allow him to come to her bed. It would just be too hard to leave or to watch him leave if it continued like this.

He paused, his thumb and forefinger hovering near the candle's flame. He looked at her with a question in his eyes.

She wanted to see him. She didn't want to be in darkness as in the past. "Please, no," she whispered.

He nodded and climbed into the bed.

"May I help you with your shirt?" she asked tentatively.

He sat up and removed it so quickly it was a blur. And then he took her in his arms, in the fashion she had grown to want more than anything. His flesh touching hers felt like two halves coming together.

"March," he whispered in her ear, "I want you."

"I want you, too," she responded.

"Are you sure? I don't want to cause you any pain."

"Please." She just could not resist him, even if he would break her heart in the end. And there was something in his eyes . . . something that spoke of such need for tenderness and love—two things she wanted to give him so very much.

It was all the encouragement he needed. With a gentleness bordering on indecision, he removed her bedclothes, and undid her simple long braid. She refused to be embarrassed by her nakedness. She had this one night to give and take before she would put a stop to something that would only become more painful as time went on.

His fingers soothed her shoulders, and drifted down her back, as she mirrored his actions. He moved her to the center of the bed, and lowered his mouth to touch her breast. She bit her lips to keep from making a sound.

There was something about the way he suckled her, and licked the crest that made her want to cry out. She tried desperately to hold back the moan in her throat.

But he must have sensed her pleasure for he

would not stop. She had no idea how much time had passed but then she felt the warm slide of his hand on her thigh.

She wanted to tell him how much she desired him, but she did not. His hand moved to her waist and cupped her breast as he licked it once again.

She shyly traced her fingers down his sides, all the way down to his buttocks. He was so solid, each muscle defined along his back and hips.

He shuddered as she brushed his ballocks.

"Dear God," he murmured. "Do that again."

She drew her fingers gently along his broad spine and drifted down to linger on his large ballocks. The sound of pleasure he made allowed her to be bold.

She touched him as she had always wished to do—without any reserve. Over and over she stroked every inch of his back, and lower, while he kissed her flesh, and ministered to her every need.

When she thought she would die from wanting, his fingers caught the back of one of her knees and drew it high. He released it only to slide his hand down to the juncture of her thighs. She could not hold back the sound in her throat any longer.

"Yes, my love," he whispered. His fingers stroked her, and she felt an embarrassment of wetness. And then he entered her with his finger, and she nearly rose off the bed.

What was happening to her? Never had she

felt the incandescent torment of sensations coursing through her body at this moment—except the night with him on the ship. Her body pulsed where their skin touched.

And he was doing something with his finger that was causing it. Inside, he was motioning for her to come closer. At that realization, a thousand shards of light burst within her. She turned her head into the pillow and released a sound of such intensity it nearly frightened her.

"Yes," he murmured. "Don't stop."

"Oh God," she moaned. "What are you doing?"

"Giving you pleasure," he said gently. "All the pleasure you deserve and want from me."

And then he lowered his body, never removing his fingers from her, and she watched in shock and wonder as he bent his head to suckle that part of her.

She could not breathe. She dared not move for fear that he would stop. He clamped his mouth on her peak, and did something unspeakable with his tongue. And at the same time, his fingers inside of her beckoned without pause.

She was dizzy from not breathing and her palms fisted the sheets below her. His free hand forced her other leg wide open.

"Yes, that's it," he rose to whisper. "Open yourself to me."

What was this? What was he doing to her? She

should never have allowed this to begin. Because now she was incapable of stopping him. It was a passion and a torment so far from what she had thought she understood.

She tried to hold herself back from the edge, but she could not. She was suddenly flying. Flying to a place too close to the sun, she was certain. She was so hot, and she burned from the pleasure of it. And it did not stop. She had never ever possessed these sensations and she was certain she never would again. As the edges of her vision began to darken, she finally took a breath and fell back down to earth.

"Take your time," he whispered. "You're still weaker than you know." He rose back up to lie beside her, and released one of her hands from the balled-up sheet to hold it within his own. His thumb brushed the back of her wrist. She had never felt so exposed and vulnerable in her life and she did not like the feeling. She preferred to be the one doing the giving.

"Please," she finally whispered. "Please come to me."

And then he was rising to mount her. At least now she knew what to expect. And yet, as he placed the large, blunt end of him against her, she realized that this would not be like either of the two times they had lain together. This was something impossible to fully understand.

He entered her gently, until she grabbed his buttocks and pulled him closer. He slid into her, in one long, slow glide, until she could not take any more of him. He angled her hips with his strong hands, and then he drove into her, every last inch inside her.

He didn't move, and she could not hear him breathe. She held very still to let him regain control.

"Why is it so good?" he murmured.

"Because it's you," she said simply. "And me."

The long slow slide and release began, and she gave every last part of herself to him and received every last part of him.

She raised one knee and he latched on to it with his strong arm, clenching it to his chest. And she reached behind to stroke his sac, which seemed to bring him to an unknown plateau. It filled her with such happiness to see him lost in passion that she could not stop the flood of a release deep inside of her. Lost with him somewhere this side of heaven, her muscles pulsed and clamped down on him.

Roman Montagu was stunned. Something he rarely if ever had been in his life.

This woman beneath him was the most beautiful vision he had ever seen. Her long hair framed an image of such intense emotion, it scared the hell out of him.

And yet, he could not have denied himself no

matter what the cost to either of them. He was caught in a maelstrom of pleasure, incapable of escape. He tried to think of anything except the touch of her fingers on his ballocks and the tightness in his lower back. He was a hair's breath away from a complete loss of control when he felt her clenching him as she strained to find release.

Using a force he had not known he possessed, he plunged still deeper inside of her and stilled. She made an inarticulate sound, which nearly undid him.

He wasn't sure how much longer he could go on. His release was poised in his shaft, inching ever closer to the end. Through sheer force of compassion he continued, thinking only of pleasing her.

And then suddenly, she stopped undulating under him.

"Wait," she whispered. "Wait."

He did as she bade. "What is it, March?"

She pushed at his shoulders, and he understood that she could not breathe with his great weight upon her. He rolled to one side and tried to keep pushing into her but she would have none of it. Relaxing totally, he allowed her to roll him onto his back, and in the process his arousal sprang free of her warm depths.

A cool breeze fluttered over his body before he realized she had moved to between his legs.

No.

She would not.

No gently bred countess would ever—

He shouted as she took him in her mouth, and cradled his ballocks with her gentle hands. He bit back another shout, horrified that he might awaken anyone in the manor.

Oh, God. It was too good. It was too damn good. She was taking him deep in her mouth and touching him everywhere with her bewitching hands. She was swirling, and giving, and driving him . . . to a place he did not know.

And then he could not stop it. And she would not let him. She moaned, and lightly, very gently took him far inside, and then paused.

He pulsed, and then tried to pull outside of her, but she would not allow it. He thrilled to the warm sensation of her mouth as he gave up all control and experienced the most profound climax of his life.

When he finally stilled, he raised his head to find her meeting his gaze. Light brown hair was tousled around her oval face, her gray eyes looking back at him with mystery and with such tenderness it suddenly made him very shy. He smiled.

"Are you all right?" he rasped out.

"Of course," she whispered.

He reached over his head for the glass of water he knew was there and offered it to her. "Are you certain?"

She drank from it. "Yes." She handed him back the glass and he returned it to the table, never letting his eyes stray from her face.

Her eyes studied him, uncertain. "Are *you* all right?"

He answered without thought. "Of course. How could I not. You are . . ." He did not know what to say. It had been the most extraordinary experience.

"Shhh . . . there's no need to say anything," she murmured.

He wasn't sure he agreed. Females were so damned complicated to understand and . . . no. Esme was easy to understand. She didn't want his compliments. She wanted his love.

He had already told her he loved her. But for some blasted reason he could not say it again now. It was lodged in his throat, under so many layers of confusion. But there was some part of him that guessed that perhaps he had only said it before due to the stress of the moment in the maze.

That was the only reason he had said it. And he did not want to feel as if he had to tell her again. Love should feel natural. No one could force it. And right now both of them needed the peaceful oblivion of sleep.

"Come here, March. Will you not let me hold you again tonight?"

She looked at him a long time before she eased into his arms.

She stayed there next to him and drifted into sleep. He smiled when she began to snore a little and then quite a lot. He realized it was the first time she had fallen asleep before him.

He was going to have to leave soon. They had made a bargain and he would stick to his end. She had an unparalleled talent and he would never hold her back.

He would give her every advantage he could afford to help her reach the pinnacle of her dreams to establish herself in the art world. Tomorrow he would arrange all the details to ensure a grand journey for her of epic proportions.

The one thing he refused to ponder was how he would feel as he watched her sail away. For some damn reason, he could not find slumber that night.

Chapter 14

Esme woke from deep sleep, to find that once again, Roman had left her sometime during the early-morning hours.

She sat up, rubbed the sleep from her eyes and yawned, only to stop in mid stretch. The muscles in her arms, normally quite strong from forever lugging about her easel and painting things, were sore. She vaguely remembered clenching the bed linen last night and sank back down onto the bed.

She pulled the covers over her head.

God.

What they had done to each other last night. It was like some sort of vivid, awful, embarrassing, fantastic dream. He had done things to her she would never have imagined, and she had . . .

well, what she had done was not anything she had dreamed of ever doing. She had just followed his lead, which had taken them on a magnificent journey to a place she had not known existed.

Esme smiled to herself under the covers, which did not make the new day go away. She threw back the bed linen, and carefully tested her sore ankle with a bit of weight.

Hmmm.

It was still a bit sore, but she ignored it and hobbled to the bell cord.

Less than an hour later, she was washed, dressed, and atop the old gelding Dobby, with her artist's gear well packed. And no one was the wiser, except her mysterious maid with the odd accent, Jacqueline Cooper, who had been instructed to inform everyone at the manor that she was starting a new painting in the direction she gave.

She settled under the shade of a tree overlooking Abshire's grand estate. He had done her a great favor by way of his advice and so she would repay him with the gift of a painting.

First she broke her fast with the lovely foodstuff Cook had packed for her. And then she laid out her affairs in the rote manner she had adopted each day before she began to create.

As the day waned in the western sky many hours later, Esme put aside her brush and gazed at her creation. It was taking shape nicely. She liked the image of the shepherd in a pasture near the manor house. It gave light to the dark, somber stones of the manor.

It would take a few more days to complete, but it would be very much worth the effort.

After she had finished packing away her things, she could not bring herself to retrieve Dobby, who had spent the afternoon munching in the pasture.

She placed a blank piece of sketching paper before her and took up her brown-pigmented pencil. Her mind took over her hand and she roughly drew a face she now knew by heart. His brushed-back salt-and-pepper hair, his square face, and strong jaw with just the hint of a cleft. His magnificent sad eyes, and his long sideburns that were so soft to the touch.

She was not a great artist, she knew, because she did not have a strong talent in any one arena. She loved to draw and paint landscapes almost as much as she loved to sketch portraits. William was forever telling her that her landscapes were perfection. But she had always secretly preferred portraiture.

As she worked, she tried to conjure up excitement about the prospect of leaving for Vienna. Perhaps she would indeed invite William to join her this time. She would not make the mistake again of departing without a maid, or more likely now two. And a footman. It would be expected of a duchess, of course.

She tried to imagine saying goodbye to Roman Montagu. She allowed all the words to flow through her brain as she worked.

She must keep it very simple, and very light. He would prefer it that way. And she would see him once or twice a year as he had suggested.

And then her pencil stopped. The sketch was complete.

She mouthed the words she would use to wish him well when she departed. It was difficult to say with any sincerity.

She tried again. And again.

And then she realized she would never be any good at it. But she would only have to do it once, act as if she had every intention of seeing him again, and then she would take her leave of him, and ensure that she never saw him again by way of travel, her art and as many commitments as she could manage. It was as Abshire had said. She had to guard what was left of her heart.

She was not the lady for him. And he certainly didn't want to be the man for her. He had not ever wanted to marry and he did not want children. He had little interest in art and less than little interest in traveling with her.

She looked at the portrait one last time and carefully placed it at the bottom of all her sketches.

She did not have the heart to tear it to pieces, but she wanted no reminder of the man who would always haunt the corners of her mind.

Roman examined the letters he had written to the owner of a shipyard and to several influential acquaintances in Vienna and in Prague. Every door she could possibly require would be open to her and she could explore, learn, and paint to her heart's content. He wanted nothing more than for her to be happy.

She had missed the early supper. A servant had informed that she was painting in some field of the estate. To his surprise, Roman could not stop his thoughts from worrying about her as he retreated to the study to prepare his eventual removal from this, ahem, bucolic retreat.

Roman sanded the words on the pages again but did not seal the letters yet. He moved back the chair from the desk in the study of Derby Manor, and for the first time realized how much he missed being in his own townhouse in Mayfair. Prinny had not allowed him to send word to his mother or his sister, and he hoped they would not worry overmuch of his whereabouts. At least he could take comfort that the Prince Regent had given his word that he would personally inform them of his well-being, but swear them to secrecy until the riots in London cooled.

He was not thick in the attics. He knew Prinny wanted his whereabouts kept secret if only to force Kress to do his bidding. At least Roman had enough sense to know that perhaps the future king had the right of it. The entire royal entourage had gone too far, and they were all of them responsible. But when Kress married, as the prince had demanded, Roman and his closest friend could continue on as before—just with much more discretion. It would all be quite simple.

Abshire's sodding words floated through his mind—*"Of course, you will have to attempt to look the other way when she takes a lover."*

He stood up, restless all of a sudden. *God.* It was not going to be as simple as he wished. The thought of Esme leaving England and starting a new phase of her life without him was . . . well, it was difficult to fathom. And the idea of her taking a lover was unbearable.

Hell. He was being ridiculous and he knew it.

Roman crossed to the French doors and stood by the long, fine white lawn under-curtains, fluttering in the breeze of the open door to the terrace. He surveyed the beauty of Derbyshire. It had been an age since he had gone to his own seat—Chardon Cross—on the eastern coast of England. There were too many memories there of Vincent.

He immediately forced his mind away from his brother. There would never be any reason to go there again. He managed the estate, and the other eight properties in the entail very easily from London, in the townhouse he had purchased the month after he had assumed the title. There were no memories there. And his mother and sister preferred Town to any other place in the portfolio of Norwich estates. They only visited their friends and acquaintances during the worst of the summer, while he usually stayed in London to focus on his scientific interests. The three of them would reconvene in Town at the beginning of the Season, when the House of Lords recommenced their debates and procedures.

It was the life he had made, and the one that fit him best. He only wished he had been able to find a suitable husband for his beautiful sister. Despite the fact that so many Seasons had come and gone, and that a constant stream of suitors of every age tried to curry her favor, she would not have any of them. This saddened his mother to distraction, although she never said a word. Instead, the three of them said all the correct things to each other, attended every important event together, and shied away from every possible memory of the time when they had been a true family at the ducal seat on the coast.

Roman had the innate sense that Esme would fit in very easily with them during the brief occasions they would attend celebrations to appear the proper family.

Roman cursed. Usually, he was much more adept at ordering his thoughts to productive ends. He should know better. He crossed back to the desk to give another go at the new pump design, and then paused.

Esme was at the threshold, looking at him, her hand raised at the edge of the door, poised to make her presence known.

"Hello, you," he said simply, and crossed the space that divided them.

"Hello," she replied shyly. "I'm so sorry I missed supper."

He smiled. "No, you aren't." He took in her paint-stained apron, which she hadn't even bothered to remove, and the blowsy nature of her simple coiffure, after a long day out of doors. She was quite beautiful in truth. "But don't worry. No one missed you. You have them all trained very well. One day you will have to tell me how you manage it, as my own mother and sister plague me to death at times." He took one of her hands in his and kissed the back of it. "Mmmmm . . . fuchsia is quite delicious."

She smiled, the worry at his possible displeasure from her absence fully gone. "It's easy," she murmured. "You just tell them that if they ever question your whereabouts you will begin to lie to them and send them in the opposite direction to where you are. And here is the important part." She paused with significance. "You say that you will stay away twice as long if they ever berate you. Although that one doesn't work well with mothers."

"Is that how you got along with your husband?" He kept his words gentle.

"My husband was a very tolerant man," she replied. "I don't know anyone else who would have put up with me. Well, no one else ever asked, to be honest with you."

"I rather think it's the other way around, March," he replied gently. "You were very tolerant of him. You were very good to put up with him."

Her face flooded with color. "You have it all wrong. He was the best of husbands. Better than anyone I know."

Something odd in his gut clenched, and for the first time he forgot to filter the words flowing in his mind. "Really? The best drinks like a fish every night? That is very odd given your reaction each time I have a glass or two of spirits. If you didn't care about it, why do you make such a fuss?" He put a hand up to stop her intention to interrupt him. He couldn't halt the outrageous words leaving him. "Perhaps you liked that he drank so that it allowed you to spend all day away from your family without a care or any guilt."

She was fast. So fast he didn't see it coming. But there was no power behind her palm as it met his cheek.

"You know nothing about my family," she said with a rush. "I probably know more about your family than you do. You are a fine one to insult. Abusing spirits might have saddened me, but he was a fine husband, who took very good care of me and everyone who depended on him at Derby Manor. He left it in a better state than his predecessor. Now, you owe me an apology, sir."

He examined her face. All the anger had left him. Her husband had been a better man than he would ever be capable of being to her. But she was living in denial. "I would have been furious if I had depended on someone and they let me down by drinking themselves to death."

Her hands were shaking by her sides. He couldn't figure out for the life of him why he was doing and saying these things to such an amazing woman. But he wanted her to fight for herself. To understand that she deserved better. Better than that miserable drunk of a husband and better than he could ever be to her.

"All right," she seethed. "You want me to tell you I was angry when he chose whiskey, and brandy, and wine over a life with me? You are bloody right I was angry. But what good is that? It never changed him and it won't change what happened. We can only live in the present, can we not? Oh, we can prepare for the future somewhat, but to be truly happy and productive we must throw away the past and live for today. Are you doing that, Montagu? Are you living in the present? Or are you living in the past—allowing it to rule your every waking moment? I don't know what precisely happened to you when tragedy struck your family, but I think I recognize a man who has decided that sharing any portion of his life with another human being—and I'm not speaking about me for I know we are united for convenience only—is too complicated, and not worth the effort. You have obviously already decided that love and happiness do not endure and the end will hurt too much, so why even attempt it?"

The shock of her words left him colder than death. He could not utter a syllable.

She looked at him with great sadness in her eyes. "I am sorry for saying it. And perhaps, I am very wrong. Love might, indeed, be too difficult to attempt or to sustain. I should not have said a word. I know better. Words do not mean very much, do they? People end up doing and feeling what they choose and nothing you can say will alter them. Nor should one try. You would like to know how I felt about the past? It is very simple. You are right. He let me down and gave up. He did not care enough in the end to fight harder for a life with me."

Her eyes would forever haunt him. They were wise and ageless.

"But other than his one flaw, and everyone has flaws, he was an excellent husband. And he at least knew the value of love, and of bringing others happiness. And at least he tried *because he knew what was important in life even if he did not have the resolve to see it through.*"

Her message was very clear. She thought he was living in the past, and wallowing in self pity, and refusing to allow anyone in his life. The problem was he didn't know how to be happy. She was suggesting he did not want to work for what was important in life. But she was wrong.

He knew what was important in life—bettering the lives of those less fortunate. And he had the brain to do it.

What he absolutely refused to see—in the darkest corner of his mind—was that one's own happiness was worth fighting for. And even if change was inevitable—and happiness or love was not permanent—he should fight for it. But he could not.

He crossed to the desk and gathered up the letters he had prepared. He handed them to her. "I am hoping these will bring you a measure of joy, Esme. I am leaving at first light. I can see how unhappy I am making you. I will follow Prinny's wishes and secrete myself at Abshire's or somewhere else for the next few weeks until I may return to London or descend to Cornwall. I've purchased a private yacht, which will always be at your disposal. My steward in London will hand select the captain and crew for you." He stopped, and then removed his gold fob and pocket watch, which he forced into her hand. "I want you to have this."

"I cannot accept it," she started. "I cannot do—"

"Please," he murmured.

She stared at the watch, indecision lighting her face. Suddenly, she pulled out of her gown's pocket a small granite-backed compass and placed it in his hand. "All right. But you shall have to take this. I used to get lost quite a bit when first I came to Derby Manor. But I don't need it anymore."

He had to lean forward to hear the next bit.

"My heart is my compass now."

He inhaled deeply and accepted the token. "By the by, your mother will never tell you, but I will. She sent out a footman to spend the day in the shadows near you. Don't for a moment think people do not worry about you. They care about you because you always try to bring everyone around you all the joy and happiness you possess innately in your heart, March. I shall be forever grateful to you for giving so much of yourself to me during that storm. I know not one other person on this earth who would have given me what you did. And I thank you for this compass. I shall always carry it with me."

"I am sorry, too. I am sorry for everything, especially striking you. I've prided myself in never harming a living thing. I can never take pride in that again." She stared at him for a long time, and then said very quietly, "It could have worked, you know, perhaps not love, but at least a deep affection. We, both of us, are very independent creatures who treasure our freedom. The freedom to do what we want, spend time apart, and to follow our individual dreams. There are not many like us. Most people look at each other like possessions, forever ordering each other about, hurting each other, trampling on each other's dreams and desires. We would not have done that. But I understand. You do not want anything other than your wild solitude. Then fly away. I truly do wish you only the best life has to offer." She stuck out her hand as if she wanted him to shake it. Like one man facing another man.

He grasped her slim hand tenderly and shook it. He was dazed by her words. What was worse was that there was some part of him that recognized that she might be right. And if there was anyone he could envision sharing a life with, it would be the woman in front of him. Why couldn't he just throw caution to the wind, grab her with both hands, and try?

He should know the answer. He really should. But he did not. He was, at heart, a wild beast who did not want to be tamed. And yet . . . she did not want to tame him. Of that he was certain. So why was he choosing solitude over companionship? Why was—

"Goodbye, Montagu," she whispered. A few moments later he was staring at the darkness in the room, where she had been.

And then life unfolded just as he had suggested to her. He took his leave of Derby Manor at dawn the next day, without another word to anyone. It was better that way. He did not go to Abshire's, as he knew he could not bear the mention of her name again, and Abshire would meddle in his affairs.

He couldn't go to London or Cornwall, and so he did the next best thing. It was an excellent idea, actually. He had places to go, and mills, and waterfalls, and dams, and reservoirs to observe. He would lead a goddamned purposeful life, even if it killed him. And he would do it alone, damn it. He could not be depended upon. He would fail other people every time. His brother Vincent was proof enough of that.

Roman urged his horse down the lane away from Derby Manor, and headed east. He didn't need to glance at the compass she had given him to verify the direction, but he did it nonetheless because it was the only reminder he had of her.

Chapter 15

After the first day, it had not been as hard as Esme had imagined it would be.

But the day he left had been unbearable. And to make it even more difficult, Verity had come to call.

"But, I don't understand," Verity said far too many times during her visit.

Esme had prayed for her cousin to finish her third cup of tea for if there was one protocol Verity always followed, it was that one had overstayed if one accepted a fourth dish of scandalbroth.

"There is nothing to understand," Esme said with a sigh. "He is gone. He has many things that occupy his time."

"But Abshire told me that the Prince Regent had ordered him not to return to London."

"He is not on his way to Town," Esme replied, swallowing her sigh this time.

"Then where did he go?"

"As I told you, I do not know precisely."

"But you are married to him, even if it is a marriage of convenience, one would think it the proper thing to do to at least inform the other where one was going just in case something of importance occurred and one needed to impart the news." Verity's words tumbled out of her mouth like a babbling brook.

Esme wanted nothing more than to impart absolutely no news to her cousin. "I'm certain he sent a missive to the Prince Regent, his steward, and his family before he left."

Verity pouted. "But you *are* his family."

"No," Esme ground out, "I am his wife. His not-so-very-real wife, in a farce of a marriage." She put up her hand when Verity made a noise to interrupt. "If you ask me one more question, then I shall be forced to demand that you tell me what has happened between you and Abshire."

Verity stared at her.

"And by the by, I like him very much. Did you know he was kind enough to pay a call when I hurt my ankle? Now are you going to tell me what precisely happened that night in London—or of your conversations since?"

Verity drained her third cup of tea and placed

it carefully in the saucer. She stood up and smoothed the wrinkles from her gown. "Do come to Boxwood for supper Thursday next, Esme. Your mother has already consented and William Topher will be very disappointed if you do not come too."

"That's what I thought," Esme replied sweetly. "Will Abshire attend?"

Verity examined the hem of her pretty new rose-colored morning gown. "I have absolutely no idea what His Grace's intentions are."

Much later, Esme's mother had tried to breach her defenses during a very private supper *à deux*, using old tactics, which failed of course, and then new tactics, which, in Esme's opinion, were more successful. Esme did not, however, succumb. She would not encourage her.

"Esme, why did he leave so abruptly? You can at least tell me that," her mother prodded as she re-arranged a vase full of fragrant roses from Derby's gardens.

"I have no idea, Mother," she replied.

"But did he not tell you where he was going in such haste? I find it a little off-putting that he did not take his formal leave of me, his new bride's own mother." She paused, indecision exposed—something Esme had never seen on her mother's face.

She continued. "Did you tell him of your ancestry? Is that why he left?"

"Mother?"

"Yes, dearest?"

"Please."

"Please, what?"

"Please let's discuss another topic. I've told you everything I know."

Her mother studied her a long moment. "You told him."

Esme sighed. "I did not tell him nor do I ever intend to. I've made up my mind. Do you think I want him to stay by my side because he believes some ridiculous curse that probably is just a massive series of coincidences?"

"You and I both know it is not a series of coincidences. It is not like you to lie to yourself, dearest. But I understand your point," her mother replied. "Yet it is a dangerous game you play, Esme. Have you not wondered how he will react if and when he learns this secret?"

"Of course I have."

"You will not be able to hide it forever, darling. Someone is bound to tell him."

"I disagree. I doubt he will ever learn of it. There are only a handful of people who know."

Her mother looked at her with doubt but at least respected her desire to change the subject. "Esme,

I've always allowed you an enormous measure of privacy, and independence. Far more than any other mother I know. I only did it as your father insisted, and you were always like him."

"And I can never thank you enough for not interfering like so many other mothers," she inserted as her mother took in more air to continue.

"But, I am certain if your father were still here"—her mother paused and Esme darted a glance at her—"he would insist that you tell me precisely everything that has happened between you." There was the smallest wobble in her mother's voice when she spoke of her late husband.

"No," Esme said with more conviction than she felt. "He would tell you to tell me to go and paint until I was ready to talk. And if I never was ready to talk, he would leave me in peace."

"Yes," her mother replied, "he had a most annoying way regarding certain things. Especially concerning you."

Her mother was trying to make her smile, she knew. Her parents had loved each other to distraction but had been as different as two people could be. Yet they had understood love was about pleasing the other, deeply seated respect and admiration, as well as a soupcon of wit. Her mother had been her father's ardent advocate while he spent the eighteen years of their marriage immersed in his art, and encouraging Esme too. And in return, her father had endeavored to please his wife in secret ways Esme had not been privy to.

"I was thinking actually . . ." Her mother paused.

Esme bit her top lip. "Yes?"

"I was thinking of going down to London. Shall we not go together?"

"I cannot."

"That's not true," her mother replied. "His Grace, your husband, may not go to Town but I specifically remember that he said that Prinny had directed that command to him alone. And since he has already somewhat broken the promise he made to the prince by leaving his honeymoon early, I see no reason for you not to go to Town with me."

"No," she replied stonily.

"Then perhaps we could go to Bellaney. You know how lovely the dower house is, and we'd rarely have to dine with Daniel in the main house."

Her third cousin, Daniel, her father's heir, was as stiff and uncompromising as a horsehair suit. "Mother?"

"Yes, my darling?"

"I've never thanked you properly for coming to stay with me here after everything," Esme said with true gratitude. "You have always been the best mother. But, right now, I can't speak of what you want to know."

Her mother stopped pretending to arrange the

roses and walked to the chaise longue on which Esme was seated. "I understand. I really do. And since you trust me when it comes to the important things, I am going to have to beg you to trust me now. I spent a little time with Norwich on two occasions while he was here, and I am acquainted with his mother and sister, too. I think, just perhaps a little, that I understand more than you know. And so, I must insist that we remain here for no longer than a fortnight, and then we are for Town."

Esme waited. She knew there would be more.

"We will wait so that there will be no wagging tongues about an abrupt honeymoon when Prinny allows the news of your wedding to spread. But we shall enjoy one week in London before you leave on your trip."

"Enjoy?" Esme asked archly.

"Or endure, if you prefer," she deferred. "Oh, and my dearest daughter?"

"Your *only* daughter," Esme retorted. It was their oldest joke.

"Either I will go on the trip with you or William Topher. I must insist. Unless of course, your husband has a change of heart."

"I would not wager a ha'penny on it," Esme replied. "I'm going out of doors to the westernmost wheat field to paint. If anyone wants to discuss anything further about my husband's departure, you may tell them I've jumped into the lake."

"Of course, I will, dearest."

Her mother was one part devil to three parts angel like many mothers. The devil in her did not relate to Esme that during the fortnight she composed and sent, via a devoted servant, a very private missive to the Dowager Duchess of Norwich, a lady with whom she had formed a fond acquaintance a very long time ago, when she and Esme's father had just married and been invited to a house party at the primary Norwich seat on the eastern coast of England.

Precisely three weeks later, Roman Montagu, the seventeenth Duke of Norwich, rode the horse he had borrowed from Derby Manor onto the lovely cobblestones of London. He rode the magnificent beast all the way to the mews behind his towering townhouse in Mayfair, handed the reins to a stable boy, and entered his own house using the servants' entrance. He knew he was being ridiculous. He had stayed away from London the perquisite number of weeks so there was no need to creep about like a thief.

He had sent another letter to the Prince Regent naming the date of his return. He had cushioned the news by adding that he would not formally announce his return, or place the news of his marriage in the newspapers, or attend any public functions. He could skulk about like the best of them.

He had returned to see to the affairs of the duchy with his steward, and to make an appearance for his mother and sister. And enough was enough. He had gathered many ideas on his travels and now he needed time in his study to continue his work.

Roman was not certain if he should be pleased or surprised that he was so easily able to enter his residence without the notice of a single servant. Why, he would be robbed blind one day.

He stuck his head in his mother's favored morning room only to find it empty. Perfect. He would retire to his study. He passed the blue room, and paused. He looked inside and it was empty too. He stood very still. Was there not a bloody soul here?

He stopped any attempt at remaining invisible and went from room to room, salon, followed by chamber, and study followed by library. He stood at the doorway exiting the library and was on the point of walking out the main entry and shouting when a flurry of voices echoed from the other side of the main doors not fifty feet from where he stood.

The door opened, and four elegantly clad females stepped over the threshold, carrying far too many hatboxes. Three footmen followed them with twice as many parcels.

Instinctively, he moved a step back into the shadow of the door.

Dear God.

It was she. March and her blasted mother had entered Norwich Hall along with his mother and sister.

"My dear Caroline," Esme's mother bubbled to his mother, "did I not tell you that Madame Fifoulard makes the most marvelous hats?"

"You did," his mother replied with more enthusiasm than he had heard in nearly two decades. "But you did not say that we would purchase all of them."

"Esme?" his sister said. "Do let's ask Madame Cooper to come to join us abovestairs. I will try not to laugh again when we try on those matching bonnets with the bumblebee pins."

"You might not laugh, but I cannot be counted on to—" Esme stopped.

She had seen him lurking in the library's doorway. Her lovely gray eyes, always so expressive, looked in his direction for a long moment before she turned to her mother.

"Mother, I need to speak to you privately for just a moment." She turned to his sister. "Please excuse me, Lily. We can try the hats in a bit. Someone is waiting to speak to you."

Three pairs of eyes met his as Esme ascended one of the pair of long winding stairs to the upper floors. Good God. She was staying here? Bloody hell, of course she was. If she was in Town, she would have to reside here. It was now her home as well as his.

He stepped forward and calmly lowered his head to accept his mother's gentle kiss. Lily was far more ebullient. She had always been the most optimistic of the three of them. She had also been the youngest by five years.

"Roman! You sly one. When did you return?"

"Just now."

She gathered his stiff form in her warm arms and hugged him to her whether he wanted it or not. Of course he wanted her to. He slowly wound his arms about her slim form and embraced her. But instead of releasing her perfunctorily as he always had in the past, he did not let go. After several moments of silence, Lily rested her head on his chest and sighed. Something eased inside of him.

"Your Grace? Oh, pardon me," the voice of his steward broke the moment.

Roman abruptly released his sister and took a step back. "Good day, Simon. I shall see you in the study shortly."

"Yes, of course, Your Grace. So sorry to have intruded."

His steward departed at the same moment as his mother-in-law came forward. "How delightful you are come."

At least he could be grateful she did not add, *my son,* as she had done on occasion in the recent past. He bowed before her. Her eyes, so very like her daughter's, studied him with kindness.

"It is good to see you, Lady Gilchrist."

"And you too, *Your Grace*." Esme's mother curtsied very elegantly and formally before him.

What on earth was going on? No one was acting as they should in this farce of a tragedy. Except his mother. She was always reserved. Except that she had sounded so animated a few moments before when they had entered without knowing he had arrived.

"Will you excuse me?" he asked. "I must have a word with Mr. Simon. Shall we reconvene in the front salon at eight o'clock and then dine? I shall have Simon inform Mr. Stephens of my arrival." He would be surprised if the butler had not already been informed.

The two mothers looked at each other, but it was Lily who spoke. "We are dining with Lord and Lady Vidington tonight, Roman." She paused. "We are invited to go to their townhouse in Portman Square."

His mother intervened gently. "I shall send a footman to inform them that you are arrived and we shall dine here."

"No," he replied. "You must all go without me. I insist. I am exhausted, really. I would prefer it. We shall dine together tomorrow—or break our fast in the morning."

The three ladies glanced at each other.

"What is it, then?"

"We are quite inundated with invitations at present," his sister said with a smile he had not seen very often. "We are to ride in the early morning with Tory Smith and her sisters. Then we promised to go to the lending library with Lindy Delmont and her family. Her brother and uncle are to escort us for ices after. Then, of course, Lady Gilchrist insists we join the crocodile of carriages crowding Hyde Park each afternoon." She stopped, obviously embarrassed.

"And then?" he asked with encouragement.

"Well, I cannot remember if we are to go to Vauxhall tomorrow night or the night after."

"The night after," both mothers said at precisely the same moment.

His mother continued, "Tomorrow night we have invited the Tulleys and Dumbartons to dine with us here before the theatre."

"I see," he said. It appeared he had worried needlessly about his mother and sister. Life went along very well without him. Actually, it appeared as if it might even be better without him in residence.

Really, it was a relief. Truly.

"Will you not join us, Your Grace?" His mother-in-law gazed at him with her perpetual sunny nature.

"Thank you, but I think I shall—"

Lily interrupted. "Oh, my brother does not enjoy frivolity, Lady Gilchrist. Except for the camaraderie of the royal entourage, of course, and then it is only on rare occasions when Kress, Candover, or Abshire wrestle him from his study."

"Thank you, Lily," he ground out, "but I should be delighted to join you at dinner tomorrow."

"And the theatre?" she wheedled.

"And the theatre if it would please you that much."

She clapped her hands and his mother smiled.

"Roman?" his mother asked.

"Yes?"

"I am so glad you have come back."

He nodded slightly. "Thank you, Mama. It is good to be home." As he retreated to the bastion of every gentleman, his study, he realized with a start that he had spoken the truth. It was good to be home. It was the first time he had even considered this house his home. He had never really had roots.

How could he have formed them when his parents had rarely been in evidence? While his father had insisted he and his wife travel extensively, he had sent Vincent, Roman, and eventually even his sister to school at a young age. Roman had been sent away to six different schools from the age of six to twenty. And he had not been allowed to attend the same schools and universities as his elder brother.

Roman glanced down at the ledgers in front of him, but did not open any of them. For the first time he wondered why his father had separated his children.

His father had had a plan for each of his offspring and Roman's had been clear. He was to focus solely on mathematics and science—even if it had not been his first choice.

He turned his attention to the magnificent white marble bust of da Vinci, a gift his mother had given him last year on the fifth anniversary of his father's death. It was the only piece of art in his study.

He was still staring at it a half hour later when his steward joined him.

Chapter 16

Esme did not have it in her to go to the Vidingtons no matter how much her mother insisted. Then again, her mother had not pushed as hard as she might have.

In fact, as Esme fiddled with the lovely food on the tray that the cook had prepared and sent up to her apartments, she decided that her mother had actually stooped to reverse ideology.

No matter. She would not have gone no matter what. It was one of the few times that she could not muster her usual optimism.

Esme finally placed the heavy, ornate silverware side by side on the plate, and left the chair in front of the small table in the room. She went to the canvases in the corner and again counted them. She had saved space by not stretching them. She would do as William had suggested and only mount them as she used them. The paints were already packed as well as the new brushes she had found in Town. Just the idea of them made her itch to paint.

She was restless. Oh, she knew why. He was somewhere in this great townhouse too. They were the only two occupants at the moment except for twenty-odd servants, who were probably wondering why they had not departed with the others. She shook her head in frustration and finally gave in to the urge by opening the new set of charcoals and opening her sketchbook to a new page.

She sat by the window, and became lost to the power of the image that took shape. It was a portrait of her father. She had drawn so many portraits of him, her first teacher. But each time she attempted a new one it gave her great comfort. It was as if she were having a conversation with him. Her questions to him were always answered by the expression of his face that took shape on the page. She liked how he was smiling in this—

A knock sounded at the door, and she immediately returned to the moment.

"Yes?"

"May I?"

It was his voice, but she had not a moment to think. "Of course."

As he entered she stood up too quickly and placed too much weight on the ankle that was almost but not fully healed. She dropped her sketchbook and caught the edge of her chair with her hand to prevent more pain.

He rushed toward her. "Are you all right?"

"Of course. Really. It's just that sometimes I forget to take a bit of care."

"How is your ankle?"

"I swear to you that it is almost perfect. I just made an awkward movement. That is all."

He gave her a long look and then bent to retrieve her sketchbook and the pages that had fallen out.

Of course the one that she had drawn of him while at Derby Manor was in full evidence along with more than a dozen others. Would the embarrassment never end?

He glanced at it and did not say a word. He picked up another one, a landscape and studied it before replacing it in her book. And then he studied each and every drawing as he carefully gathered them together.

The last one was the one of her father, nearly complete. He examined it for a long while, his eyes squinting.

She handed him her spectacles she had hastily removed, just like she did whenever he was in her presence.

He accepted them without comment and put

them on the end of his broad nose. "Your father?"

"Yes," she replied quietly.

"You are very like him, except for your eyes."

"I know. I liked his eyes best of all."

"You have your mother's eyes."

"Yes. And you must have your father's eyes."

"No one has ever suggested that," he replied, ill at ease.

"There are no portraits of your father here. But you must take after him."

He stiffened. "Not as much as my brother did." He paused. "March . . . it is good to see you."

"Thank you," she replied. She wasn't sure when she had felt this shy in her entire life.

He placed the book in her hands. "Tell me, how are you?"

"I am good. Excellent, really." She stopped then rushed on. "I am so sorry you returned to find me and my mother installed here without any advance warning. It is just that my mother wrote to yours without informing me. It seems they were acquainted long ago and your mother insisted we stay here when we decided to come to Town."

"It's perfectly correct, March. You should always stay here when you are in London."

"I would not have agreed had I thought you were coming back so soon. I only came to purchase goods before I leave. We are to sail very shortly."

"I am so glad," he replied. "March, you have a very great talent. Especially with portraits. Don't let anyone tell you otherwise. And I am certain this trip will be everything you hoped it could be and perhaps more."

"Your mother is very excited about it too. We are going for part of the time to a place where she apparently spent some time one summer many years ago."

"My mother?" He appeared stunned.

"Oh, I'm so sorry. I guess she did not have time to relay it to you, but she asked if she could accompany me. I've never seen my mother so relieved. She was originally supposed to journey with me, but her heart wasn't in it. She accompanied my father to so many museums in his lifetime that I think it secretly bores her to pieces. She was delighted to switch roles with your mother and chaperone your beautiful sister, during the social whirl of the upcoming Season."

He did not respond and so she filled the void, as she was always wont to do.

"I should warn you that I do believe they have formed a wager. Your sister's future husband is about to be found come hell or high water." Esme could not think of another thing to say to fill the silence and so she stopped.

"My mother is going with you?"

He obviously hadn't understood. "Yes. She is

quite enchanted with the yacht you so very kindly purchased. Your sister tells me that she has never seen her mother this excited about anything. She even went so far as to interview the captain and every last potential member of the crew, along with your steward."

He closed his eyes and sagged against the wall.

"Oh, I am so sorry," she whispered. "Are you worried about the idea of her sailing?"

"No."

"Then what is it?"

He exhaled and heaved himself upright. "I've just realized I've made a grave mistake."

She waited.

"I'd forgotten how much my mother loved to travel. My brother did too. She was forever sending me letters to my school or university from points across Europe and beyond. But it has been a long time since she went anywhere beyond England. I should have arranged this for her long ago."

"Well then, this will be lovely for her. I am so glad." And Esme was. She had adored his mother nearly on sight.

She would not tell Roman, but they had visited every last museum in Town during the time since she had been here. And at every entertainment, they had sought out and studied each privately owned piece of art.

"Oh, I almost forgot." She retrieved an unsealed

missive from a drawer in the bedside table and handed it to him. "This was delivered yesterday by a footman from Carleton House. It was directed to both of us so I took the liberty of opening it. I hope you do not mind. I was worried it was something important from Prinny."

He opened the missive and quickly read it. "So we are still not to announce our wedding."

"Correct. One can hope that news from people and servants who know the truth in Derbyshire will be slow traveling from the north."

He smiled. "And Prinny is gone south toward Cornwall in secret?"

"It appears so."

"Well, since Candover has gone with him, at least it appears an answer to my wager with Abshire will be forthcoming."

"What wager?"

"The one in which I wagered that my poor, dear friend, the Duke of Kress will be soon wed, very likely against his will."

A coldness invaded her veins. "It appears the same unhappy fate awaits all of you, then." She turned and walked toward her bed, refusing to limp in his presence. "I wonder who will be next. Abshire's goose will be cooked, don't you think?" She hoped there was no trace of bitterness in her voice.

"March?"

"Yes?" She would not turn around. Instead she rearranged the bedcover.

"I've done it again, haven't I?"

She turned to look at him across the chamber. "I beg your pardon?"

"I'm no good at this. I told you."

"What are you talking about?"

"I've trampled on your sensibilities again, haven't I?"

"No," she said. "I just don't know the rules for a marriage of convenience."

He walked over to her and took her hand and kissed her knuckles. "Neither do I."

She took a deep breath. "Then we shall just have to decide on them together."

"All right. What do you propose?"

"Well, I would like as I mentioned before, that we treat each other with respect and kindness above all else. The way we would treat our best friends in the world. What would you propose?"

"It is rather what you said only more. That we only think of what will bring the other the most happiness."

"That is very important," she breathed, "especially for best friends."

He stepped a bit closer. "Can you think of any other ideas?"

"Yes." This was going to be difficult to say aloud.

"What is it?" he asked gently, tilting her chin up to gaze steadily into her eyes.

His eyes were so very blue, even in this low light. She would always drown in his eyes.

"We shall always have to take care not to do two things."

"Yes?"

"We must never have relations again as you do not want an heir, or let any level of intimacy hamper our independence."

He removed his hand from her chin and bowed his head. "You are, of course, right. As always, March. I suppose I shall bid you good night, then."

He walked to the door of her room and departed, gently closing the door behind him.

"Good night, you," she whispered.

Roman made good on his promise and attended dinner the following evening, and the theatre after that. He took care to pay more attention to his mother and sister.

But during the day, he had a breakthrough in his plans for the waterworks. All the hours of computations, all the many days studying water wheels after the first one that had inspired him in Derbyshire, came to fruition. He tilted back his chair in his study and looked at the long scroll of paper completely unfurled across his desk.

It would work.

He had not a single doubt.

It would take years to build, of course. And it would first have to be examined by any number of other experts, and debated in the House of Lords, and monies appropriated by Prinny, and so on, and so forth.

But it would one day revolutionize basic, everyday life in London.

God. He could not believe he had actually done it.

He had a sudden desire to tell someone. But there was not a single one of his friends in town. Kress was in Cornwall, Candover on his way south with Prinny, and Abshire languishing in Derbyshire. He really was not all that close to any of the other members of the entourage.

He dropped the chair back to all four legs and shook his head. He knew that none of the gentlemen he had thought to have a word with were really the one person he most wanted to tell.

It was March.

Of course it was she. She had said it all last night. They were, and always would be, the best of friends.

But he was too shy to go to her. He could not understand why. He had no reason to be reticent with her.

Instead, he did what he knew best. He said not a word. Better he spend a few days planning the political steps it would take to see this plan implemented in the fastest, most efficient way possible.

Yes, it was better to keep his excellent news to himself. He didn't want anyone to feel obligated to celebrate.

The afternoon before they were all to go to Vauxhall began with the arrival of an unexpected guest. A man whom Roman had never hoped to have to lay eyes on again.

William Topher arrived at the Norwich townhouse in Wyndam Square with a gleam in his eye and a letter in his hand.

All the residents of the townhouse were gathered in the large walled garden in the rear, where a light repast had been laid out under the dappled sunlight of a small stand of white-trunked birch trees. March had wanted to paint a portrait of his mother in the afternoon sun. His mother wore an expression of such serene happiness that Roman could not stop looking at her. The last time he had seen such an expression had been when Vincent was still alive, and they had all been sailing for the day. He stopped the remembrance abruptly and focused on the servant who approached.

"Your Grace?" A footman came forward. "There is a visitor asking for Her Grace, but if you will pardon me for saying so, I do not think he is referring to your mother."

Roman nodded. "I shall see to—" He stopped short at the sight of William Topher walking toward them. The man had had the gall not to wait for the footman to return to invite him to the garden. He was the most insufferable man alive.

"William!" Lady Gilchrist suddenly exclaimed with a warm laugh. "What has brought you to Town?"

March put aside her brush and rushed forward to meet her mentor. "William, it is wonderful to see you," she said warmly. "Lily? Your Grace?" She beckoned his sister and mother to come forward. "Do let me present to you my longtime mentor, Mr. William Topher."

He bowed with a flourish.

"William, I am delighted to introduce Her Grace, the Duchess of Norwich, and—"

Roman's mother interrupted with a correction. "The Dowager Duchess of Norwich, sir."

His wife blushed and looked at his sister. "And this is Lady Lily Montagu, His Grace's sister."

"I am honored beyond words to meet you both. The reports of great beauty at Norwich Hall pale when faced with it in person."

His mother beamed. "Thank you for the compliment to my daughter, sir."

He smiled like a weasel. "I was speaking of you, Your Grace."

Lily clapped her hands. "Oh, Esme was correct. I like you very much, sir."

"Do call me William. I shall die a happy death if we can all be intimates."

Roman looked at all four of the ladies surrounding his wife's sodding mentor and decided the world had gone mad. Did they not recognize a simpering sycophant when they saw one? He shook his head in disgust.

"Ah, Your Grace," Topher said bowing toward him. "I did not notice you against the shade of the tree. It is such a great honor and pleasure to see you again. I promise not to disturb this tranquil repast *en famille,* very long. I just have very important news to impart and then I shall decamp to the room I have taken at the hotel near the docks."

"Nonsense, Mr. Topher," his mother instantly said. "You must stay here. Will he not, Roman? This townhouse has nearly a dozen empty bedchambers."

Five pairs of eyes looked at him expectantly.

Where was a duck when one needed one?

It took every ounce of self-control to modulate his voice. "Of course you must stay with us. Delighted to accommodate you, Topher."

The man's eyes brightened. "I do apologize to arrive without notice. Terrible of me, isn't it?" He could not meet Roman's eye. "But you see, the thing of it is, a letter arrived for me from Vienna." He nodded his head and his eyes almost bulged with excitement. "Yes, yes, yes . . . it contains the most marvelous news. It is as I hoped, although with a slight alteration. It concerns you, Esme."

"What is it, William?"

"The exiled Duc d'Orleans very much liked the works of yours I secretly sent to him."

"What?" Esme said, shocked. "Why would you have sent my work to the duke?"

"Do you not remember that I have a regular correspondence with his daughter, whom I taught the year before I came to know you, my dear?"

"But how does that signify?" Esme asked, still taken aback.

"Well," William began, "his daughter wrote to me and suggested her father was looking to commission a rendering of his new grand estate. I immediately proposed you, and promised I would be on hand also to guide you. But, and I hope you will pardon me for saying so, after I sent your portfolio, he changed his mind as many great men do." Topher's eyes darted to Roman in a most unguarded fashion. "For some odd reason, the duke now wants you to paint a portrait of himself, instead of the castle. Imagine, Esme! While it is vulgar to discuss payment, the amount he suggests stunned me to near speechlessness."

Too bad Topher was only *near* to speechlessness, Roman thought darkly.

"What?" No less than three of the ladies said it at the same time.

"I am so glad I caught you before you sailed, Esme, I mean, Your Grace. I will, of course, have to go with you now. This is the most important piece of work you will ever attempt. But, never fear. I will be there to help you."

Roman shook his head. He would *never* trust the man. There was something about his manner. And he was certain—all jealousy aside—that the artwork Esme produced in the presence of Mr. Topher was not as good as the work she created on her own. Had not anyone else noticed it?

He cleared his throat. "March? I should like a word with you in private."

She swiveled her head toward him, her gray eyes excited beyond recognition. "Of course." She crossed the space between them and Roman offered his arm, which she accepted. They walked toward the mews, where their words would not be overheard.

"What is it, Montagu?"

"First, I congratulate you. You have unparalleled talent. And now you have an important first commission which shall prove it to the world." He felt guilty. He should have arranged a way for her art to be displayed before now. He could have helped her more in her artistic endeavors instead of allowing that toad, Topher, to do it. "And I also want to tell you that I was wrong all those weeks ago when I suggested that artists are dreamers with little value. I was a fool to think it and I can't even tell you why I had formed such an irrational opinion. Just the expression on my mother as you painted her likeness confirmed what an idiot I've been."

She grasped his face between her hands and stroked his sideburns in the manner that sent a flood of tenderness through him. "Thank you, Montagu. Your approbation means a great deal to me." Her eyes were shining with happiness.

"But there are two things I must add."

"Yes?" Curiosity did not mar the happiness in her expression. She was so beautiful right now. So vibrant, so happy, so alive. But it would not last when he spoke the truth to her.

"First, while I hate to admit that your dear Mr. Topher is right about anything, he was correct to suggest that payment is vulgar for people of our class. What do you plan to do about it?"

"Thank you for asking my opinion, Montagu. Most husbands—in truth or in name only—would play the tyrant and demand obeisance to their decisions."

"We have always had a gentlemen's agreement, March. I shall always treat you as an equal."

"I shall accept any monies proposed with the understanding that they will be set aside as a donation to the city from our family to help in the creation of your water project when you complete it."

Our family. Whose family was she referring to? Something in the back of his throat prevented him from replying. This was the perfect opportunity to tell her his news. But he would not take away the excitement of her moment to shine. "That is very kind. The people of London will be grateful when and if the project is seen through."

"I've never been more certain of anything in my life. You will accomplish it. I know you will, Montagu. And I assure you that I am thinking only of you when I suggested the monies be donated to your work. In any case, it will be but a mere drop—I'm sorry for the metaphor—of what will be needed, I'm certain." She was gazing steadily at him in that forthright manner of hers. "Was there something else you wanted to say?"

He was no good at communicating with finesse. And so he said what had to be said. "Do not trust William Topher to guide your talent any longer, March."

Her jaw dropped. A few moments later she collected herself and stood up very straight. "You have never liked him."

"You are correct."

"You got off on the wrong foot. I realize his way

with people can be off-putting, but his character and his heart are in the right place."

"Our opinions are at odds, March." He paused, desperate to find the words to convince her. "There is sometimes a moment—a very awkward moment—when a student's ability surpasses a teacher's. A poor mentor is blind to it. A great teacher recognizes it and knows when to step away."

She stared at him, all color leaving her face.

"Do not take him with you to Vienna."

"I see. And so I am to go without the person who arranged for my first commission? But I may take your mother?"

"Of course you should take my—"

She interrupted. "But essentially, I am to meet the Duc d'Orleans alone, negotiate the commission, paint his portrait without any direction from a man who has devoted a good portion of his life guiding me?"

This was the moment he had dreaded when he opened this discussion. It was when he would either do what a man should do when he loves a woman—something a husband would do for a most beloved wife—or he would not. He should offer to go with her. He should be there to reassure her and to advise her. His project was finished. He knew Prinny would embrace his plan with tears of joy—and orchestrate the entire financial undertaking. If anything would win over the hearts and minds of an unhappy populace, it was the promise of something so basic and necessary to every person's life here in the city—clean water. And he would be back in time for the construction.

Roman knew he should just get on that blasted yacht with her and go. Instead, he met her gaze and blinked. "Topher cannot even recognize that your forte is portraits, not landscapes. He might even be jealous of your talent."

"Jealous? You believe *William* is jealous? Of me? How ridiculous. Perhaps you do not like the idea of a gentleman traveling with me. Is that it?"

"Of course not," he lied. "Look, even the Duc d'Orleans deduced after seeing your work that you are a superb portraitist."

She did not accept his argument. He could see it in her eyes. "March, I realize I do not have the right to tell you what to do, considering . . . But, I hope you know I will always have your best interests at heart."

She did not form a reply as the man Roman least wanted to see walked toward them.

"Esme," Topher said on his approach. "I do apologize for interrupting. But the hour grows late and I must pop down to that marvelous shop near Bond Street to replenish my own art supplies to prepare for our trip. Shall we not go together? I should like to advise you on a few things such as the exact shade of Orlean's flesh. What say you?"

Roman held his breath.

She looked between the two men.

"If you don't mind, William, I would like to finish the portrait of Her Grace today before the light changes. Perhaps we can go tomorrow if you are willing to wait. Otherwise, really, I will not be put out at all if you decide to go alone."

"Absolutely not," Topher blustered. "Of course, we will go tomorrow. Just now I took the liberty of studying your likeness of Her Grace, and it is lovely, my dear. Perhaps the mouth and nose need a bit more work, but other than that? The gloss on the hair is extraordinary as always." He paused. "It really is too bad that the Duc d'Orleans does not want you to do the landscape for him. His portrait is sure to be a difficult commission."

Esme glanced at Roman. "William?"

"Yes, my dear?"

"I've not thanked you for arranging this first commission. I am, as always, very grateful to you."

William bloody Topher smiled like the victor that he was.

Chapter 18

In which, dear reader, we skip Chapter* Seventeen *as Roman Montagu would prefer it and he should have a say in his own story, should he not?

Vauxhall at night was always something to behold, Esme thought as she entered the small boat that was to carry the Norwich party to the famed gardens. She was seated in front of the oarsman, all alone while the others were seated behind. This was by far the most beautiful way to see the approach. Everyone from the Norwich townhouse in Wyndam Square had taken the boat, except, of course, Roman Montagu. He had taken a carriage, and his mother had thanked him by suggesting that it might very well rain and they would all crowd in the carriage with him for the journey back.

Esme had not hesitated to go by boat. Oh, she knew she would have to have a private word or three with her husband. They had been interrupted. But now was not the moment. And she needed time to think and reflect on what he had said. She trusted him. Blindly, for some ridiculous reason. There was not a single doubt in her mind that when it came to her passion in life, he would be her greatest champion.

But aside from her father, William Topher was the man who had taught her everything she knew. If she had talent, it was William who had nurtured it. It was William who had pushed her to new heights. And she liked to think that she had a backbone, and knew how to form her own opinion. There had been times when she had disagreed with William's advice, and she had created pieces the way she had wanted.

Since her private words with Roman in the rear garden, she had been trying to remember all the many canvases in her possession. Which were her favorites and what had been William's suggestions during their creation.

Of one thing she was certain. If they had ever had a difference of opinion, William had never had any malice or jealousy. He was not that way. No matter what her husband thought. The only question was whether William's guidance was indeed of great benefit to her now. Or was she just depending on him because she didn't have the courage to trust her own instincts at times?

She studied the way the light of the many lanterns in the night-darkened trees of Vauxhall bounced off the water's wavelets as they approached the dock. Perhaps her husband was correct. Perhaps she did not require a teacher any longer.

She made ready to exit after her mother stepped onto the dock with William's aid.

"My dear," her mentor insisted, stretching out his hand to her. "Do let me help you. Is your ankle bothering you at all?"

"Not in the least."

"Good. Then I shall claim the first dance, if I may?" William smiled in the darkness. "But first there must be strawberries, no? I long for the famed strawberries of Vauxhall almost as much as I miss the watered-down lemonade and rataffia. It has been an age since we were here. When was it?"

She thought back in time. "It must be nearly three years now."

"How could I have forgotten?" he replied. "Although I remember why we did not return to Town sooner. I did not find the artists we met or the lectures we attended particularly inspiring. We do better when it is just the two of us in Derbyshire, don't you think, my dear?" His large, beautiful brown eyes stared directly into hers. He then turned abruptly toward her mother.

"Dear Lady Gilchrist, do take my other arm. I am quite overwhelmed," William continued. "For the first time in my life I find I wish for four arms, to escort you all!"

Lily giggled.

Her Grace smiled. "I do hope Norwich is here already. He was kind to make all the arrangements for a box."

They made their way past the small docks where others arrived as they had done. They crossed the wide lawn, and exclaimed over the beauty of the evening. A breeze rustled the leaves of the trees near the dancing area, and the wilderness of large oaks, and elms, and pines in the paths beyond.

Roman met them at the entrance to the boxes. He looked more handsome than Esme had ever seen him. He had carefully combed back his graying hair from his beautiful forehead. All of the Norwich family had the same jet black hair, which became gray far earlier than was typical, his mother had once mentioned. Only Lily had managed to evade the trait.

Roman stood in front of a tree lit with lanterns. His silhouette showed his great, wide shoulders and his slim hips to advantage. He stepped forward and she could see the piercing pale blue of his eyes.

She had fallen in love with him. No. It was worse than that. She loved him as she would love no other. It didn't matter what he felt for her, it didn't matter that he was unable to love her as she loved him. He was the man for her. And no matter where life would take her, even if it was far, far away from him, she would love him.

She removed her arm from William's as they drew near. Her husband caught up her hand and kissed the back of it. "You are very beautiful, tonight, March," he said for her ears only.

"Thank you," she replied simply.

"I hope you still feel kindly enough toward me to allow me the honor of the first dance?" His eyes were twinkling.

"Oh dear," William interrupted with a hint of a smile. "You are too late, Your Grace. She has promised it to me. And I don't know if you are aware, but Esme never, ever goes back on a promise. Do you my dear?"

Roman's eyes changed.

She kept her eyes on her husband. "William is correct. I did promise him the first dance. But I would be very grateful if we may dance the second?"

He smiled. "I have always admired a person who keeps their promises. As well as ladies who are not afraid to ask a gentleman to dance."

"Perfect," Lily said with a laugh. "Then, brother dear, will you dance the first with me? It has been an age."

They settled on the pale cushioned benches in the box her husband had reserved for them. The night was only a little cool, and Esme was grateful when he placed a shawl on her shoulders. "Thank you. I had thought I'd forgotten it."

"You did," he said, "but I saw it on my way out and brought it for you."

The strawberries were as small, and sweet, and delicious as Esme remembered. The libations were another story.

Couples strolled the long allées throughout the evening. One could get lost along the paths whether one chose to or not. There was a reason parents took great care in the chaperones they chose for their daughters on the nights they visited Vauxhall. There were far too many stories of forced marriages that were all due to the romantic atmosphere of the gardens.

Esme's mother and father had never worried for her. At least there was one benefit to being plain. And her father's limited means had not tempted any blackguard. The Gilchrist fortune had not been as grand in her early years as it had become in later ones.

The orchestra struck up the notes to a minuet, and William claimed her hand the same time her husband claimed his sister's. They were so handsome together, and it was very obvious how much Lily adored her brother. She watched them out of the corner of her eye while they were deep in conversation as much as the dance would allow.

William performed the steps to the intricate dance to perfection. He was in his element. And not for the first time, Esme wondered why her mentor had never married, or shown any interest in courting a lady.

He had a stipend, and after ten years at the estate, he had been deeded the small, unentailed house originally built for Esme's mother, who in the end had preferred the dower house on the property of her late husband, Esme's father.

The dance ended and they began the walk back to the box.

"William?"

"Yes, my sweet?"

"We've always spoken very frankly with one another, haven't we?"

"Of course. That is the way between mentor and student."

"I would ask a favor of you."

"Anything, my dearest girl."

"I'm undecided about the trip to Vienna."

He halted, forcing her to stop short. "Whatever do you mean? You must go. Don't tell me that dried-up stick of a husband-in-name-only has a medieval streak!"

"No, not at all. He would like me to go."

"Then what is it?"

"I might choose to go alone."

William appeared a tad stunned. But gradually,

oh so slowly, he smiled like a cat who found the cream. "Lord. Finally. I was wondering how long it was going to take."

"What ever do you mean?"

"I've been waiting and waiting, dearest. And it was beginning to appear as if I might never earn my retirement."

"Sorry?"

"Esme, my dear, you are the love of my life—not in the way you might think. Every teacher dreams of a student such as you. Someone who is so brilliant, so naturally gifted, with such a great desire to absorb everything. You had only one flaw."

"I did?"

"Yes. But only a very little of the flaw. You had moments, fleeting moments of doubt about your abilities. Yet a great artist must have a certain level of arrogance to succeed. You could not accept that you had such a raw and perfect talent. I want you to fly away. Fly to Vienna and paint that damned portrait without any interference from me. I shall write to the Duc d'Orleans and tell him. And as for me? I am going to enjoy the Season with your mother and the very lovely Lily Montagu, who has begged me to stay in Town, and then I am going to sit in front of a huge fire all winter long in Derbyshire and relish the sentiments of a job well done. And then . . . Well, perhaps I shall choose a wife." He waggled his eyebrows.

"Oh, William!" She wrapped her arms about her handsome teacher and kissed him on the cheek.

He kissed her right back. "Now do you understand why I consider you the love of my life?"

A growl erupted. "Take your bloody hands off my wife, you scoundrel!"

Esme quickly removed herself from William's embrace. The next minute, her dearest teacher in the world was flat on his back, gasping like a freshly landed trout.

A small crowd of people gathered. Esme's mother pushed her way past the shocked onlookers.

"Esme? Are you all right? What on earth happened? Why is William on the ground?"

"Because I punched him," Roman Montagu, the Duke of Norwich, replied, more agitated than Esme had ever seen him.

"And why would you ever do that, my son?" her mother asked.

A few shocked sounds began as soon as *my son* left her mother's lips.

"Because he was pawing and making love to *my wife*," he ground out.

"Montagu," Esme said with great calm, "apologize to William immediately. You have misunderstood. It was a very innocent action, not what you think. You have it all wrong."

"Your Grace?" A middle-aged man with a very

poorly made wig stepped forward. He was familiar to Esme. *Very familiar.*

"Yes?" her husband answered.

"I do beg your pardon, but I feel it my duty to warn you that the bushes along the edges of the waterline are prime breeding areas for ducks."

Esme studied the bewigged man and suddenly remembered. He was reputedly the infamous columnist from the *Morning Post*. The one who had started the mayhem after the debauched evening of the royal entourage.

Hushed whispers erupted all around. By the sound of it, there was not a chance of any measure of doubt now. By next morning, the whole of London would know three things:

1. The Duke of Norwich was married to her.
2. He had punched another man who had just danced with her.
3. He was obviously still cursed. And there would never be a good time to reveal her ancestry to him.

Montagu stepped toward her and William, who was still gasping and clenching his stomach. The crowd took a step backward and made not another sound. Goings-on like this were too important to miss a thing.

He stretched out his hand and offered it to William.

William looked at it with blatant fear, then chanced a look at her. She nodded mutely, and William accepted his aid. Her former teacher stood up, incapable of speaking, and brushed the dirt off his evening clothes.

"Mr. Topher," her husband said gruffly, "do accept my apologies."

"Accepted, Your Grace," William rasped.

"All right, everyone," Esme's mother said with laughter threading her musical voice, "the fireworks are over. Now it is time to see the other fireworks. Come along, William, I would have a word, if I may?"

The rest of the evening at Vauxhall passed without incident. Except for the fact that Esme could feel, oh, about two hundred pairs of eyes in her direction, she had a lovely time.

The only person who did not look at her was her husband.

His turn would come.

The return to Norwich Hall in Wyndam Square was done silently. The six occupants in the barouche might have had enough social backbone to enact *joie de vivre* in front of the curious eyes of a goodly number of their peers at Vauxhall that evening, but they did not even try to keep it up in the close confines of the carriage.

Roman, Lily, and his mother were seated on one bench, and March, Lady Gilchrist, and William Topher, who was quieter than a rabbit, were on the other.

A few kisses, and a great number of "good nights" were performed for the benefit of the servants in the front hall, and then each of the six retreated to their corners, er, apartments.

Roman performed his evening ablutions with his usual orderly precision, aided by his valet, who was not only meticulous, but also something far more important—silent.

He knew he would go to her tonight. She was scheduled to sail with his mother the day after tomorrow. This was the only time he knew he could speak to her without interruption.

He did not want her to misunderstand his intentions, and so he instructed his valet, Mr. Tanner, to lay aside his dark blue velvet dressing gown, and instead he donned the clothes he would have worn the next morning. Again, his valet, who had been in his employ for as long as he could remember, said not a word. At the last minute, he accepted the silver flask his man offered with knowing eyes.

He waited until all sounds of Tanner retreating belowstairs faded.

Roman glared at himself in the looking glass he used to shave each morning and wondered who in hell was the old man staring back at him. His hair had turned a shade grayer during this summer that would not end. His eyes looked tired and drawn. He shook his head and headed for the door. Lord, he was becoming vain in his old age. That could not be a good sign.

He walked purposefully, and silently, along the carpeted hall toward her chamber. He hoped she was not already in her bed.

Roman knocked on her door and listened keenly.

"Mother?" her voice called behind the door.

"No. It's me." Why was he so bloody nervous? He added the obvious. "Montagu."

"Come in," she said.

He opened the door to find her just leaving her bed, her back to him as she straightened the covers, fluffed the pillows, and placed a book on her bedside table.

She removed her spectacles as she turned to face him. She appeared very much like a young girl to him. Her hair was down, not in her usual evening braid. She carefully placed her small gold-rimmed spectacles on top of the book.

"Hello, you," she said softly.

"Good evening," he replied.

The two then spoke at the same moment.

"I've come to apologize, I had no right to—" he said.

"I am sorry for speaking so freely in front of—"

They paused before Roman spoke again. "I haven't seen you wear your spectacles in some time."

She shrugged her shoulders and looked embarrassed. "Oh, I wear them still while reading and painting. I just try not to wear them in public. I'm not too proud to admit I've become vain in my declining years."

He threw back his head and laughed.

"And just what is so funny?" she retorted, her hands on her hips.

"First, you are not in a decline. Second, I had the exact same thought not two minutes ago while standing in front of a looking glass. You were right. We are very much alike."

"The best of friends are," she said.

"Is that what we are, March? The best of friends?" He thought he saw a hint of sadness pass over her expression before she evaded his gaze.

"Why are you here?"

"Why are you changing the topic?" he murmured.

"I will answer, if you go first."

"All right. I really am here to apologize. I realize what a fool I have made of myself. I don't know what came over me, March. Like you, I have never struck another person in my life. Never had a reason to, to be honest. And now it will be all over the newspapers, and Prinny will again be furious. But more importantly, I don't want to cause you any embarrassment, or any pain or unhappiness."

"It was an innocent mistake," she admitted. "And I know why you misunderstood. Look, I just want to tell you that you were partially right. You were wrong in thinking that William had any improper intentions regarding me or my art. His opinions might differ from yours or other people, but he has an excellent eye. Although you were right when you suggested that I no longer needed a mentor. And William was delighted when I told him I was going to Vienna without him. Apparently, he has been dreaming about his dotage for a long time."

"Good for him. I'm sorry it had to begin with a left hook."

She smiled. "I think he will enjoy the notoriety. He has never had anyone take him as seriously as you did—aside from our acquaintances in the art world."

Silence descended on the pair of them abruptly.

Without thinking, he pulled the flask out of his pocket. He offered it to her and her eyes darkened with worry.

"No, thank you," she said.

"March, please tell me you do not still think I drink to excess."

She shook her head. "Of course not. I've never seen you three sheets to the wind, except perhaps a bit dipped the night of the storm."

"You must put away your fear then. Would you like to taste it?"

"I never drink."

"May I?" he asked with kindness.

"Whatever you like."

He would not if she would not. He placed the flask beside her book.

They both stared at it.

After a few moments she retrieved it and drank from it.

She sputtered and coughed. And handed it to him.

"A bit less next time," he said with a grin. He took a swig and replaced it on the table. "Now, that wasn't so terrifying, was it? Now you can cross that fear off your list."

"Yes," she said slowly. "You are right. And I will. There is nothing to fear about spirits. If anything, one should blame the man, not the method of corruption."

He nodded. "You are entirely correct. And you and I do not have obsessive natures, except where our work, our passions are involved. Do you agree?"

She didn't answer. "So are *you* ever going to cross a fear off your list?" Her eyes were owlish, and her lips plush in the candlelight.

He was indeed becoming an idiot in his old age. He should have seen this coming. "You're not going to suggest I get on a ship again, are you?"

"No, I didn't say that."

"But that is what you want, isn't it?"

"No," she said gently. "I would never ask anyone to do something they don't want to do. Everyone has to make their own choices in life."

He reached behind her and took another mouthful from his flask. He offered it to her and she accepted it. This time she did not cough when she drank. Her eyes watered just a little but she held her own.

"Don't worry. I'm leaving, Montagu," she said handing him back the flask. "I just want to thank you for everything you've done for me. You've helped me understand many things, and helped me to grow. I hope I've done the same for you." She took back the flask and took another drink. This one long and deep.

He extracted his flask from her fingers. "March, did you eat anything at Vauxhall?"

She shook her head—a little too many times. "Only a few strawberries. Why?"

"I wouldn't have any more, if I were you."

"Oh, so first you want me to drink and now you want me to stop. Make up your mind, Monta—Montaguuuu." She laughed.

He should shoot himself. What was he thinking

to offer her spirits? Thank God he spied a plate of biscuits and a cup of milk on her dressing table. He fetched them and forced her to eat every last crumb.

"So, you . . ." she paused, most likely still affected by the spirits, but suddenly very serious. "Are you ever going to tell me about your fear? Your brother drowned, is that it?"

Bloody hell. This was the last thing he wanted to discuss. But he knew he owed her this much. He'd allowed her a little too much brandy, and he had never answered any of her questions in the past. He just did not ever reveal anything about himself to others. It was of no use to anyone. Talking of oneself was, at its base, selfish and boring to boot.

"Yes, he did. Many years ago," he replied, hoping that would satisfy her.

"Why is your mother not afraid to travel?"

He exhaled. She was not going to let him off the hook, excellent fisherman that she was. "Well, first, she isn't cursed, and second, she wasn't on the ship when it sank."

She blinked twice. "And?"

"And I was with him. It was just us two. A squall set in, and we hit a reef."

She stared at him. Waiting.

"And the sailboat sank. We climbed up the mast. I couldn't hold on to Vincent, and he drowned."

"What do you mean, you couldn't hold on to him? Was he hurt?"

"Yes."

He could see how hard she was trying to think despite the spirits.

"Were *you* hurt?"

He paused. "Not really."

"Roman Montagu, were you or were you not hurt? How badly? And what was wrong with your brother?"

He hated this. He really did.

"My arm was broken and he had hit his head."

"Was he unconscious?"

"No."

"So you were trying to hold on to him with only one hand? And he slipped from your grasp?"

"No."

"Well, then what was it?"

"I—I let him go."

She stared at him, those gray eyes of hers studying him. "You did nothing of the sort. Maybe it seemed that way. He slipped from your grasp—that's all. Obviously you were near to death yourself."

He felt ill. "You were not there. That's not what happened."

"I see."

She didn't believe him. No one had. Everyone had told him he was blameless. But not one of them had been there when the wave had crashed over them, and he had let go.

"March . . ." he whispered. "I will let you down. I always let people down."

She came over to him and grabbed his collar and dragged him down an inch so they were eye to eye. "Don't you dare," she said intently. "Don't you dare be the second man in my life to let me down."

"March," he ground out. "You cannot count on anyone. You know that already. And people have to choose if they want to be relied upon. What is your true fear? That you will be alone?"

"No," she replied quickly. "I enjoy being alone far too much, as well you know."

"So what is it, then?"

"Love," she said, her expression filled with sadness. "I don't think I really know what it is after all—or how to give or receive it in the right fashion. My father always said it was the most important thing in life. And I'm a complete failure at it."

"Oh, March . . ." He didn't know what to say. She was the most loveable person he knew.

He pulled her into his arms and kissed her. He kissed her plush mouth, and he pressed his lips against her forehead. He kissed her eyelashes and tasted her salty tears.

He couldn't tell her what she wanted to hear, but he could show her. He poured out all the love she deserved in his actions.

He tugged at his neckcloth, and undressed in haste as he brought her to her bed and got into it with her. She said not a word, but every now and again, a tear ran down her face.

She was so fragile to him. He didn't want to hurt her. And yet, it was ridiculous. She was an incredibly strong woman, physically; and her inner spirit was honest and true. He knew she would be perfectly fine without him. Actually, she would be far happier in the end, even if she didn't see it now. But, at this moment, while she was still here, he wanted to treat her with all the love and care she deserved.

He stroked her arms, and her legs, and brought her night rail over her head as he stroked her sides. He knew she loved her breasts to be touched and so he stroked them and suckled them and pushed away her hands when she tried to minister to him.

This had to be for her. Only for her.

He took her slowly. First with his fingers, and then with his mouth, and his tongue. She loved when he stroked her with his fingers and took her in his mouth. And he reveled in every inarticulate small sound she made. For so long he lavished attention to every last inch of her until she begged him to stop. She would not take her full pleasure.

It was as if she was waiting for him.

And so finally he gave her what he instinctively knew she wanted. He closed the space between their bodies and they were flesh to flesh. He entered her slowly, but without pause.

She was so warm, and so soft and wet. He felt her love wash over him and it cleansed his spirit as it had the last time.

She raised her knees off the bed and hugged him closer to her. It was the simplest and oldest of motions, but she was in raptures within moments. He was deep, ever so deep inside of her and he could feel the intensity of her pleasure as he triggered it again and again.

She couldn't seem to stop. Like the rolling of the waves off the coast, she kept pulsing about him, her face buried in his chest. Not a sound did she make.

Suddenly, he couldn't hold on any longer. A pure rush of sensation, starting at the base of his back, swept through him, sending shocks of intense pleasure where her skin touched his.

He could not stop. He could not pull out. He was powerless to even move an inch. The most potent undulation pumped through his arousal, until he had given all of himself to her. And she had been right there with him, her body milking his, her arms like bands around him, as if she were melded to him.

He dropped his head to her forehead, breathing hard. What had he done? God. He had never, ever allowed himself to find release in a lady's body.

"Montagu?" she said with startling clarity.

He lifted his head and looked into her beautiful gray eyes. "Yes?"

"I love you. I know you don't want to hear it. And I know you don't want this love I feel. But I can't *not* tell you anymore. You are the most amazing person I have ever met and you deserve all the love I have—even if it is imperfect. I can't leave without telling you . . . I love you."

"So do I," he replied gently. "I am only sorry I am not the man for you."

She stared at him for a long time. "It's the reverse, Roman. You *are* the man for me. I get to decide who is for me and who is not. It is obvious that it is I who am not the woman for *you*."

He was done with words. They didn't help. And they would only sting. And so he said nothing. Instead, he rolled to the side and cradled her in his arms as he had done all those nights when she had been hurt in Derbyshire. She was warm and safe in his embrace and he would keep her there until morning light if she would let him.

He knew he was being selfish and he knew he was hurting her. But she moved closer to him, laid her head on his chest, and said not another word either.

Neither of them slept. He could feel her even breathing, but not the light, sweet snoring he had come to enjoy.

How on earth was he going to let her go?

Chapter 19

Esme sat with her mother in her chamber the morning she was to set sail, a large breakfast tray in front of them on the low marble-covered table. For once, her mother was not wearing the mysterious lovely smile Esme wished she possessed.

Instead, her mother buttered triangles of toast, and carefully placed a dollop of apricot preserves on each piece. Preparing food is what her mother had always done when she was worried about her only child.

And Esme did what she had always done when her mother worried. She forced herself to eat every last bite, even if it tasted like sawdust.

"You will promise me three things, Esme."

"Anything you like, Mother."

"Four things, actually."

"Yes?"

"First, you will write to me at least twice a week. It is only fair." Only the odd swallowing motion gave her mother's sensibilities away.

She took the small silver butter knife from her mother's hand and returned the half buttered toast point to the plate. And then she inched closer on the chaise and took her mother in her arms.

"I shall miss you dreadfully," Esme whispered.

Esme felt her mother's gentle hands stroking her hair, and she closed her eyes, drinking in the sensation.

"As I will miss you, my darling."

"What are the other things you would like me to promise?" She inched closer, enjoying the warm scent of her mother's lily of the valley perfume.

"That you will grab on to your life, and paint to your heart's content. Creating art always brought your father profound happiness and it does the same for you."

"I know," Esme murmured into her mother's shoulder.

"Esme, you are destined to become the greatest artist of this century. This commission is only the beginning."

She didn't reply. Instead she eased away from her mother's arms and smoothed the fabric of her new pale blue lace morning gown. Between her mother, Lily, and her mother-in-law, Esme had been forced to endure more shopping expeditions in Bond Street environs than she ever had in her entire life. She appeared every inch a duchess now—just when there was no need.

"And third," her mother continued, "I want you to try to forget him. I know you love him. I also think he loves you. But, he is a desperate case, and he is inflexible, Esme. I've observed him. And his mother has hinted about a few things. He does not like to surround himself with others. He does not want to intimately share himself with people. Oh, he will always provide for his family. And he takes great joy in their happiness, but that is all. You cannot expect anything truly intimate with a man like this."

"Mother, you know I would never force anyone to do anything—especially to try to love me," she said, forming a false smile. "In fact I think you know that I tend to fade into the scenery if someone even hints they do not enjoy my company. I might have hoped he wanted me as I cared for him. But he does not. It is very simple and you are right. I will forget what might have been." She didn't add that it would take forever plus one day to forget a single moment with Roman Montagu. "I'm very good at that, as you know."

"You are, my love. Almost too good at times. You

are the strongest female I know, Daughter—you got that trait from me by the way." Her mother picked up her toast again and recommenced buttering it. "But you are also the one with the greatest heart and the most tender sensibilities—that is from your father. You must not let what has happened affect your joy in life. Please."

"You mustn't worry, Mother. I will be perfectly fine. You know that. I will throw myself into my art and that will be the end of it. I am determined to be happy."

"Very good," her mother said.

"What was the fourth thing?" She might as well get it out of her all at once.

"The fourth thing?"

"Yes, you said there were four things."

"Well . . ."

"Mother?"

"Yes, my love?"

"What do you want? Is there a fourth thing or not? I should call for Madame Cooper. It's time to go."

"I want you to, um . . . You know I am not *always* perfect at these sorts of mothering things, Esme. Fashion, yes. The rest? Not as good." She paused, her mind obviously at work. "It's just that I would like you to not quite give up. Oh, I know it doesn't make any sense. I told you to try to forget him. But I don't think you should quite give up. More time is needed, I am convinced. Will you do that, my love?"

"Mother?"

"Yes?"

"I love you, I really do."

"Of course you do. I always give the very best advice."

Esme smiled. She had always admired her mother's confidence. "I've promised you four things. It is your turn to promise me one thing. I want you to stop worrying. I am about to have the time of my life and I might not return. I know you and Lily will do very well here. And I also wanted to ask you to visit me. Perhaps next summer? When do you—"

"Esme, darling, I heard you distinctly ask me to only promise you one thing. That is two things. I will only promise you the first one—to not worry. But you must return here. One year, two years, maybe a little more. But then you must come back to England."

"We'll see," Esme replied and got up to call for her maid. It was past time to go.

Esme tried to hurry everyone on the front white marble steps of the Norwich townhouse. But it was not easy. Lily was not good at saying goodbye, and neither was Esme's mother. When she was finally settled in the first carriage with Her Grace, she was relieved. She had known he would not see them off. But one never really knew. It was better this way. Really, it was.

And then there was another moment of anxiety as they boarded the magnificent large yacht. It was a heavy vessel, built for safety and comfort—not speed.

Perhaps he would be there to say goodbye.

But he was not.

The captain welcomed them, and the crew busied themselves about the yacht with warm smiles of shy welcome. Esme climbed down the stair to the cabins, but at her door, her mother-in-law stopped her.

"Esme?"

"Yes, ma'am?"

"Caroline, please."

"What is it?"

"He is very like his sister."

"Sorry?"

"My son is no good at bidding farewell to anyone. He is far too sensitive. The only difference between them is that where Lily cannot let go, he cannot even put in an appearance."

She would not play the innocent. She liked this grand lady far too much. "It's far easier this way. Please there's no need to worry."

"But that's what mothers do. It begins the day our first child is born."

"Pardon?"

"Worry. We cannot help it. Even if it accomplishes nothing."

Esme smiled. "Caroline?"

"Yes?"

"I have a present for you."

"You do?"

"Yes. It's waiting for you in your cabin."

"What is it?"

"I can't tell you. It would ruin the surprise. Shall we meet on the deck in say an hour? I shall be dying to know what you think."

The clouds of concern faded from her mother-in-law's eyes. "What a perfect idea."

As she watched Caroline leave her with a new lightness in her step, it filled Esme's heart with happiness. Mothers might worry, but worry was useless. Seeing joy radiating from someone's face via distraction was the best way to erase it. She didn't need to be there when her mother-in-law opened the package filled with supplies for a budding artist. If Caroline Montagu, the Dowager Duchess of Norwich, was not an artist in the making, Esme would eat her brand-new tubes of paint—fuchsia and all.

Somewhere very deep inside of Roman, he knew what was going to happen. His entire godforsaken life had been nothing but a tragedy mixed with an ironic smidge of comedy from time to time.

The barometer in the west library was dropping by the minute. Of course it was. He refused to think about it. Instead, he focused on the selection of a book about art that he would have his steward send to March and his mother.

There were storms every other day off the coast. The Atlantic Ocean was a vast wilderness of watery danger. There had never been any doubt that they would encounter a storm or two along their voyage.

It was just that the barometer was dropping too quickly. And they had just departed. He had seen the crew cast off the lines, from a distant vantage point, and the yacht would be expertly sailed by a man who was as good a sailor as Admiral Nelson.

When the storm hit, they would most likely be in the exact same area *The Drake* had been the night they had been caught. It was a notoriously treacherous spot.

His sister entered the little used and smaller of the two libraries.

"Good afternoon, Lily."

His sister was in better spirits than just after March and his mother had departed. She looked so beautiful, Roman thought. Even more ravishing now at five and twenty than she had been at eighteen during her debut season. She was dressed to go out of doors, a dainty parasol dangling from one arm.

"You'll need something a tad more durable if you are going out and about."

"Whatever do you mean?"

"It's about to storm."

She crossed to a window and gazed outside. The clouds were ominous.

"It doesn't look *too* bad. I don't think it will start for another few hours. I'll only be out for an hour or so. Katie Harrington wants to show me the new mare her brother bought for her birthday."

"The barometer is dropping."

She walked over to glance at it. "So it is."

She looked at him, and he was again reminded how similar she was in appearance to Vincent. She was the beautiful, idealized feminine form of him.

"Are you worried? About Esme and Mama?"

"No," he replied instantly. "Not at all. I'm more worried about your visit with Miss Harrington. Is her brother still pining for your favors?"

"Charles? You must be joking. He married Cynthia Pendrey two seasons ago."

"Right. Well, then. I've not had the pleasure of turning down a proposal for you in quite awhile. Who is the current favorite?" He smiled. "Just so I can be prepared."

She stared at him with Vincent's eyes. "Actually, I've only just begun to consider eventually wedding someone now that you have indeed married.

Although, I'm not certain a marriage of convenience meets the terms of our agreement."

"What agreement?"

She stared at him. "Have you forgotten our conversation of six years ago?"

He blinked. A conversation? They'd had some sort of . . . Oh, God. "Lily, do not tell me you were serious."

She was as still as a fashion plate in one of those magazines ladies favored. "I knew you didn't believe me then. I was wondering how long it would take before you thought to confront me though. Longer than I thought, in the end."

"Are you telling me you refused a dozen suitors because of that ridiculous, juvenile conversation?"

"No, it was more like two dozen. They stopped coming to you for permission as I think they realized that unless I desired it, you would not agree to it."

He was so far out of his depth, he felt as if he were drowning.

"Just because I was only nineteen did not mean I was not serious."

"Are you telling me you refused all those gentlemen because I said I would never marry?"

"Yes. I told you I would not unless you did," Lily reminded him. "If you would not grab onto happiness with someone, I wouldn't either."

"But that is ridiculous."

"No. You are ridiculous, Roman. I don't care if it's because of the curse or because of Vincent. But it is finally done and you married the nicest person in the world. But now you've let her go. So I am giving up on you. Officially. This season, I am going to try to find the man for me." She paused and looked beyond his shoulder. "Well, now you've done it. I'm late for my friend and it has started to rain. I'm going to send a note to cancel, go up to my room, and try to remember why I love you."

She turned on her heel and left. And once again, he found himself dazed and flummoxed by yet another woman. There was a reason he preferred the company of gentlemen. Where was a member of the royal entourage when one needed him?

It had not taken long at all, Roman realized in retrospect. At the first clap of thunder, he dashed a note to Abshire's steward, informing that he was taking advantage of his friend's standing offer to use his prized yacht. He then directed his staff to bring 'round a carriage and retrieve a few personal effects. He shouted instructions about the management of his project to his steward, Simon, and shocked his butler, Mr. Stephens, and valet speechless by demanding they accompany him as he prepared to go.

Damn it all to hell. Was he ever to have a moment of peace? He was on the point of leaving the townhouse when Lily and Lady Gilchrist pounced on him from the salon nearest the door.

"Where are you going?" Lady Gilchrist asked, trying but not succeeding at hiding the hopeful expression in her visage.

"You know very well where I'm going, madam."

"Vienna is lovely this time of year, I hear," she replied owlishly. To her credit, his mother-in-law refrained from any sort of display of overly familiar affection. He could not say the same for his sister.

Lily ran into his arms and hugged him fiercely. He tried to disentangle himself but gave up when she would not leave off. Finally, he kissed the top of her head and she released him, with a lopsided smile. He donned his great coat and gloves, looked at the two ladies in front of him one last time, and departed without another word.

Roman made his way to the docks in the deluge, and for the first time in his life did not think of the curse that had dogged his innermost thoughts since the day his father had died five years ago. He didn't care about it anymore. He knew where his path lay, all stupid ducks be damned.

On the bench opposite him in the carriage, Stephens and Tanner were smiling in a way Roman had never seen. The driver found Abshire's slip and within a half hour they set sail, on the fastest small yacht in English racing history.

"Lord, I never thought I'd see the day we'd have this chance again, Your Grace," his butler said, his thinning hair gone all to hell in the wild wind. He was letting out sail as Tanner tended the cleat. These two men had been crew to Norwich vessels during his father's day. And Roman was at the helm, just as he had been all those many years ago.

For the oddest reason he could not fathom, not an inch of fear bloomed. Oh, he might die tonight. He might die tomorrow. He might even die within the hour—and it might be by duck. But, by God, he was going to live this life of his again. He wanted all of it. Not just math and science, and helping better the lives of others. He was going to embrace everything life had to offer and stop letting fear rule any part of it.

The shoals off the coast were treacherous, but he, Stephens, and Tanner knew well the dangers involved. Roman scanned the maps in Abshire's cabin and could navigate with the best of them. It was what he and Vincent had done every chance they could get during the summers they were on the familial estate on the coast.

He glanced at the small granite compass Esme had given him that he would always carry, and prayed he would overtake them within three hours if they were lucky.

And when he did find her—even if he had to

sail all the way to the Italian coast? Why, he would tell her that if she would still have him, he would never again spend a night away from her—his freedom be damned. He *wanted* her to depend on him. He *wanted* to be the man for her—to be her great champion—if she would give him one last chance.

For six hours they sailed. The ominous waves crashed over the port side, and Roman pushed the limits of the yacht despite the gale.

And finally, just as he decided that he was a complete idiot and that attempting to find another vessel in the middle of a storm in the vast Atlantic was a fool's errand, he saw a dark shadow beyond the sheets of rain that had finally begun to fizzle.

He pointed toward the other vessel and gained Stephens's and Tanner's attention. "Ship ahoy!"

The two men shouted with excitement. All of them were wet to the bone yet not one of them would ever complain. Of that Roman was certain. It was because these two men cared. They cared what happened to him even if they rarely uttered more than a polite yes or no to him.

He suddenly felt very humble before them.

Stephens clapped him on the back with his great bear-like arms. "I knew it! I knew we'd find 'em, Your Grace!"

Tanner grinned like a young boy. Roman had rarely ever seen the man smile before.

"Thank you," Roman said into the wind. "I will never be able to thank both of you enough. Double rations of rum all 'round!" They would wait to celebrate, of course, but it was only right to promise a pirate's celebration in a moment like this.

They sailed through the night on the larger vessel's tailwind. There was not a chance of boarding the other in such weather, but Roman took great comfort knowing she was in his sights.

And as the skies cleared in the hours before dawn, and he saw the glimmer of the stars, he prayed one last time that everything would be all right.

She might not want him after everything he had said and done. She might very well have hardened her heart and given up on him. She might not want to depend on him for anything. He had certainly spied a measure of pride in her—as she should have. She might have decided that, indeed, he was not the man for her.

As the dawn broke, the waves calmed, and soon enough they drew alongside the other craft. Roman charged Stephens and Tanner to sail Abshire's sleek yacht back to London.

With a minimum of effort, Roman transferred to the other vessel, and climbed the knotted line to the top railing and swung himself over. The captain of the other yacht welcomed him. The man knew well enough to order his crew to busy themselves and disappeared himself within moments.

His mother was waiting for him on the opposite railing. March was not in evidence. His heart plummeted as he approached his mother and kissed the cheek she offered.

And then her arms were wrapped around him and she would not let him go. She was crying.

He had only ever seen her like this once. The day Vincent had died. He gently guided her to the prow of the vessel for privacy. "Mother . . . I'm sorry."

"Hush," she said, accepting his drenched handkerchief. "You came."

"I'm sorry for all the unhappy years. I should never have closed myself off, especially from you and Lily. I've been a coward—"

"Stop," she said with such force, he did as she bade. "It is I who have been a coward," she whispered, unable to look at him. "I promised I would never tell you. I promised him so many times. It was the only thing he demanded, and the only way he would forgive me. But I should have told you immediately after he died. It's just that I had too much pride and worried about your opinion of me. And so I just conveniently never told you."

He stilled. "What are you talking about?"

"Your father made me promise I would never tell you."

He closed his eyes.

"You were not his child. He acknowledged you, of course. I am so sorry, Roman. So very, very sorry. We never will tell anyone else. But you had to know. And, and . . ."

"Who was he?" He could barely hear his own words.

She finally looked at him, tears streaming down her face. "A very great man. The man I loved with all my heart. We met the summer my parents took all my brothers and sisters and me for a tour of Italy. My father would not let me marry him. And our family returned to London immediately. But I never forgot him even when my parents arranged my marriage two months later. I had no choice, Roman. It was an alliance between two great families, as you know."

"And?"

"I had Vincent more than a year after the wedding. But I always pined in secret no matter how hard I tried to forget." His mother paused and then continued, her voice so low Roman had to bend closer to make out the words. "And then he came to London to find me. He had hoped I was still unmarried. And then . . . well, the unforgivable occurred, while Norwich was gone off with his friends." She stopped, uncertainty in her sad eyes.

"Tell me," he said gently.

"It was the greatest of sins, Roman."

"I don't care," he said. "And I fully understand.

Father was unbearable. We all knew it. Even Vincent could not always coax him out of his ill temper, despite the fact that my brother was our father's favorite. And . . ." He stopped, unable to finish the sentence. He still found it nearly impossible to discuss his brother.

His mother grasped the sleeve of his coat. "I hope I have done the right thing in telling you, Roman. At least you will finally comprehend why your father was cool toward you. He even went so far as to quash the budding artistic talents you possessed at a very young age. And I felt helpless to stop him. But now you know why. Norwich even refused to love Lily. He never trusted me after you. But don't think I was unhappy. He at least liked to travel, which I loved too. And so we went about our marriage as most do. But there was never any love between us, Roman. He was a man who did not want love. Yet, I wanted something very different for you, and Lily, and Vincent."

Roman stared at his mother, her head bowed forward in complete embarrassment. "Who was he?" he asked quietly.

She appeared wistful. "Mendamos. Louis Mendamos. You take after him. Very much so."

A flood of shock and uncertainty washed over him. Good God.

"The Italian sculptor?" he could barely form the words.

"Yes. I told you he was a very great man. We met while I was visiting one of the museums in Rome, where his works were exhibited."

He couldn't move. Couldn't speak.

"It's the reason I named you *Roman*."

He tried to work past the knot in his throat. Who in hell was he? His entire life had just been wrung from him, twisted, and handed back to him in an altogether different form. He didn't know whether he should be happy to know that the taciturn man who had acknowledged him was not his true father, or whether he should be sad that he was the product of a passionate affair of his beloved mother. Roman looked at the uncertainty and worry in his mother's expression, and knew what to do. He took her in his arms. "Thank you for telling me. I will always love you for it." He paused, his mind still reeling. "Is he still alive?"

She looked away. "I don't know. I did not follow his whereabouts after he begged me to go away with him and I refused. I could not leave Vincent behind. I just could not. I did not go to museums afterwards on purpose. Nor did I hold on to any hope. Norwich forgave me in his own way. I owe him for it. And after he died, it was only right to honor his memory by not seeking out Louis. It was a long time ago, Roman. I only want peace now. I am grateful, however, to Esme for allowing me to relive the joy I found in seeing great art."

At the mention of her name, Roman's heart swelled. "Mother, I must go to her. See her straightaway."

"Of course. And you must tell her what I just told you. I trust her without question and I know she will not think less of me for it. She is the one for you, Roman. I only wish you had met her a decade ago." His mother went on tiptoe and kissed first one cheek and then the other. "She is waiting for you in her cabin. You know which one. You chose it for her. And I forced her to go below when you were coming up the rope ladder." His mother smiled. "Don't look so worried. I shouldn't tell you, but it was all I could do to restrain her from jumping overboard when she saw your approach. She knows nothing about playing the reserved, cool-as-you-please game of most ladies I know."

"That is precisely why I love her," he returned.

Chapter 20

The newest Duchess of Norwich paced the small cabin, hope alternating with impatience. It was absurd. Why was he here?

It could not be bad news. No, Caroline would have immediately come below to tell her. So, what could it mean? Why was he here? And why was everyone taking so long to come to her?

He could not be here for her. Esme refused to allow hope to blossom more than a small sprout.

And then there was a light tap, and he entered without waiting for her answer. He took up so much space, and now he was crowding toward her, his blue, blue eyes tracking her every movement.

"March?"

It was so unfair. Just the sound of the deep

rumble of his voice sent shivers up her spine. "Yes?"

"A change is in order."

"It is?"

"Yes."

"But first I have something to tell you."

"You do?" She breathed. "Tell me."

"The night before last, you said you got to decide if I was the man for you."

"I did."

"But you did not give me the same choice," he said. "Esme *Montagu*?"

"Yes?"

"You are the woman for me."

Oh, her heart was pounding, and she was furious that her eyes were stinging. She refused to cry. "I am?"

"Yes. You are not only the woman for me, you are the one and only woman with whom I was meant to spend a lifetime. If you will still have me, we will live it together. Through the good times and through the bad times. We can always seek solitude when needed for your painting and my work, but we will also have happiness shared, if you choose to have me. Will you? Still have me?"

She burst into tears. "Oh, I'm so sorry," she said, desperately trying to regain her composure. "I am just so surprised. I mean, of course, I will have you. I am already yours and you know it."

He finally reached for her and she ran into his arms.

She began, "Montagu . . . I lo—"

He interrupted her. "No, my love. You must allow me to play the besotted husband." He stared into her eyes. "I love you," he said simply. "And I shall always love you. You may depend upon it."

The balm of his words made her heart feel light for the first time in many weeks. And her head felt just right cradled in the crook of his shoulder as he gathered her closer.

"I also have other news," he said, and kissed her head.

"I have something I must tell you, too," she murmured. She very much feared he would take back all he had just promised as soon as she told him. But she knew why she had not. She had not wanted him to stay with her via a misguided reason or effort. Esme had dreamed that he might one day love her for herself alone.

He looked at her quizzically after the long silence. "What is it?" His expression was so serious.

"You go first," she said, hoping he could not detect the fear in her voice.

"All right. I actually have two pieces of news."

"Yes?"

"Yes. The first is that I finished the project. It is waiting for Prinny's return along with a very long list of suggestions to see to before construction can begin."

"Oh, but then you must return to—"

"No, you did not understand," he stopped her. "We are not returning. We are going to Vienna for you to paint. The most important part of my work is done. Prinny must arrange the political maneuvering for the monies. We will return for the construction, but only after your commission is fulfilled. March?"

"Yes?"

"I cannot bear the idea of spending a night away from you ever again, my love."

Her heart was beating very fast.

"Do you feel the same?" His eyes searched hers.

"Of course I do," she whispered as she stroked his face. "But you must want to be in London more than anything right now to see your plans realized." How was she going to tell him? How was she going to be able to bear the look of revulsion he was sure to sport when she told him her ancestry?

"Esme, you must tell me what *you* want."

She could tell he was trying very hard to keep his expression blank.

He continued. "Would you prefer to be alone for several weeks or months to create this masterpiece? I have already told you my feelings, but your sensibilities are even more important to me."

"Ummmmm . . ."

"The truth if you please."

She forced herself to speak. "Roman, I have something very important to tell you. And then, if you still feel the same, we can take these decisions together."

"There is nothing you can say that will alter my feelings and decision." He smiled and he suddenly appeared years younger to her in his absolute happiness.

She swallowed and glanced at the floor. "Perhaps, but I will understand if you want to resume our prior arrangement after . . . after I tell you."

He gazed at her with expectation, but did not hurry her. When she could not make herself open her mouth again, he finally closed the gap between them and again held her in his embrace. She drank in the warm and familiar scent of him. Oh, how she wanted and needed his arms.

"It doesn't matter, Esme," he insisted. "Nothing can be as bad as you think. I am here and will always be here to help you if you will allow it, darling."

She closed her eyes. "My mother's maiden name is Mannon."

His arms immediately stiffened.

"I am the last direct descendant of the lady who cursed your family. My full name is Esmeralda Mannon Morgan March. I should have told you a long time ago."

The strong, warm comfort of his body against hers disappeared and she opened her eyes to face him.

"You forgot *Montagu*," he said with a gleam in his eye.

"Pardon me?"

"It's your hearing again?" he suggested with a smile.

"No. But I don't think you—"

"Esme, I don't care who your family is or was. I just want you to be my family now. Will you?"

A tide of relief and warm happiness flowed through her. "But you're not afraid of the curse?"

"No, and I shall tell you why. But first, I should ask if you know if the curse applies only to Norwich dukes with the first duke's blood in their veins."

"Why would you ask such a question?"

"Can you not guess, my love?"

She studied him. "The version of events told to me by my grandmother suggests that the first Esmeralda cursed every Norwich heir and duke who possessed Norwich I—the Duck Hunter's—blood."

His smile was blinding. "Excellent news, my darling. I'm delighted to inform I am probably not cursed at all."

"That is good because I dreaded having to warn you that the captain brought his collection of duck calls on this yacht. I would stay very far away from his cabin if I were you."

He threw back his head and laughed, his fears obviously gone far, far away. He grabbed her in his arms and swung her in a circle before he herded her onto her small bunk. "May I tell you why the curse will not plague me?"

"It only matters that you believe it, Montagu. But I should also warn you that according to my grandmother, I have no power to remove the curse. I think you know I would if I could."

"Shhh . . ." he held a finger to her lips. "No, I won't have you worry," he insisted. "Let me tell you why." And so he told her what his mother had revealed to him.

Esme swore ten times over that she had always suspected he was an artist at heart because of his designs, his mathematical genius, and the way he had expertly painted seabirds that day on the Isle of Wight. Within a quarter hour, she proposed a dizzying number of artistic endeavors the both of them could explore together.

It was a very long time before anyone on board saw the Duke and Duchess of Norwich again.

Every last person on the ship celebrated.

With the captain's duck calls.

In the end, there was a small detour to their destination.

His wife had commented on the lines of worry she had spied on his face the morning after they reunited. She sat across from him at the mahogany table in the cabin, trimming a quill as he dressed.

"Who are you writing to?" He wanted nothing more than to remove the boots he had just put on, pick her up, and take her back to the small bunk.

"To my mother and to Verity," she said, not looking up from her handiwork.

He sighed and drew out a chair opposite to sit with her. "I must write to Kress straightaway to relieve his worry concerning his fortune."

She raised her eyes from the page and looked at him.

"What is it, my love?" She reached across to stroke his sideburns.

This calmed him in some mystical way no scientific theory could ever explain. She evoked such peace in him whenever she touched him. "I've fulfilled Prinny's directive of waiting, and I must inform Kress. I must return his fortune. I owe him twice over, for if he had not forced the wager that made me board *The Drake*, I would never have found you," he said, catching her hands in his, "the love of my life."

She smiled with such happiness radiating from her face. "But it will take weeks for a letter to reach him if you post it from Vienna. We must instead go to him now. Penzance is not so far. If we stay but a day or two, it will only add a week at most and I am not to see the Duc d'Orleans for at least a fortnight after the day we were supposed to arrive. And I'm certain your mother will not mind if we take a slight detour."

He eased her lovely light brown hair away from her face, which had grown so very dear to him. He prayed they would have many more years in front of them—enough to fill up every reservoir of happiness they possessed.

Instinctively, he knew that the love they shared today was but a hint of the grand passion that would build throughout the rest of their lives. He could not imagine that his love for her could grow more, but it had become clear in the last few days that he knew nothing about how passion fueled the hearts of eternal lovers.

He had been reticent yesterday when he had told her about his true father. But in her signature fashion, she had built on it by saying she liked him better for it. With her excitement and her every praise of the sculptor whose blood ran in his veins, his sense of self had grown. And she had gently insisted they try to find him when they arrived in Italy.

"Esme?" he said, rising from the chair.

"Yes?" she replied, not looking up from her letter.

Roman circled the table and came behind her.

He gently brushed aside her soft hair and pressed a kiss to her warm, lilac-scented long neck. She immediately turned and Roman removed the quill from her fingers.

Esmeralda Mannon Morgan March Montagu needed no further hint. She took matters into her own bewitching hands—a trait Roman was beginning to love. As they whiled away the hours lost in each other's embrace, Roman finally understood what had eluded him for so long. Love was not to be feared.

"My darling," he whispered in her ear as she gently caressed his face.

"Yes?"

"Thank you."

She slowly rose onto one elbow. "For what?"

"For being so patient and so kind. You are the greatest woman I have ever known. Your capacity to love and accept others for who they are is unparalleled.

"You know I've always considered myself a failure at love," she whispered. "And I've always felt more at ease giving love instead of receiving it."

"I guessed that long ago," he replied. "But your instincts were far better than mine. After my brother's death, I embraced solitude, never wanting to depend on anyone, nor have anyone depend on me. Love was never an option. But you have shown me this is not the way to happiness.

And you, my love, had better be prepared for the result. I intend to shower you with all the love you deserve and more for the rest of our lives." He paused. "Which will be very, very long since I am depending on you to cast a spell on our longevity." He paused with a grin. "One can hope it will not involve waterfowl."

She smiled hugely and kissed him for all she was worth. It would take him many, many happy years to find out that she did, indeed, have a talent inherited from her ancestor.

Their approach to St. Michael's Mount was done an hour before dawn. Moonlight reflected off the beautiful, ancient granite walls of the towering former abbey. Norwich shook his head as he stared at it from the railing.

Kress would surely be climbing the walls in boredom within this wreck of a castle, even if it was magnificent. His half-French cohort was the latest member of the royal entourage, and he was a gentleman who detested anything to do with countrified living. Kress was a man who lived for the glitter and jaded amusements of Town.

Norwich pulled Esme closer to him as they stood side by side. She was nearly his height and he adored the way they could gaze into each other's faces without a crook in either of their necks.

"Who will be there?" The luster of her hair gleamed in the lowlight.

"I'm not at all certain. Kress, obviously. The question is whether Candover or Prinny has joined him. As you know, the both of them were secretly on their way southward. I understood from Candover it was to 'save Kress's bloody absinthe-soaked neck.'"

She laughed.

He loved to see his bride so happy.

And then they were arrived and the lines were secured by the waiting men at the small port of the mount. Roman helped his mother and Esme descend the gangway, and they made their way up the steep incline to the ancient fortress, the last bastion near the tip of Land's End.

A massive Cossack footman allowed them inside without a word. The man did not even make them wait by decamping to inform his master of their arrival. Surely, they were all abed at this hour. But, apparently, no. The huge man looked them over from head to toe and then motioned them with the crook of his fat finger to follow him.

Kress's great-aunt, a grand French countess who was either blind or not—a question that he and Kress had debated privately between them for the last two decades—had always surrounded herself with the oddest assortment of servants. This footman was all the proof Roman needed that he would find her here.

Esme, Roman, and his mother were escorted into a massive stone chamber, some sort of ancient dining hall with a huge fireplace filling one side. A small group of people turned upon their entrance.

Roman had the joy of seeing the jaw of his oldest friend in the world, Alexander Barclay, the very newest Duke of Kress, drop open in shock.

"I knew it," Kress sputtered. "You're too damn stubborn to die, Seventeen. As I always told you, that curse does not apply to you."

Isabelle Tremont, the Duchess of March and the only female in the royal entourage, rushed forward and hugged him. Roman was so surprised by her exuberance that he could do nothing but clasp her to him gently. He had had no idea she would truly care if he lived and breathed or not.

"Oh," she exclaimed. "Where have you been? Does Prinny know? You must have crossed paths with him. You've missed him. He is on the road to London. He will be so relieved to learn of your well-being."

"I have your fortune, Kress," Roman said quickly, not wanting another minute to lapse before he could ease his friend's mind. "I did not win the wager. I lasted not a full day on that blasted vessel."

Kress glanced at Candover, who said not a word.

Kress's eyes narrowed. "You knew, didn't you?" He looked ready to do bodily harm to Candover. "Is there no bloody code in this damned royal entourage? There should be a code. And the first rule should be, 'One shall always immediately tell the other if they know where their sodding fortune is.' "

Candover calmly replied, "I beg your pardon, she's standing next to you."

Roman noticed a very pretty lady, just a half step away from Kress. She was clutching a very odd and very ugly bouquet of half-dead flowers. And on her hand the most enormous diamond and sapphire ring resided.

Kress's jaded brown eyes filled with pride. "You're a bit late to the celebration, Norwich. May I present the lady I married one half hour ago? My wife, Roxanne Newton Barclay, the Duchess of Kress. Roxanne, *cherie*?" Kress addressed the lady beside him with more tenderness than Roman had ever beheld in his oldest friend. It almost eased the shock Roman felt upon learning the news that the one man aside from himself who had been determined to avoid leg-shackling had fallen as hard and as fast as he had.

Kress's eyes did not stray from his bride. "May I present Roman Montagu, the Duke of Norwich, *cherie*? As well as his mother, Her Grace, the Duchess of Norwich, and—"

"Actually," Roman's mother interrupted. "I'm

delighted to inform that I am now quite officially the Dowager Duchess. Roman?"

He gently squeezed Esme's waist in a highly improper and intimate fashion. She looked so very happy beside him and his heart swelled. "I'm honored beyond measure to introduce *my* wife, Esme Montagu, the new Duchess of Norwich, to you all." It was his turn to endure the shocked expression of his friend. Roman continued smoothly. "March? My good friend, Alexander Barclay, the Duke of Kress, and Isabelle Tremont, the Duchess of March, who—"

The petite duchess was examining Esme and interrupted him. "Oh, Esme and I know each other very well, Norwich. Do you have any idea how lucky you are to have captured this lady's interest? She has a talent unparalleled. Oh, Esme, I am so pleased to see you! It has been an age. Have you seen the latest exhibition at the Royal Academy?"

Esme embraced her friend before Isabelle turned to Norwich again. "But why do you address Esme as 'March'? This is all going to be highly confusing—sort of like the ridiculous number of alias names that have been floating around the Mount the last month. You should have been here, Norwich." She then paused for a moment and backtracked. "But the name 'March'? That's my title. Although, James?"

"Yes?" Candover looked at the pretty duchess with the same casual indifference that he always employed. It spoke of anything *but* disinterest.

"Perhaps, you should address me as such. I mean, I've always thought it highly unfair. Why is it that all of the rest of the entourage address each other by their titles and I must forever be Her Grace, or Isabelle?"

Candover emitted a pained sigh.

Esme dropped a curtsy as Kress bowed to her, and then accepted a warm welcome from Kress's wife, Roxanne, and finally straightened for Candover's chaste, cousinly kiss on her cheek. Everyone did their duty to Roman's mother, who appeared overjoyed by events.

Kress and Roman glanced at each with raised brows.

Kress spoke first. "I want an afternoon—no, an entire day with the lady who managed to tame the wild beast. March, is it? May I have the pleasure of your company tomorrow, or rather, today, now that the sun has come up?"

"Not on your life," Roman replied before his wife could utter a sound. "Unless, of course, I am permitted the honor of an afternoon with that lovely creature next to you. Your Grace? What say you?"

Roxanne Barclay smiled hugely. "Why, I would be deligh—"

"Absolutely not," roared Kress. "He is not to be trusted. He is not—"

Roxanne interrupted Kress. "You say that about everyone in the entourage. Abshire, Candover, Barry, and especially . . . *Sussex*."

Kress was quite obviously not pleased by the mention of the most charming, handsome duke in their exclusive circle and it amused Roman to no end. He had thought Kress and Sussex got on well enough together. Apparently, not where Kress's bride was concerned.

"If you had seen them the night of Candover's wedding debacle, *cherie*, you would know why," Kress replied, more embarrassed than usual.

"But I thought none of you could remember a thing," Isabelle inserted.

"We don't need to remember," Candover ground out.

"I like your friends very much," Esme said, turning to Roman.

"I had hoped you would, March," he replied, his heart expanding as he looked at her. He still couldn't believe she was next to him. He doubted he would be able to let her out of his sight for at least a fortnight. It was a good thing they would be boarding that yacht again within a day or so.

"Norwich?" Isabelle repeated. "Are you ever going to tell me why the name 'March'? She was Lady Derby and now she's your duchess."

"It was my first husband's family name," Esme answered for him.

"But now you are a Montagu," Roxanne said gently.

"Yes, well, it will not do for me to address her thusly as that is how she addresses me," Roman replied.

Esme tilted her head to look at him. "Well, you could use Morgan or Mannon," she said shyly.

Fate, indeed, was nothing but a very odd duck. He smiled to himself.

All at once, he felt Esme's hand reach for his. "Or whatever name you like."

Kress grinned. "I would advise a name with a number. Seventeen never pays attention to anything unless it involves numbers."

"Perhaps you should do the same, *mon vieux*," ground out Roman. "I was not the sodding idiot who lost an entire fortune not a week after it had been entrusted."

Kress's wife Roxanne diplomatically interrupted. "The name Esme or Esmeralda signifies great beauty, does it not? Mannon is also lovely. Why cannot you use either?"

Candover, who had been as silent as he always was, replied. "Esmeralda Mannon was the infamous lady who cursed the first Duke of Norwich. She didn't care for his engagement gift of a dozen bloody ducks. Esme is her direct descendant."

Roman started. "You knew?" For the first time in their acquaintance, Norwich would have liked to bloody Candover's nose. In fact, he might very well do it this—

"Of course, I knew. But I didn't want to spoil the enjoyment of the day you would finally figure it out on your own." He looked at Esme and winked. "Was it as ghastly as I can imagine, cousin?"

All the fight went out of Roman as he looked down to see the great humor flooding his wife's face. He stroked her jaw with one finger. "Well, was it?"

She darted a look toward Candover. "Ghastly isn't the word I would choose, cousin. But then, I am surprised by the audacity of such a private query. Curiosity is not usually a word I would choose to describe you."

"She is definitely one of us," Roxanne announced to Kress. "I shall arrange for the front chambers to be made up for our new guests, darling. And I shall wake all our other guests, as a grand double wedding celebration is in order. Will that suit you, March? Pardon me, is it Esmeralda, or is it to be Mannon?"

All eyes focused on Roman.

Mannon . . . It was perfect for her. She was, after all, in his scientific mind—100 percent completely undecipherable, impossibly talented, complicated, and bewitching sensual woman, with her quiet, ordered mind and immense depth of character and heart.

"Esmeralda Mannon Morgan March Montagu?"

"Yes, my love?" Her eyes were shining.

"Mannon?"

"Yes," she agreed, her smile soft. She was lovelier than she had ever appeared to him.

"I have three things to say in front of all these people, who I would have liked to have been with us on the day we wed—apart from your cousin who was our witness."

Kress sent Candover another black glare for not telling him he knew Roman was alive all these past impossible weeks.

"What things?" she asked.

"First, I promise never to go hunting or to give you a dead duck." He paused. "Second, I promise to take great care of your heart and your talent. And lastly? You may depend upon me always. For anything and everything. I will not let you down."

"I know you won't, my love," she replied with great love radiating from her expression.

And with that, the members of the royal entourage cheered. They also all secretly wondered . . .

Who was next?

Now you know what happened to Roman Montagu, the Duke of Norwich, the morning after the most extravagant royal bachelor party of all time. But what about his friend Alexander Barclay, the Duke of Kress?

Alexander Barclay, the Duke of Kress, cannot for the life of him remember anything after the party. Only one thing is certain, his fortune is missing, and the Prince Regent and his royal entourage are facing humiliation and worse in the press. The prince commands all the dukes to mend their ways, and Kress is forced southward to reform and rebuild a castle fortress.

The first time Kress lays eyes on Roxanne Newton Vanderhaven, she is hanging on to the side of a cliff with waves crashing far below. After saving her, he reluctantly agrees to hide her in his ancient, crumbling castle on St. Michael's Mount until she can figure out why her husband, the Earl of Paxton, abandoned her on the cliff. And along the way, sparks fly. . . .

Turn the page for an excerpt from *The Duke and the Deep Blue Sea*, the first book in the Royal Entourage series by Sophia Nash.

Now available from Avon Books!

A new duke always had hell to pay.

Oh, it had been all well and good when Alexander Barclay, now the newly minted ninth Duke of Kress, had walked into White's Club in Mayfair and been pounded on the back by a blossoming number of friends a fortnight ago.

And it had been *very* good last week when he had met his new solicitors and removed from his cramped and moldy rooms off St. James's *Street* to palatial Kress House, Number Ten, St. James's *Square*.

However, it had gone from the first bloom of bonhomie with the *crème de la crème* of the most privileged societal tier in the world to near pariah status overnight. Alex's avalanche from grace had all started last eve at the Prince Regent's Carleton House, where he provided the spirits to toast His

Grace, the Duke of Candover's last evening as a bachelor.

His own induction into the circle that same night, he could not remember.

Alex should have known better. Had not the sages throughout history warned to be careful of what one wished? Barons, viscounts, marquises, and earls would have given up their last monogram-encrusted silver spoon for entrée into the prince's exclusive circle, and all for naught as one had to be a duke of England to be included. For two centuries, the dukes in the peerage of Scotland had pushed for inclusion in the royal entourage to no avail. And one did not speak of the Irish dukes' efforts at all.

Yes, well. Being a duke was anything but entertaining right now. More asleep than not, Alex shivered—only to realize his clothes were wet, and even his toes were paddling circles in his boots. Christ above, he would give over a large portion of his newfound fortune if only someone would lend him a pistol to take a poorly aimed shot at the birds singing outside like it was the last morning the world would ever see.

Sod it . . . What on earth had happened last night? And where in bloody hell was he?

The fast clacking of heels somewhere beyond the door reverberated like a herd of African elephants. A sharp knock brought stars to the insides of Alex's eyelids before the door opened.

"Hmmm . . . finally. Thought we'd lost you," shouted a familiar feminine voice.

Footsteps trampled closer and Alex pried open his eyes to find a blurry pair of oddly golden peepers and coils of brown hair floating above him. Ah, the young Duchess of March, the only female in the prince's entourage. Alex wished he could make his voice box work to beg her to stop making so much noise.

"Although, you," she continued, looking at Alex's valet stretched out on a trundle bed nearby, "are not Norwich. Come along, then. The both of you. Prinny is not in a mood to wait this morning—not that he ever is." Isabelle displayed the annoying habit of tapping her foot as she stared at Alex.

When he did not move, Isabelle had the audacity to start pulling his arm. Dislocation being the worse of two evils, Alex struggled to regain full consciousness and his feet as his man did the same with much greater ease.

Ah, at least he had one question answered. They were still in the prince's Carleton House. *Thank the Lord.* Any debauchery that might have occurred had at least remained within the confines of these gilded walls. There had been far too much gossip lately of the immoderation of their high-flying circle.

"Look, if we're not in His Majesty's chambers

within the next two minutes, I cannot answer as to what might happen," the duchess urged. "Honestly, what were you and the rest thinking last night? There must have been quite a bit of devilish spirits to cause . . ."

He held up his hand for her to stop. Just the thought of distilled brews made him wince.

"Must have been the absinthe," his valet, Jack Farquhar, said knowingly. "Englishmen never have the stomach for it."

"You're English," Alex ground out, his head splitting.

"Precisely why I never imbibe. But you . . . you should be *half* immune to that French spirit of the devil incarnate."

Isabelle Tremont, the Duchess of March, had a lovely warm laugh, but right now it sounded like all the bells of St. George's at full peel.

"We *must* go. You too." She nodded to Jack Farquhar, before she continued. "Kress, do you have the faintest idea where Norwich is? Were you not with him during the ridiculous bachelor fete? You two are usually inseparable."

Alex made the mistake of trying to shake his head with disastrous results. "Can't remember . . ." As the duchess pulled them both forward, Alex's toes squished like sponges inside his now not so spanking white tasseled Hessian boots.

The effort to cross the halls to the Prince Regent's bedchamber felt like a long winter march across Europe to St. Petersburg. Alex looked sidelong toward his soon-to-be dismissed valet. "Absinthe, *mon vieux*?"

"'Twas the only thing in your new cellar . . . eighteen bottles. Either the last duke had a partiality for the vile stuff or his servants drank everything but that—in celebration of his death."

To describe the pasty-faced, hollowed-eyed jumble of gentlemen strewn around the royal bedchamber as alive was a gross kindness. Four other dukes—Candover, Sussex, Wright, and Middlesex—as well as the Archbishop of Canterbury formed a disheveled half-circle before Prinny's opulent, curtained bed where the future king of England reclined in full shadow.

"Your Majesty would have me recommence reading, then?" The pert voice of the duchess caused a round of moans. "I'm sorry, but Norwich and Barry cannot be found, and Abshire is, umm, indisposed but will arrive shortly." She blushed and studied the plush carpet. "As His Majesty said, there should be no delay in a response to these outrageous accusations." She waved a newspaper in the air.

Alex swiveled his head and met the glassy-eyed stare of the bridegroom, the Duke of Candover, who turned away immediately in the fashion of a cut direct.

"Uh . . . shouldn't you be at St. George's?" Alex would have given his eyeteeth for a chair.

"Brilliant observation," Candover said under his breath.

"Late to the party, Kress." The Prince Regent's voice was raspy with contempt. "Haven't you heard? Candover has been stood up by his bride on this wedding morning. Or was it the other way around, my dear?"

"It appears both, Your Majesty," the duchess replied, scanning the newspaper with what almost appeared to be a hint of . . . of *delight*? No, Alex was imagining it.

"Lady Margaret Spencer was tucked in an alcove of the church, but her family whisked her away unseen when Candover did not appear after a ninety-minute delay," Isabelle read from the column.

"Why wasn't I woken?" Candover grasped his wrenched head in obvious pain.

"James Fitzroy," the duchess replied, disapprobation emanating from every inch of her arched back, "you should know. Your sisters and I woke to find every servant here on tiptoe. You, and the rest of you"—her eyes fluttered past the prince in her embarrassment—"commanded upon threat of dismissal or, ahem, dismemberment that you were not to be disturbed."

"I remember that part very well," inserted Jack Farquhar.

In the long pause that followed, Alex imagined half a dozen ways to dismember his valet. He was certain that every duke in the room was considering the same thing.

"Continue reading, Isabelle." The royal hand made a halfhearted movement.

"Let's see," the duchess murmured, her eyes flickering over the words of the article. "Uh, well, the columnist made many unfortunate assumptions and . . ."

"Isabelle Tremont, I order you to read it," ground out the prince.

"Majesty," she breathed. "I—I just can't."

John Spence, the Duke of Wright, who at seven and twenty was the youngest of all the dukes, chose that moment—a most opportune one—to sway ominously and pitch forward onto the future king's bed. Without a word, the Duke of Sussex hauled Wright off the royal bedclothes and laid the poor fellow, who was out stone cold, on the floor.

Alex strode forward and grasped the edges of the paper from the pretty duchess's nervous fingers.

"Ah, yes, much better," the Prince Regent said sourly. "Might as well have the man"—his Majesty's hand pointed to him—"who is to blame for the ruin of us all, read it."

Head pounding, Alex forced his eyes and mouth to work. "'In a continuation of the regular obscene excesses of the Prince Regent and his *royal entourage,* not one of the party made an appearance at St. George's earlier this morning, with the exception of our Princess Caroline, darling Princess Charlotte, and Her Grace, the young Duchess of March. His Majesty's absence and that of the groom and groomsmen caused all four hundred guests to assume the worst. And, indeed, this columnist has it on the very best authority, partially one's own eyewitness account, that not only the august bridegroom, His Grace, the Duke of Candover, but also seven other dukes, one archbishop and the Prince Regent himself, were seen cavorting about all of London last eve on an outrageous regal rampage. Midnight duels, swimming amok with the swans in the Serpentine, a stream of scantily clad females in tow, lawn bowling in unmentionables, horse races in utter darkness, wild, uproarious boasting, and jesting, and wagering abounded. Indeed, this author took it upon himself to retrieve and return to White's Club their infamous betting book, which one of the royal entourage had had the audacity to remove without even a by your leave. In this fashion we have learned that the Duke of Kress lost the entire fortune he so recently acquired with the title, although the winner's name was illegible . . .'" Alex's voice stumbled to a halt.

"Happens to the best of us," the Duke of Sussex murmured as consolation. That gentleman was as green about the gills as Alex felt.

"And the worst of us," mumbled the Duke of Middlesex, as he finally gave in to the laws of gravity and allowed his body to slide down the wall on which he was leaning. He sunk to the ground with a thud.

"Don't stop now, Kress. You've gotten to the only good part." Candover leaned in wickedly.

Alex had never tried to avoid just punishment. He just wished he could remember, blast it all, what his part had been in the debacle. He cleared his throat and continued, "'Even the queen's jewels were spotted on one duke as he paraded down Rotten Row. Yes, my fellow countrymen, it appears the English monarchy has learned nothing from our French neighbor's lessons concerning aristocratic overindulgence. As the loyal scribe of the Fashionable Column for two decades, you have it on my honor that all this occurred and worse. I can no longer remain silent on these reoccurring grievous, licentious activities, and so shall be the first plain-speaking, brave soul to utter these treasonous words: I no longer support or condone a monarchy such as this.'" Alex stood very still as the last of the column's words left his lips.

At precisely the same moment the other dukes cleared their throats, and one valet tried to escape.

"If any of you leave or say one word, I shall cut off your head with a . . ."

"Guillotine, Majesty?" Isabelle chirped.

In the silence, a storm brewed of epic proportions.

Thank the Lord, the chamber's gilded door opened to divert His Majesty's attention. The Duke of Barry, a Lord Lieutenant of the 95th Rifle Regiment, stepped in, almost instantly altering his unsteady gait with expert precision. Only his white face and the sheen of perspiration on his forehead gave him away. Mutely, he stepped forward and laid a dueling pistol on the foot of the cashmere and silk royal bedclothing.

"Dare I ask?" His Majesty's voice took on an arctic edge.

Barry opened his mouth but no sound came out. He tried again. "I believe I shot a man. He's in your billiard room, Majesty."

The Duke of Abshire entered the royal chamber behind Barry with the hint of wickedness in his even, dark features marred by a massive black eye. Known as the cleverest of the bunch, good luck had clearly deserted him on this occasion.

"I thought you were leaving, Abshire. Or do you need me to show you out?" Candover's usually reserved expression turned thunderous.

Alex leaned toward Sussex, and almost fell

over before righting himself. "What did I miss?"

"Trust me," Sussex whispered. "You do not want to know. You've got enough on your dish, old man."

Alex raised his eyebrows at Sussex and missed Abshire's dry retort directed at the premier duke, Candover. There was no love lost between those two. Then again, Candover's remote, holier-than-thou manner grated on just about everyone.

Middlesex, still on the floor, tugged on Alex's breeches and Alex bent down to catch the former's whisper. "I heard a lady shouting in chambers next to mine, then two doors slammed, and Candover came out rubbing his knuckles."

Alex shook his head. Could it get any worse?

The black-haired duke, Abshire, clapped a hand on the shoulder of the most respected and most quiet duke of the circle, Barry. "Is he dead?"

"Yes," Barry replied.

"Are you certain?" Sussex asked, eyes wide.

"I think I know when a man is breathing or not."

"But there are some whose breath cannot be detected," Middlesex croaked.

"Rigor. Mortis," Barry replied.

An inelegant sound came from the duchess's throat.

"Please forgive me, Isabelle," Barry said quietly. "Your Grace, I do not know the man."

"Just tell me you locked the chamber when you

left it," the prince said dryly. When Barry nodded, the prince continued darkly. "I had thought better of you, Barry. What is this world coming to if I cannot count on one of England's best and brightest?" The prince, still in full shadow, sighed heavily. "Well, we shall see to the poor, unfortunate fellow, as soon as I am done with all of you."

"Yes, Your Majesty," Barry replied, attempting to maintain his ramrod posture.

"Now then," His Majesty said with more acidity than a broiled lemon. "Does not one of you remember what precisely happened last night?"

"I remember the Frenchified spirits Kress's man"—the Duke of Sussex looked toward Jack Farquhar with pity—"brought into His Majesty's chamber."

"I must be allowed to defend . . ." Farquhar began and then changed course. "Yes, well, since three of you locked me in a strong room when I voiced my concern, I cannot add any further observations."

"Is that the queen's coronation broach, Sussex?" the imperial voice demanded suddenly.

The Duke of Sussex, now pale as the underbelly of a swan, looked down and started. Hastily, he removed the offending article and laid the huge emerald-and-diamond broach on the end of the gold-leaf bed frame, beside the pistol.

Alex just made out Middlesex's whispered

words below. "Very fetching. Matches his eyes to perfection."

Alex felt a grin trying to escape as he helped Middlesex to his feet.

"Just like the wet muck on your shoulder compliments your peepers, Middlesex," retorted Sussex.

Ah, friendship. Who knew English dukes could be so amusing when they dropped their lofty facades? Last night had probably almost been worth it. It was too bad none of them could remember it.

"Well, at least the columnist did not know about the unfortunate soul in the billiard room," Isabelle breathed. "Did you all really swim in the Serpentine? I declare, the lot of you are wetter than setters after a duck. I would not have ever done anything so—"

"You were not invited," the Duke of Candover gritted out.

"And whose fault was that?"

"Enough," the Prince Regent roared. The royal head emerged from the gloom and Alex's gasp blended with the rest of the occupants' shocked sounds in the room.

His Majesty's head was half shaved—the left side as smooth as a babe's bottom, the long brown and gray locks on the right undisturbed. None dared to utter a word.

Prinny raised his heavy jowls and lowered his eyelids in a sovereign show of condescension.

"None of this is to the point. I hereby order each of you to make amends to me, and to your country. Indeed, I need not say all that is at stake." His Majesty chuckled darkly at them. "And we have not a moment to spare. Archbishop?"

A small fat man trundled forward, his head in his hands, his gait impaired.

The future king continued. "You shall immediately begin a formal answer to this absurd column—to be delivered to all the newspapers. And as for the rest of you—except you, my dear Isabelle—I order you all to cast aside your mistresses and your self-indulgent, outrageous ways to set a good example."

"Said the pot to the kettle," inserted Sussex under his breath.

"You shall each," His Majesty demanded, "be given your particular marching orders in one hour's time. While I should let all of you stew about your ultimate fate, I find . . . I cannot. I warn that exile from London, marriage, continuation of ducal lines, a newfound fellowship with sobriety, and a long list of additional duties await each of you."

"Temperance, marriage, and rutting. Well, at least one of the three is tolerable," the Duke of Abshire on Alex's other side opined darkly and discreetly.

Alex could not let this farce continue. "Majesty,

I appreciate the invitation to join this noble circle of renegades but—"

"It's not an invitation, Kress," the Prince Regent interrupted. "And by the by, have you forgotten your return to straightened circumstances if this column is correct? You shall be the first to receive your task."

"An order is more like it," the Duke of Barry warned quietly. The solemn man wore a distinctive green military uniform that reminded Alex of his own dark past. A past that would infuriate the Prince Regent if he but knew of it.

Prinny glanced about the chamber in an old rogue's fit of pique. "Kress, you shall immediately retire to your principal seat—St. Michael's Mount in Cornwall. Since a large portion of the blame for last evening rests squarely on your shoulders, I hereby require you to undertake the restoration of that precious pile of rubble, for the public considers it a long neglected important outpost for England's security. Many have decried its unseemly state."

A departure from London was the very last thing he would do. He hated any hint of countrified living. The cool lick of an idea slid into his mind and he smiled. "But, according to that column, I've no fortune to do so, Your Majesty."

Prinny's face grew red with annoyance. "You are to use funds from my coffers for the time being. But you shall repay my indulgence when you take a bride from a list of impeccable young ladies of fine lineage and fine fortunes"—Prinny nodded to a page who delivered a document into Alex's hands—*"within a month's time."*

Candover made the mistake of showing a hint of teeth.

Alex Barclay, formerly Viscount Gaston, with pockets to let in simpler times, felt his contrarian nature rise like a dragon from its lair, but knew enough to say not a word. The ice of his English father's blood had never been very effective in cooling the boiling crimson inherited from his French mother.

"And you, my dear Candover," the prince continued, "shall have the pleasure of following him, along with Sussex and Barry, for a house party composed of all the eligibles. While you are exempt at the moment from choosing a new bride, as homage must be paid to your jilted fiancée, I shall count on you to keep the rest of these scallywags on course."

Candover's smile disappeared. "Have you nothing to say to His Majesty, Kress?" The richest of all the dukes coolly stepped forward to face Alex and tapped his fingers against a polished rosewood table in the opulent room seemingly dipped in gold, marble, and every precious material in between. The rarefied air positively reeked of royal architects gone amok.

When Alex's silence continued, all rustling around him eventually stopped. "Thank you," Alex murmured, "but . . . *no thank you.*"

Candover's infernal tapping ceased. "*No?* Whatever do you mean?" A storm of disapproval, mixed with jaded humor erupted all around him.

Oh, Alex knew it was only a matter of time before he would capitulate to the demands, but he just hadn't been able to resist watching the charade play out to its full potential.

The Prince Regent's face darkened from pale green to dark purple. It was a sight to behold. "And let me add, Kress, one last incentive. Don't think I have not heard the whispers questioning your allegiance to England. If I learn there is one shred of truth to the notion that you may have worn a frog uniform, I won't shed a single tear if you are brought before the House of Lords and worse. Care to reconsider your answer?"

It had been amusing to think that life would improve with his elevation. But then, he habitually failed to remember that whenever he had trotted on happiness in the past, there had always, *always* been *de la merde*—or rather, manure—on his heels in the end.

The only question now was how soon he could extricate himself from a ramshackle island prison to return to the only world where he had ever found peace . . . London.

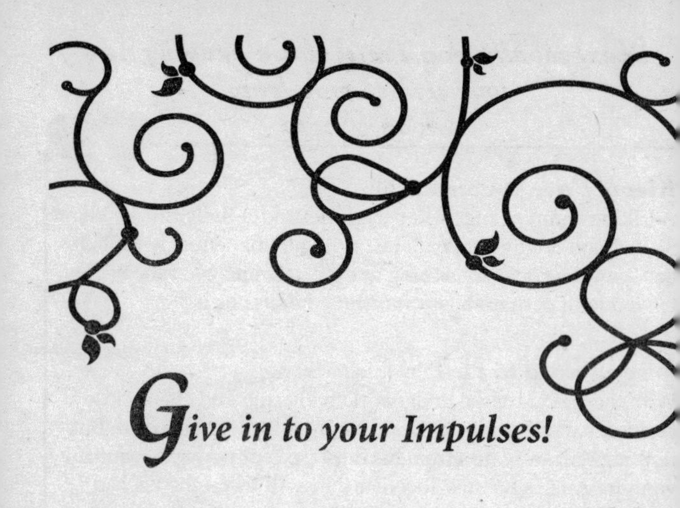

AVONIMPULSE